REYKJAVÍK NIGHTS

Also by Arnaldur Indriðason

Arnaldur Indriðason

REYKJAVÍK NIGHTS

Translated from the Icelandic by
Victoria Cribb

Harvill *Secker*
LONDON

Published by Harvill Secker 2014

2 4 6 8 10 9 7 5 3 1

First published with the title *Reykjavíkurnætur* in 2012
by Vaka-Helgafell, Reykjavík, www.forlagid.is

First published in Great Britain in 2014 by
HARVILL SECKER
20 Vauxhall Bridge Road
London SW1V 2SA

A Penguin Random House Company

global.penguinrandomhouse.com

A CIP catalogue record for this book is available from the British Library

ISBN 9781846558122 (hardback)
ISBN 9781448189809 (ebook)
ISBN 9781846558139 (trade paperback)

Penguin Random House supports the Forest Stewardship Council® (FSC®),
the leading international forest-certification organisation. Our books carrying the FSC
label are printed on FSC®-certified paper. FSC is the only forest-certification scheme
supported by the leading environmental organisations, including Greenpeace.
Our paper procurement policy can be found at
www.randomhouse.co.uk/environment

Typeset in Minion by Palimpsest Book Production Ltd,
Falkirk, Stirlingshire

Printed and bound in Great Britain by
Clays Ltd, St Ives PLC

REYKJAVÍK NIGHTS

1

There was a green anorak in the water. When prodded, it stirred, turned a slow half circle and sank from view. The boys fished at it with their poles until it floated up to the surface again, then recoiled in horror when they saw what lay beneath.

The three friends lived on Hvassaleiti, in the residential blocks lined up along busy Miklabraut all the way down to the expanse of waste-ground known as Kringlumýri. To the north the waste-ground was overgrown with nettles and angelica; to the south lay a large area of open diggings, deep gashes in the earth, where the inhabitants of Reykjavík had excavated peat by the ton to heat their houses during the First World War when fuel was in short supply. They had drained and laid tracks across the marshy ground before embarking on the largest scale peat extraction in the history of the city. Hundreds of men had been employed in cutting, drying and transporting it to the city in wagons.

After the war, when imports of coal and oil resumed, the

abandoned workings gradually filled with brown groundwater and remained like that for many years. Later, in the fifties and sixties, when the city expanded to the east and new suburbs rose on Hvassaleiti and Stóragerdi, the area became a playground for the local children, who built rafts to sail on the largest ponds and wore cycle tracks up and down the various hills and mounds. When the temperature dropped in winter, the icy pools came into their own as skating rinks.

The three boys had knocked up a new raft, using off-cuts of timber from a nearby building site. It consisted of two sturdy crossbars, some sheets of polystyrene and a serviceable platform made of planks from a concrete mould. They propelled it with long poles, which they inserted into the murky water and used to push off from the bottom, since the pool wasn't very deep. Although they wore rubber boots and did their best to keep dry, it was not uncommon for kids to fall in. Then they would return home with their knees trembling from the cold and at the thought of yet another telling-off – or worse – for turning up like drowned rats again.

They punted along gingerly in the direction of the Kringlumýri road, trying not to rock the raft in case it shipped water or sent them overboard. There was quite a knack to this: like tightrope walking, it required cooperation, skill, and not least a cool head. The boys took their time to find their balance before finally daring to push off from shore, aware that if they stood too close together on one side they risked capsizing.

In the event, the maiden voyage exceeded expectations. They were pleased with their new craft, which slipped along easily, and they made several trips back and forth across the deepest part of the pond. The rumble of traffic reached them from Miklabraut in the north, while the view to the south was dominated by the geothermal-heating pipeline that supplied hot water to the tanks on top of Öskjuhlíd hill. This was another of their playgrounds, where they sometimes came across small, hard balls the size of hens' eggs. They had puzzled over these until one of their fathers explained that they were golf balls. People must have been practising on the waste-ground by the pipeline, he said, adding that Reykjavík's golf course had once been located on the eastern side of Öskjuhlíd, not far from Kringlumýri. In those days the area had been known as Golfskálatjörn or 'Clubhouse Pond', though he thought it unlikely the balls had been lying there that long.

They were making good headway when the raft encountered an obstacle. One corner dipped into the dark water, and they came to a standstill. The boys quickly restored the equilibrium by shifting to the opposite side, and gradually the platform rose up again, though not all the way. It must have caught on something heavy. On previous excursions they had found a variety of junk in the brown depths; rubbish that had been thrown into the pits, such as the broken bicycle that jutted up in one spot. Some of this junk, like the polystyrene, had come in handy for raft building, but this hindrance, whatever it was, seemed more immovable. They guessed it must have snagged on a nail sticking out of one of the crossbars.

Warily, they tried pushing backwards, and discovered that it took all their strength to move their vessel. The debris dragged along with them a short way, then the raft suddenly broke free, its corner shooting up out of the water, almost causing them to overbalance. They managed to steady it again, thanking their lucky stars that they hadn't got drenched, then turned their attention to the thing that had been pulled up to the surface.

'What is it?' asked one, poking cautiously with his pole.

'Is it a bag?' asked his friend.

'No, it's an anorak,' said the third.

The first boy prodded harder, jabbing the object until finally it moved. It sank from view and they fished around until it floated up again. Then, by slow degrees it turned over, and from under the anorak a man's head appeared, white and bloodless, with colourless strands of hair. It was the most gruesome sight they had ever seen. One of the boys let out a yell and tumbled backwards into the water. At that, the precarious equilibrium was lost and before they knew it all three had fallen overboard, and they waded shrieking to the shore.

They stood there for a moment, wet and shivering, gaping at the green anorak and the side of the face that was exposed above the water, then turned and fled as fast as their legs would carry them.

2

A report came over the radio about a disturbance at a house in the Bústadir district and they accelerated onto Miklabraut east-bound, then crossed Háaleiti and took Grensásvegur south. It was long gone three in the morning and there was little traffic on the roads, though they passed two taxis heading for the suburbs, before almost colliding with another vehicle which crept up from Fossvogur and into their path at the Bústadavegur junction. The middle-aged man at the wheel had apparently failed to notice how fast the police van was travelling and had judged it safe to pull out.

'Is he crazy?' shouted Erlendur as he swerved violently round the vehicle before continuing along the road.

'Should we pull him over?' asked Marteinn from the back seat.

'Leave him,' said Gardar.

Glancing in the rear-view mirror, Erlendur saw that the car was now crawling west along Bústadavegur.

Gardar and Marteinn were law students temping for the summer. Erlendur quite enjoyed working with them. Both had Beatles haircuts, fringes flopping over their eyes, and large sideburns. At present the three of them were riding in a lumbering police van, a black-and-white Chevrolet, slow but reliable, equipped with a small holding cage for prisoners in the back. They hadn't bothered to turn on the siren or the flashing lights, which was probably why they'd nearly collided with the car, but they didn't need to for a domestic incident in the early hours. Sometimes Gardar liked to activate the whole system and drive like a maniac, though, just for the hell of it.

They parked outside the house, put on their white caps and climbed out into the light summer night. Though overcast and drizzling, it was mild. There had been a fair amount of drunkenness in town, but nothing serious until now. Earlier they had stopped a motorist on suspicion of drink-driving and taken him for a blood test. After that they had been summoned to a brawl outside a crowded nightclub, followed by another at a rundown house in the west end, where five men of assorted ages, a ship's crew from out of town, rented a couple of rooms. A shouting match with their neighbours had ended in blows, in the course of which one of them had pulled a knife and managed to stab another man in the arm before being overpowered. When Erlendur and company arrived to put an end to the fight the man was so enraged he was foaming at the mouth, so they cuffed him and took him to cool off in the detention cells at Hverfisgata. The others had sobered up with the arrival of the police and gave conflicting accounts of how it had all started.

They rang the doorbell of the terraced house. There was no sign of any disturbance, yet according to the police radio a

6

neighbour had rung in to report a noisy row at this address. They knocked on the door, tried the bell again, then conferred. Erlendur wanted to force an entry but was overruled by the two law students. The neighbour was nowhere to be seen.

While they were arguing, the door abruptly opened and a man in his early forties appeared. He was in his shirtsleeves, his flies were undone and his braces were dangling from his waistband. He had his hands in his pockets.

'What's all this about?' he asked, surveying them each in turn, apparently surprised to receive a visit from the police. They couldn't smell alcohol on his breath, but neither, it seemed, had they got him out of bed.

'We've received a complaint about noise at this address,' said Gardar.

'Noise?' repeated the man, squinting at them. 'There's no noise here. What . . . who's been complaining? You mean someone called the police?'

'Do you mind if we come in a minute?' asked Erlendur.

'In?' echoed the man. 'In here? Someone's been having you on, boys. You shouldn't fall for prank calls.'

'Is your wife up?' asked Erlendur.

'My wife? She's out of town. Staying at a summer cottage with friends. I don't see . . . There must be some mistake.'

'Perhaps we were given the wrong address,' suggested Gardar, glancing at Erlendur and Marteinn. 'We'd better check with the station.'

'Excuse us,' said Marteinn.

'No problem, boys. Sorry there's been a mix-up but I'm alone in the house. Have a good night.'

Gardar and Marteinn headed back to the van with Erlendur

following in their wake. They climbed in and Marteinn radioed the station, only to receive confirmation that they had the right address.

'But there's nothing going on here,' said Gardar.

'Hang on a minute.' Erlendur got out of the van. 'There's something odd about this.'

'What are you going to do?' asked Marteinn.

Erlendur retraced his steps and knocked on the door. After a short interval the man opened it again.

'Everything OK?'

'Could I use your toilet?' asked Erlendur.

'Toilet?'

'Just quickly,' said Erlendur. 'I won't be a minute.'

'I'm sorry, it's . . . I can't . . .'

'Can I see your hands?'

'What? My hands?'

'Yes, your hands.' Erlendur gave the door a determined shove, forcing the man to retreat before him into the house.

Barging in after him, Erlendur threw a quick glance into the kitchen, opened the door to the toilet opposite it, then dashed into the passage, opening more doors and calling out. After a brief protest at this extraordinary behaviour, the man stood, passive, in the hall. Erlendur strode back past him into the sitting room, and there he found a woman lying motionless on the floor. The room was a shambles – overturned chairs, fallen lamps, an ashtray stand on its side, curtains ripped from their rails. He ran to the woman and stooped over her. She was unconscious, one eye had sunk into her face, her lips were split and blood was oozing from a cut on her head. She appeared to have knocked herself out on the stand as she fell. Her dress was rucked up over

8

her hips and from the old bruise on her thigh he deduced that the violence had not begun this evening.

'Call an ambulance,' he bellowed to Gardar and Marteinn, who had materialised in the doorway. 'How long has she been lying here?' he demanded of the man, who was still standing, immobile, in the hall.

'Is she dead?'

'She could well be.' Erlendur did not dare touch the woman. She had a serious head wound and the ambulance men would know what to do before moving her. He grabbed the torn-down curtains and spread them over her, before ordering Marteinn to handcuff the husband and take him out to the van. The man no longer saw any reason to keep his hands in his pockets. His knuckles were bleeding from the assault.

'Do you have any children?' asked Erlendur.

'Two boys. They're in the country.'

'I'm not surprised.'

'I didn't do it deliberately,' the man said as he was cuffed and led out. 'I don't know . . . I didn't mean to go for her like that. She . . . I didn't mean to . . . She . . . I was going to ring you. She fell against the ashtray stand and didn't answer and I thought maybe . . .'

His words dried up. The woman emitted a faint moan.

'Can you hear me?' Erlendur whispered, but she did not respond.

The neighbour who had called the police, a man in his early thirties, was now outside talking to Gardar. Erlendur joined them. The neighbour was saying that he and his wife had heard rows from time to time but nothing as bad as tonight.

'Has it been going on long?'

'I really couldn't say. We've only lived here just over a year and it . . . like I said, you sometimes hear shouting and stuff being thrown around. It makes us very uncomfortable because we don't know what to do. It's not as though we really know them, even though we're neighbours.'

The wailing of sirens grew louder and they saw an ambulance turn into the road and approach the house. It was followed by a second patrol car. The other neighbours, woken by the commotion, now appeared at their windows or doors, and watched as the woman was carried out on a stretcher and the police van pulled away slowly with her husband locked in the back. Soon peace was restored and the residents returned to their beds, curious about the disturbance in the middle of the night.

Apart from this, the night shift was uneventful. As Erlendur was leaving work, he saw the wife-beater waiting for a taxi outside the police station. He had been released after questioning, free to go, as the incident was considered closed. His wife's condition was not critical; in a few days she would be discharged from hospital and no doubt return home to him. She probably had little alternative. There was no support network for women who suffered domestic abuse.

Before leaving, Erlendur had flicked through the incident report and noted that a middle-aged man had driven into a lamppost in the Vogar district and written off his car. He had been alone and highly intoxicated at the time. Erlendur guessed from the description of the vehicle that it was the one which had nearly crashed into them on Bústadavegur.

For a moment he stood looking up at the ultramodern building of the police headquarters on Hverfisgata, then strolled down to the seafront on Skúlagata, gazing first north to the flat-topped mass of Mount Esja, then over at the mountains to the east. The sun shone high above their peaks. It was early Sunday morning and the tranquillity that had descended over the city did much to exorcise the ugly tumult of the night.

As he walked, his thoughts returned once again to the tramp who last year had been found floating in one of the flooded workings on Kringlumýri. For some reason the case continued to haunt him. Perhaps because the man had not been a complete stranger. Erlendur had been on patrol nearby when the report came in, so he had been first on the scene. In his mind's eye he saw the green anorak in the water and the three boys who had gone out on the raft.

Erlendur knew that in the year that had elapsed since the man drowned Reykjavík CID had uncovered no evidence of suspicious circumstances. Yet he was also aware that the death of a homeless man had not been given high priority. They had other fish to fry and, besides, it looked like an open-and-shut case; the assumption was that the tramp had stumbled in and drowned by accident. No one seemed interested. Erlendur wondered if that was because the man had not mattered to anyone. All his death meant was one less vagrant on the streets of Reykjavík. And perhaps his death was that straightforward. But, then again, perhaps not. Shortly before the man died, Erlendur had heard him allege that someone had tried to set fire to the cellar in which he lived. Nobody had believed him, Erlendur included, and now it troubled him that he had not listened to the man, merely brushed him off with the same indifference as everyone else.

3

One evening not long afterwards, on his night off, Erlendur walked over to Kringlumýri. It was not the first time his feet had led him in that direction. With little to occupy him outside work, he took pleasure in wandering the streets on fine summer evenings, round Tjörnin, the small lake in the centre of town; through the west end and out to the Seltjarnarnes peninsula, or south along the shores of Skerjafjördur to the cove at Nauthólsvík. Occasionally he would drive out of town in his old beaten-up car, park somewhere remote and go hiking in the mountains. If the forecast was good, he would take along a tent and provisions. Although he didn't think of himself as a serious outdoorsman, he had joined the Icelandic Touring Club. He received their annual publications but didn't take part in any of their organised trips. The experience of trekking to the hot springs at Landmannalaugar had taught him that travelling with a bunch of relentlessly hearty people was not for him. Such forced jollity could quickly become oppressive.

He hadn't met that many women either, but then that wasn't really a priority. On his rare forays into the Reykjavík nightlife he had been put off by the noise and rowdiness. Then one evening at Glaumbær, back before the place burnt down, he had met a young woman called Halldóra. She was chatty, knew her own mind, and took a frank interest in him. Sometime later, on a night out at Silfurtunglid with the boys from the force, he ran into her again and she asked him to come home with her. Afterwards she phoned him, they met up, and now they were in a relationship of sorts.

As Erlendur walked through his own neighbourhood of Hlídar, past Hamrahlíd College, where they offered adult education courses, he wondered yet again whether he should go back to school. He had completed his compulsory education but left before the sixth form. When his family moved to Reykjavík he had been put in the lowest class at his new school. His ability was never even tested; it had simply been assumed that since he came from a poor background, was recalcitrant and uncooperative, he must belong with the slow kids. Unhappy about the move, unhappy with city life, all he had really learned was to hold his tongue. The upshot was that he lost interest in formal education, defied his teachers and any kind of authority, and quit at sixteen. He had already been working during the summers, and after that last winter at school he moved out of the home he shared with his mother and into a rented flat. His mother, Áslaug, earned a pittance, and he himself did little better when he took a job at the fishery.

Erlendur glanced up at the college building, tempted by the new opportunities for adult education. Twenty-eight was not too old to resume his studies, and anyway he would need to pass his final school exams if he wanted to go to university. He was interested in history, particularly the history of Iceland, and could envisage giving up police work at some point to dedicate himself to research.

He broke into a jog across busy Kringlumýrarbraut. Every now and then over the past year he had found himself drawn back to the diggings, though he hardly knew why. The water that had collected in the hollows was shallow, brown and devoid of life; 'ponds' was too good a name for them. Today there were a couple of rafts out and the place was alive with kids riding bikes up and down the hills. Two small motorcycles tore up the dirt track at the furthest point, the roaring and backfiring of their engines carrying to Erlendur through the quiet evening air.

The tramp had been found where the water was deepest. They calculated that his body must have been there for two days before it was noticed. Since the pathologist concluded that he had died on the spot, the police inquiry had focused on determining whether there could have been any foul play. The level of alcohol in his bloodstream indicated death by natural causes. There were no signs of a struggle, and no witnesses had come forward. Nor were there any traces of suspicious activity at the scene, such as tyre tracks or footprints, though there had been a delay between his drowning and the start of the investigation, and in the interim the ground had been trampled by children playing. In the absence of new evidence, the inquiry soon ran out of steam and the case was closed.

During his first months in Traffic, Erlendur had encountered the victim on several occasions. His name was Hannibal and he was a homeless man whom the police had picked up for a variety of reasons, though mainly for being drunk and disorderly. The first time he crossed Erlendur's path was in the depths of winter. Hannibal had been sitting, hunched forward, on a bench in Austurvöllur Square, his numb fingers cramped around the neck of an empty *brennivín* bottle. It was bitterly cold. Convinced the man would die of exposure if they left him where he was, Erlendur had said he wasn't having that on his conscience, and after a bit of dithering the officers had decided to take him back to the cells for the night. They helped him into the police van, where he came to his senses. It took him a while to work out what was going on, though the situation was familiar to both parties, but when he did he began to thank them profusely, the dear boys, for taking such good care of him. He asked for his bottle but was informed that he had emptied it. Could they spare him a drop of booze, then? The question was directed at the rookie, Erlendur, whom Hannibal had not seen before and guessed was more likely to be a soft touch. To begin with, Erlendur ignored him, but when Hannibal kept repeating his question, he told him to shut up. The tramp's gratitude swiftly evaporated.

'You bloody arseholes, you're all the same.'

On the second occasion, Erlendur had come across him lying at the foot of 'the Tin', as they called the corrugated-iron fence around the Swedish fish factory on the northern side of Arnarhóll. Tramps used to seek refuge there from life's hardships and from the bone-piercing frost that accompanied the northerly gales. Hannibal was blue with cold; he sat propped against the corrugated iron, legs outstretched, wearing the usual tattered green anorak, completely dead to the world. Erlendur was on his way home from the centre of town when he caught sight of him. He hadn't intended to interfere at first, but on closer inspection he grew worried. The frost was tightening its grip and the north wind swept ribbons of snow along the ground to collect at the tramp's feet. Although well kitted out in a down jacket, hat and scarf, Erlendur was finding it hard enough to keep out the bitter chill himself. He tried calling the man by name but there was no reaction. He called again, louder, but Hannibal might as well have been a statue. Erlendur went right up and poked him with his foot.

'You all right, Hannibal?'

No response.

Erlendur knelt down and shook the man until his eyes opened a crack, but Hannibal did not recognise him or know where he was.

'Leave me alone, you bastard,' he mumbled, trying to beat him off.

'Come on,' said Erlendur. 'You can't lie here in this cold.'

He hauled the man to his feet, which was no easy task since he was quite a weight and far from cooperative. It took all Erlendur's strength just to heave him upright before he could help him down the slope. But the movement cleared Hannibal's head a little and he was able to direct Erlendur through the centre of town to a small building round the back of a house on Vesturgata. There he gestured to a narrow flight of steps leading to the cellar. He could hardly stand, so Erlendur gave him a hand down the stairs. The door was secured only by a simple wooden latch, like on a cowshed. Erlendur lifted this and Hannibal pushed the door open, reached in a hand and, finding the light switch, turned on a naked bulb hanging from the ceiling.

'This is my refuge from a cruel world,' he said and tripped headlong over the threshold.

Erlendur restored him to his feet. The refuge was less a flat than a small storeroom for a variety of junk so unremarkable that no one was expected to steal it, judging by the ineffectual latch on the door. Lengths of piping and bald tyres mingled with rusty tubs, plastic containers and tangles of useless netting, while on the floor was the filthiest mattress Erlendur had ever seen. A threadbare blanket lay rumpled on top of it, and strewn all around was an assortment of empty bottles which had once contained alcohol, medicine or cardamom baking extract, along with the kind of small plastic methylated spirits containers you could buy from the chemist's. There was a throat-catching stench of decaying rubber and urine.

Once Erlendur had helped the man to bed, he was eager to get out as quickly as possible, but Hannibal rose up on one elbow.

'Who the hell are you?'

'Take care now,' Erlendur replied, backing out through the storeroom.

'Who are you?' Hannibal demanded again. 'Do we know each other?'

Erlendur hesitated in the doorway. He had no desire to get involved in a conversation but neither did he wish to appear disrespectful.

'The name's Erlendur. We've met before. I'm a policeman.'

'Erlendur,' repeated Hannibal. 'Mind's a blank, mate. Got anything for me?'

'Like what?'

'Could you spare a bit of loose change? Doesn't have to be much, you know. A few coins would do. I'm sure you could spare some, a flush bloke like you, who gives a helping hand to the likes of me.'

'Won't it just go on booze?' Erlendur asked.

Hannibal twisted his mouth into a smile of sorts.

'I won't lie to you, Erlendur, my friend,' he said, very humble now. 'You may find it hard to believe but it's not in my nature to lie to people. I just need a tot of gin. That's all I ask for in this godforsaken world. I know it won't sound like much to you, and I wouldn't pester you, my friend, if it wasn't such a little thing.'

'I'm not giving you money for gin.'

'How about a drop of meths, then?'

'No.'

'Oh, well then,' said Hannibal, lying back on the mattress. 'In that case you can bugger off.'

The roar of the motorbikes receded as they vanished in the direction of Hvassaleiti. The kids poled their rafts to shore and dragged them onto dry land. Erlendur looked south towards the pipeline. It had emerged during the inquiry that Hannibal's presence in Kringlumýri was due to his having found a new home, if you could call it that. The summer he died, he had been evicted from his cellar after being accused of starting a fire, though he had stubbornly protested his innocence. Forced onto the streets, he had sought refuge in the casing around the heating pipeline. A slab of concrete had broken off in one place, leaving an opening large enough for him to crawl inside and warm himself against the hot-water pipes.

It was to be Hannibal's last home before his body was discovered in the flooded pit. He had slept there in the company of a few feral cats that were drawn to him much as the birds had once flocked to St Francis of Assisi.

4

Erlendur was standing on the brink of the pool where Hannibal had met his end when a boy tore past him on a bicycle, spun round and rode back. Although a year had passed since they had last met, Erlendur recognised him immediately: he was one of the kids who had found the body.

'You're a cop, aren't you?' said the boy, braking in front of him.

'Yes, hello again.'

'What are you doing here?' asked the boy. He was as plucky and self-assured as Erlendur remembered; ginger hair, freckles, a look of mischief. But he had grown. In only a year he had gone from being a child to a teenager.

'Just taking a look around.'

The boy had been the leader of the trio. They had all raced off to his house to inform his mother of their discovery. Realising they were in earnest, however far-fetched their tale, she had completely forgotten to scold them for coming home soaked again, and instead called the police straight away. The other boys had run home for a change of clothes, then they had all cycled back down to the diggings. By then two police cars and an ambulance had arrived. Hannibal's body had been recovered from the pool and was lying on the ground, covered by a blanket.

When the report came in, Erlendur had been on traffic duty on Miklabraut. As soon as he reached the scene, he had waded into the water and pulled the body ashore. Only then did he see it was Hannibal. It had given him a turn, yet Hannibal's death had seemed strangely inevitable. The police had been shooing away the boys, along with the other onlookers who had gathered, when they piped up that they had found the body. After that they were taken to sit in one of the patrol cars and later questioned closely about their discovery.

'My dad says he drowned,' the boy observed now, leaning on his handlebars and looking over at the place where Hannibal had lain suspended in the water.

'Yes,' agreed Erlendur. 'I expect he fell in and couldn't save himself.'

'He was just an old alky.'

'It must have been a bit of a shock for you and your friends to find him like that.'

'Addi had nightmares,' said the boy. 'A doctor came round to his house and all. Me and Palli didn't care.'

'Do you still play here on rafts?'

'Nah, not any more. That's kids' stuff.'

'Ah, right. Did you by any chance notice the man down by the pipeline last summer? That you can remember?'

'No.'

'Anyone else notice him?'

'No. We used to play there sometimes but I never saw him. Maybe he was only there at night.'

'Maybe. What were you doing up by the pipeline?'

'You know. Looking for golf balls.'

'Golf balls?'

'Yeah. There's a bloke from those houses who's always practising shots.' The boy gestured to some rows of terraced houses on Hvassaleiti. Dad says there used to be a golf course by the pipeline, near Öskjuhlíd, and we sometimes find old balls.'

'I see. And what do you do with them when you find them?'

'Nothing.' The boy prepared to pedal off. 'Just chuck 'em in the water. I ain't got any use for them.'

'"I *haven't* got any use for them".'

'Yeah, OK.'

'And "OK" isn't good Icel—'

'I've got to go home now,' interrupted the boy and, climbing onto his saddle, was off before Erlendur could finish his sentence.

Erlendur followed the track between the old workings and up the hill towards the heating conduit. The pipeline was fifteen kilometres long and ran from the geothermal zone in the Mosfell valley north of the city, skirted the suburbs, then finally discharged into the huge hot-water tanks that crowned Öskjuhlíd. Inside the concrete casing ran two fourteen-inch steel pipes booming with naturally heated water. Although insulated, these had still emitted enough warmth to provide comfort for Hannibal during the last days of his life.

They had not yet repaired the hole in the casing. Erlendur contemplated the broken-off slab of concrete lying in the grass and wondered what had caused the damage. An earthquake, perhaps, or frost.

The opening was large enough for a grown man to crawl through with ease. He noticed that the grass around the entrance was flattened, and when he poked his head inside he saw that someone else must have had the same idea as Hannibal. A blanket had been dragged in there. Two empty *brennivín* bottles and a handful of methylated spirits containers were scattered under the pipes. Not far beyond them he could make out a shabby hat and a mitten.

The gloom intensified as Erlendur peered further inside. As his eyes adjusted, he was jolted by the sight of a mound deep within the tunnel.

'Who's there?' he called.

There was no answer, but the mound suddenly came to life and began to move in his direction.

5

Erlendur nearly jumped out of his skin. Panicking for an instant, he backed out of the opening and stumbled away. A moment later a head popped up, followed by the rest of a man who crawled out of the hole and hunkered down on the grass in front of him. He wore a ragged, dark coat, fingerless gloves, a woolly hat and large rubber galoshes. Erlendur had seen him before in the company of other Reykjavík drinkers, but didn't know his name.

The man said good evening as if he were accustomed to receiving visitors there. From his manner, you would think they had met in the street rather than crawling around in a concrete pipeline. Erlendur introduced himself and the man replied that his name was Vilhelm. His age was hard to guess. Possibly not much over forty, though given the missing front teeth and the thick beard that covered his face, he might have been ten years older.

'Do I know you?' asked the tramp, regarding Erlendur through horn-rimmed glasses. The thick lenses rendered his eyes unnaturally large, giving him a slightly comical look. He had an ugly, hacking cough.

'No,' said Erlendur, his attention drawn to the glasses. 'I don't believe so.'

'Were you looking for me?' asked Vilhelm, coughing again. 'Did you want to talk to me?'

'No,' said Erlendur, 'I just happened to be passing. To tell the truth, I didn't expect to find anyone here.'

'Don't get many passers-by,' said Vilhelm. 'It's nice and quiet. You don't have a smoke, do you?'

'Sorry, no. Have you . . . May I ask how long you've been living here?'

'Two or three days,' said Vilhelm, without explaining his choice of camp. 'Or . . . What is it today?'

'Tuesday.'

'Oh.' Vilhelm's cough rattled out again. 'Tuesday. Then maybe I've been here a bit longer. It's not bad for the odd night, though it can get a bit nippy. Still, I've known worse.'

'Do you think your health can cope with it?'

'What the hell's that got to do with you?' asked Vilhelm, his body racked by another spasm.

'Actually, I'm not here completely by chance,' Erlendur continued, once the man had recovered. 'I used to know a bloke who dossed down here like you. His name was Hannibal.'

'Hannibal? Oh, yes, I knew him.'

'He drowned down there in one of the ponds.' Erlendur waved towards Kringlumýri. 'Ring any bells?'

'I remember hearing about it. Why?'

'No reason,' said Erlendur. 'I suppose it was just an unlucky accident.'

24

'Yes, unlucky all right.'

'Where did you know him from?' Erlendur took a seat on the concrete casing.

'Oh, just around and about, you know. Used to bump into him on my travels. A really good bloke.'

'You weren't enemies, then?'

'Enemies? No. I haven't got any enemies.'

'Do you know if he had, or if there was anyone who might have wanted to harm him?'

Vilhelm stared at Erlendur through the thick lenses.

'What do you want to know for?' His shoulders shook with another coughing fit.

'No particular reason.'

'Come on.'

'No, honest.'

'You reckon maybe he didn't drown all on his own?'

'What do you think?'

'I haven't the foggiest.' Vilhelm rose to his feet and flexed his back, then came and sat down next to Erlendur on the casing. 'You couldn't spare a little change?'

'What do you want it for?'

'Tobacco. That's all.'

Erlendur took out two fifty-króna pieces. 'That's all I have on me.'

'Thanks.' Vilhelm was quick to palm them. 'That'll do for one packet. Did you know a bottle of vodka's getting on for two thousand krónur these days? I reckon the lot who run this country have lost the plot. Totally lost the plot.'

'The pools down there aren't very deep,' Erlendur remarked, returning to his theme.

Vilhelm coughed into his gloves. 'Deep enough.'

'You'd have to be pretty determined to drown in one, though.'

'I couldn't say.'

'Or drunk,' Erlendur persisted. 'They found a fair amount of alcohol in his blood.'

'Oh, Hannibal could drink all right. Christ!'

'Do you remember who he was hanging around with most before he died?'

'Not with me, at any rate,' Vilhelm replied. 'Hardly knew him. But I spotted him a couple of times at the Fever Hospital. In fact, that's the last place I saw him; he was trying to get a bed but they said he was drunk.'

No more information was forthcoming. He said he was planning to spend at least one more night by the pipes, then he would see. Erlendur tried to dissuade him, asking if it was really his only option. At this hint of interference, Vilhelm told him to bloody well leave him alone. Erlendur left after that. He was pursued by the sound of coughing as he stepped up onto the conduit and followed it west through the light arctic night as far as Öskjuhlíd, before jumping down and heading home to Hlídar.

Hannibal had no doubt tested the limits of the shelter's ban on alcohol more than once. Perhaps that was why he had taken refuge in the pipeline at last, an outcast, free from all interference, removed from human society.

6

Towards the end of their shift Erlendur, Marteinn and Gardar were sent to escort a runaway prisoner back to jail at Litla-Hraun. Two days earlier the fugitive, who was serving a two-and-a-half-year sentence for drug smuggling, had felt the urge to nip into town and had escaped without much effort. Although only twenty-five, he was well known to the police in connection with drugs, alcohol smuggling, theft and forgery. At twenty he had spent several months inside for a series of burglaries. Subsequently, he had been caught with a significant quantity of cannabis at Keflavík Airport, high as a kite after four days in Amsterdam. The customs officials had him on a watch list but they would have stopped this gangly hippy, with his beard and long hair, anyway. It transpired that he had hardly even bothered to hide his stash. The goods were wrapped in a pair of jeans inside a brand-new sports bag.

After his latest escapade, he had given himself up at the police station on Hverfisgata, and now Erlendur and company ushered him out to the van. The man was garrulous; he must have got hold of something good before handing himself in.

'Why did you run away?' asked Marteinn as they drove out of town.

'It was my mum's birthday. The old girl's fifty!'

'Was it a big do?' asked Gardar.

'Yeah, hell of a party, man. Loads of booze.'

'Was she pleased to see you?' asked Marteinn.

The police had been watching his mother's house but had failed to catch him.

'She was over the moon!'

'And you had no trouble giving them the slip?'

'At Hraun? Nah. I more or less walked out.'

'You know they'll increase your sentence.'

'It'll be bugger all. Anyway, it's not so bad inside. Mum had an important birthday, man. No way was I going to miss that!'

'No, of course not,' said Marteinn.

The van climbed laboriously over Hellisheidi with the fugitive chatting all the way back to his cell, about life in the nick and the other inmates; about the local football team and the rubbish season they'd been having, and how his English team wasn't doing much better; about this crap film he'd seen on TV while in hiding; the coffee shop he had visited in Amsterdam; prison food; a steakhouse in Amsterdam. Nothing was off limits.

They were thoroughly fed up with him by the time they dropped him off at Litla-Hraun. Later, as they were trundling back into town, there was an alert about a young girl who had gone missing. She had left her home in Reykjavík three days earlier and not been heard of since. She was nineteen years old and when last seen had been wearing jeans, a pink peasant blouse, a camouflage jacket, and trainers.

'Remember the lad who woke up the other side of the country in Akureyri – last year, wasn't it?' said Marteinn. 'He went for a night out in Reykjavík without telling anyone. When they hadn't heard from him for four days, his parents called the police. They were a respectable family. He was in a newsagent's when he saw a picture of himself in the papers.'

'What about the woman who went for a few drinks at Thórskaffi?' said Gardar. 'She was never found. That wasn't so long ago.'

'Out with friends, wasn't she?' said Marteinn. 'And never came home.'

'That's right. She was going to walk back.'

'Wonder what happened to her.'

'Threw herself in the sea, surely?'

'Hey, Erlendur,' said Marteinn, 'wasn't that around the same time as your tramp drowned?'

'*My* tramp?' Erlendur had not heard that one before, though he had told them of his encounters with Hannibal and the indifference of the investigating officers. 'Yes, it was around then.'

Their shift was ending. All they had to do was return the van and go home, when a notification came through about a burglary in Vogar.

'Shit!' exclaimed Gardar. 'Do we have to take it?'

They were the closest vehicle, so Erlendur swung off the main road into the residential streets. As they approached the house in question they caught sight of a figure sprinting away. The man paused for a split second when he saw the police van, then dodged into the next-door garden. Erlendur braked violently. Gardar hurtled out with Marteinn on his heels. Within minutes they had run the man down, wrestled him to the ground, then bundled him into the van.

They discovered a watch and some jewellery on him. He had also been observed discarding a large object when he first spotted them. While Gardar and Marteinn were chasing the thief, Erlendur had gone to investigate the loot left lying in the road and discovered that the burglar had made off with the family fondue set.

7

As it happened, Erlendur was well acquainted with the facts of the woman's disappearance from Thórskaffi, since stories of people going missing held a particular fascination for him. He devoured news reports on everything from poorly equipped ptarmigan hunters failing to return home from the mountains at the appointed time, to travellers in the interior who had not been heard of for days, or youngsters, like the girl in the pink blouse, running away from home. Most turned up eventually, alive or dead, but some were never seen again, despite large search parties and rescue units combing the countryside for days. The missing left a series of unanswered questions behind them.

Soon after Erlendur joined the police, he had begun to trawl through the archives for cases, old and more recent, in Reykjavík and the surrounding area. For years he had been reading up on tales of travellers going astray or surviving ordeals on the country's high moors and mountain roads. His digging in the police records was merely an extension of this interest.

Only rarely were these missing-persons cases attributed to criminal action, but then Erlendur's interest was personal rather than professional. He spent hours leafing through reports of cold cases and familiarising himself with the circumstances of a variety of disappearances and unsolved crimes, though the latter did not have the same appeal. There were exceptions, however, such as Hannibal's demise, though whether there had been anything suspicious about that was disputable. In this instance it was his acquaintance with the victim that had aroused his curiosity.

One case in particular exerted such a powerful hold on Erlendur's imagination that he had immersed himself in the details to the extent of visiting the sites in question. One day in 1953 an eighteen-year-old girl, a pupil at the Reykjavík Women's College, had been due to meet her friends at a cafe much frequented by students on Lækjargata in the centre of town. Although they had originally come from different schools, the four girls had all started in the same class at the college and become good friends that first winter. They hung out together and signed up for all kinds of extracurricular activities. They had been meeting to plan an evening's entertainment for their class. When only three of them turned up the girls were not unduly annoyed; they simply assumed their friend was ill since she had been absent from class that morning. They phoned her house from the cafe to find out how she was. The girl's mother answered and it took her a minute or two to grasp what they were talking about. 'We just wanted to know how she's feeling,' explained the friend. The girl's mother was puzzled by the question: her daughter wasn't ill; she'd gone to school.

The girl almost invariably took the same route to the college. It was a fifteen-minute walk from where she lived in the west of town, via Camp Knox, the area of Nissen huts built by the American occupying force during the war, which later became a source of cheap housing for Reykjavík's poorer families. From there she headed east along Hringbraut to Fríkirkjuvegur where the college was located. On other days she used to catch the bus, but the driver had failed to notice her among the passengers that morning. As it tended to be the same small group of people every morning, he claimed to know the girl by sight. So either she had walked in or hitched a lift with someone she knew. It would not have been the first time. And although she had never been known to accept a ride from a stranger, this could not be ruled out either. But nor could it be established with any certainty, since no one had come forward to say they had given her a lift.

It was always possible that she had never intended to go in that day, that she had met up with some unknown person, with disastrous consequences, or had, alternatively, been bent on taking her own life in such a manner that her body was never found. She had not, as far as anyone was aware, had a boyfriend or gone out on dates or kept some relationship secret from her parents. And she had always been conscientious about her attendance. Could she have killed herself? There was no hint of any personal problems that could have pushed her to the brink of despair; on the contrary, she was popular and outgoing. But, then again, she had vanished during the blackest months of winter, and the darkness could take its toll on people's mental health, so suicide could not be entirely ruled out. Indeed, the fact that her body never turned up suggested that it may have been swallowed without trace by the sea.

Erlendur had traced the girl's route to school on foot, though much had changed in the intervening years; the Nissen huts were long gone and new buildings had risen in their place. On another occasion he had caught the bus to Fríkirkjuvegur. He had also stood in front of her old home in the west of town. She had been an only child. He saw the garden where she had played, the door she had walked through. He lingered only briefly, no more than a minute or two, but it had been long enough for his eyes to drink in the sadness.

The fate of the Thórskaffi woman was shrouded in the same mystery. Admittedly her friends had voiced suspicions of depression, though the woman had never confided in anyone, and unhappiness in her marriage. Her husband had flatly denied this, however, while conceding that he had been aware of mood swings and maybe low spirits. He had reported his wife missing early on Monday morning, by which point he had not heard from her since Saturday evening when she had gone out with friends from the estate agency where she worked. When she did not return home the following day, he had rung round her colleagues, but it was no use: some had only the haziest recollection of how the evening had ended.

They had gone out for dinner at Naustid to celebrate the firm's fifth anniversary. Spouses were not invited and in their absence everyone had let their hair down and consumed copious amounts of alcohol. They had stayed at the restaurant until late, then someone had suggested moving on to Thórskaffi, a busy nightclub where a popular band was playing. Once there, the group had gradually dispersed, either calling it a night or running into other friends. No one had noticed when or with whom the woman had left. The last person she was known to have talked to was the oldest employee of the firm, a receptionist in her fifties. The receptionist had offered to share a taxi but she had said no thanks; she was going to stay on a bit longer and would probably walk home as it would do her good to clear her head. She lived in the new neighbourhood at the western end of the Fossvogur valley but said she didn't mind the distance.

Later, when interviewed by the police, none of the other customers at Thórskaffi could recall much about the missing woman. Her colleagues had seen her chatting to a handful of other people, and two of these had come forward when the search was at its height. One was an old college friend who had been there with his wife. To them she had not appeared drunk, merely in high spirits, as they reminisced about their school days. The other witness was a woman she had known since her teens. A little later this friend had observed her talking to a man she did not recognise and could only describe in the vaguest terms since it had been dark in the club.

The search had yielded no results. The woman had simply vanished into thin air and the subsequent investigation had uncovered little that might explain her fate, apart from the detail that three years previously she had cheated on her husband. The circumstances had been so similar that when she failed to return home her husband had initially assumed that she had been up to her old tricks again. After the first occasion she had insisted it was the only time she had been unfaithful; it had been a moment of madness during a rough patch in their marriage. He had no reason to doubt her words.

One theory was that she had either bumped into her old lover or gone home with a new man, and that something had happened and she vanished without trace. When questioned, the former lover swore blind he had not met her that evening. The man her friend had seen her talking to had never come forward.

Yet in spite of this they saw no reason to treat the woman's disappearance as a crime. Suicide was deemed more likely.

A single detail had struck Erlendur as he read the file one evening when he did not feel like going straight home after his shift. Two of the people interviewed had mentioned that the woman had been mad about jewellery.

Erlendur started awake, worried that he had overslept. He had been having a nap as he sometimes did before going on duty. Relieved to discover that it was still early, he got up and prepared for yet another night shift. He had lain there for a long time that evening, brooding over the fates of the girl from the women's college and the woman from Thórskaffi, and wondering if his decision to join the police had been precipitated by his fascination with stories like theirs.

8

The Fever Hospital on Thingholtsstræti, a handsome, two-storey wooden building dating from the nineteenth century, was the first purpose-built hospital in Reykjavík. For the past four years, however, it had played a new role, providing shelter for the city's homeless; a hot meal, washing facilities and a bed for the night if they wanted it. Discipline was strict. The doors were locked at a respectable hour and the occupants had to be out by a set time in the morning. The rule that they had to be sober throughout their stay was non-negotiable.

The men seeking admittance ranged from humbly grateful for anything they might receive after a tough spell on the streets, to those who were argumentative or even drunkenly aggressive. The last group were turned away. Some of the men were in good shape, others so frail that the staff took them straight to hospital.

One evening, Erlendur dropped by before work, just as they were refusing entry to a man who was bundled up in a thick winter coat and woolly hat despite the summer heat. He was arguing with a member of staff, who then took the man's arm and led him out. In the faint hope of arousing pity, the drunk protested, though not very vehemently, that he could not face another night in the Nissen hut.

'Come back when you've sobered up,' the staff member said. 'You know the rule, my friend. It's perfectly simple.'

He closed the door and turned to Erlendur.

'Looking for someone?'

'No.'

'You're not seeking admission?' The man's tone made it clear that Erlendur looked far too fit to require the services of the Fever Hospital.

'Got many residents at the moment?'

'No, five, though we can expect more tonight.'

'That's not many, is it?'

'Not compared to last Christmas,' said the man. 'We were bursting at the seams. Put up something like thirty men. Christmas is always busiest.'

'I'm after information about a homeless man who died suddenly about a year ago. Name of Hannibal. Jog your memory at all?'

'Hannibal? You mean the fellow who drowned in Kringlumýri?'

Erlendur nodded.

'I remember him well.' The man was middle-aged, a little plump, his beard neatly trimmed around his mouth. 'He used to drop in from time to time. Yes, I remember Hannibal all right. Strange fellow. Did you know him?'

'We were acquainted,' Erlendur replied, without elaborating. 'Did he stay here often?'

'He wandered in off the street every now and then. Last time I saw him I had to turn him away for being drunk and making a nuisance of himself. I gather he was sleeping up by the hot-water pipes towards the end.'

'That's right. Not far from where they found him in Kringlumýri.'

'Poor man.'

'So he was sober the times he stayed here?'

'Had to be – we don't allow any drinking.'

'Did you talk to him at all?'

'No, not that I recall. Just went over the rules with him, as I always do.'

'Did he come here often when he was sober?'

'From time to time, as I said, but usually he was in such a state that we couldn't admit him. There were maybe two or three occasions when he was allowed to stay. No more. Then he had to leave in the morning like everybody else.'

'Did he associate with any of your regulars? Can you remember?' asked Erlendur.

'Not off the top of my head. But it's not a big community.'

'Community?'

'Reykjavík's drinkers.'

'No, I suppose not, though they certainly make their mark on the town.'

'That's nothing new. Most of them know each other. I vaguely remember him complaining that someone had tried to set fire to him. Can that be right?'

'The cellar where he was sleeping caught fire, yes. The owner reckoned he'd started the blaze himself by accident. Did he tell you different?'

'Well, as far as I remember, he was extremely resentful about how he'd been treated. The incident's stayed with me because that was the last time I saw him. He was fuming about being evicted. Does that fit?'

'Sounds right. The cellar was a total dump but at least it was a roof over his head. Did he mention being blamed for the fire?'

'No, just ranted on about it – he was the worse for wear and didn't hang about long. In my line of work you hear so many sob stories and excuses, so many complaints and accusations about everything under the sun that in the end you stop listening.'

When Erlendur left the Fever Hospital shortly afterwards, the drunk man was still standing in the street outside. To combat the unsteadiness of his legs he had propped himself against a fence from where he hailed Erlendur.

'You pissed too?'

Erlendur stopped and considered the man in his thick winter coat and hat; the grimy hands, the wrinkles etched deep in his face. He could be either side of fifty.

'No, I'm not pissed.' Erlendur went over. 'Won't they take you?'

'Arseholes,' said the man.

'If you sober up, they'll give you food and shelter. They can't have everyone wandering around drunk though, can they?'

The man gave him a look of contempt; clearly this was unworthy of a response.

'You wouldn't by any chance remember a guy called Hannibal? Used to come down here.'

'Hannibal?' the man said sharply.

'Yes.'

'I knew Hannibal. Why are you asking?'

'I –'

'He was drowned like a dog.'

'What do you mean?'

'What do I mean? I mean someone went out there and drowned the poor sod.'

'Why do you say that?'

'I just know.'

'Did you see it?'

'No, I didn't. But I saw plenty of other things.'

'Why are you so sure, then?'

'How else did he drown in that puddle? Eh? You tell me!'

'So you –'

'Me? No, wasn't me. I had nothing to do with it.'

'So what did you see?'

'Eh?'

'You said you'd seen plenty of other things. What did you mean?'

'I see things,' repeated the tramp. 'And I know things too. Don't you go thinking I'm some kind of fool, mate. I'm no fool, let me tell you.'

'Do you know things about Hannibal?'

'Oh, leave me alone. Why don't you talk to that stupid prick Bergmundur? He knew Hannibal better than me. Saw him in the square only yesterday. Back on the bottle, the bloody fool. Not for the first time,' he added, with an oddly censorious expression, as if he himself never touched a drop except on special occasions.

Little was to be gained from the couple who used to live above Hannibal's cellar. Erlendur had finally tracked them down to a grotty rented place near the swimming pool in Laugardalur. They had been out the night of the fire yet were convinced that Hannibal was responsible. Not that they spoke badly of him. In fact, they showed sympathy for his plight.

'We didn't mind him sleeping there,' explained the woman whose name was Málfrídur. She had a puffy red face, a large splayed nose and a big mouth, which was prevented from closing properly by protruding teeth. Her husband, who was waiting by the stove for the coffee to percolate, also looked like a drinker: grubby vest, braces hanging down over his trousers, bare feet. The flat was dirty and there was an unpleasant smell whose source Erlendur could not identify. Burnt offal, he suspected.

'We liked the bum,' said the man, pouring coffee into some glasses.

'Sad what happened to him,' added Málfrídur.

'He didn't have any enemies that you were aware of?'

'No,' said the man, 'but it's tough on the streets. Wasn't the poor sod drunk when he fell in?'

'Do you believe he started the fire himself?' asked Erlendur.

'Yes, it was just him being clumsy, wasn't it?' said Málfrídur, her mouth hanging open.

'Mind you, he blamed the brothers next door,' her husband pointed out.

'Yes, but that was a load of nonsense,' said Málfrídur. 'They had no motive.'

'Any idea why he accused them?' asked Erlendur. 'Had he got on the wrong side of them?'

'No, the brothers had nothing to do with it,' insisted Málfrídur.

'I didn't like them,' remarked her husband. 'Never did.'

'That's different.'

'Why didn't you like them?' asked Erlendur, looking at the man.

'They wouldn't so much as give you the time of day, even though we were neighbours. And they were mixed up in some kind of shady business, if you ask me. Selling home-made spirits – that sort of thing. Turned their noses up at us. I went round once; asked if they'd sell me some booze – I'd noticed a constant stream of people coming and going from their place. Late at night, mostly. All sorts. They denied they had any, but I know they were lying.'

'Was Hannibal aware of this?'

'Haven't a clue. We never discussed it. Then all the comings and goings stopped. I don't know if it had anything to do with me going over there. They were nasty pieces of work, those brothers.'

'They used to be glued to their telly all evening,' said Málfrídur.

'Oh?'

'Yes, it was on every night. We could see from our window. They were telly addicts, if you ask me. Total addicts.'

'Then they moved out,' said the man.

'Yes, soon after that business with Hannibal,' added the woman. 'And we haven't laid eyes on them since.'

9

Erlendur stood at the Grensásvegur–Miklabraut junction, directing traffic round a three-car pile-up. Two police vehicles and two ambulances had been called to the scene, along with a fire engine to cut an injured driver from the wreckage. An estate car had cannoned into the back of another, smaller vehicle, forcing it through a red light and into the box junction where a van had smacked into its side. The van had been travelling fairly fast, so the car had rebounded into Grensásvegur, where it rolled over. The impact had hurled the driver of the van through the windscreen and he was now lying in his own blood on the tarmac. The driver of the car that had rolled over was still trapped under the steering wheel. Meanwhile, the man who had originally caused the accident was sitting in one of the police vehicles, suspected of driving under the influence. He was bleeding from a gash on his head. His wife too was clearly the worse for wear. Gardar said she was something of a madam: his efforts to prevent her walking away from the scene had resulted in an angry altercation. Blood was trickling from her forehead onto the mink coat draped around her, and she was swaying slightly in her high heels. Finally Gardar persuaded her to accompany him back to where her husband was sitting, shoulders bowed, in police custody.

It was just after midnight on Friday and there was still a fair amount of traffic on the city's main artery. Erlendur's position in the middle of the busy junction was not immediately life threatening, but there was always an element of unpredictability at this hour. Their very first job that evening had been to pull over a drunk driver on Skúlagata after they noticed him changing lanes at breakneck speed. Despite being almost incoherent when they helped him out of the car, he had insisted that he was stone-cold sober, then had passed out en route for a blood test.

The three wrecked vehicles were towed away. Once the ambulances and fire engine had departed as well, they were able to reopen the junction to traffic. Then, as they were driving away, a call came in about a fight at Röðull on Nóatún. A drunk man had attacked a bartender, then started terrorising the other customers before being overpowered by two bouncers, who were now waiting for the police.

When they reached the club, they found a long queue.

'Fancy-dress, is it?' someone called out as they elbowed their way through the throng. They were met by a doorman who showed them through to the kitchen where the troublemaker was lying face down on the floor, restrained by two burly men, while the other staff bustled around them.

'I'll kill you!' the man blustered. 'I'll kill you, you fucking pigs.'

The head bouncer launched into an explanation of what had happened. Refused a tab at the bar, the man had completely lost it and slashed the bartender in the face with a broken glass. The victim had been driven straight to Casualty, spouting blood. The bouncers had recognised the perpetrator as an occasional customer, known for his obnoxious behaviour. They'd thrown him out a couple of times when women had complained about him, but they didn't know his name.

'He's one of those dickheads who walks in here and thinks he owns the place,' said the head doorman. 'It'll be good to get rid of the prick. He's barred from now on.'

Marteinn clicked a pair of handcuffs onto the man's wrists and, with Erlendur's help, hauled him to his feet.

'I'm going to sue those bastards for assault!' the man stormed. His stretch on the kitchen floor had only made him feel more aggrieved. 'They attacked me. Dragged me in here. Threw me on the floor. I'm going to sue them.'

'It's touch and go whether they'll be able to save Kiddi's eye – he's our bartender,' the bouncer told them. 'He'll definitely want to press charges against this tosser.'

Accompanied by a tirade of abuse, they escorted the man outside, through the crowd to the police car. A few of the people in the queue tried to interfere, mouthing off about stupid pigs and police oppression. Inured to such insults, they paid no attention.

Afterwards they took a coffee break at the station. The shift had been no better or worse than usual so far. Car crashes, drunk drivers, bar brawls – it was all part of the job, like the insults of the onlookers.

Much to Erlendur's irritation, Gardar and Marteinn had spent most of the night arguing about the British rock group Slade. They had heard on the news that there was a chance the band might perform live at the Laugardalshöll concert hall that autumn.

Gardar was desperate for tickets. Earlier that summer Procol Harum, one of Marteinn's favourite groups, had played at the University Cinema. He had attended the first of their three gigs and was so blown away that he had been lost for words. He had been humming 'A Whiter Shade of Pale' almost non-stop ever since. But his enthusiasm had fallen on deaf ears, so now when Gardar started going on about Slade, Marteinn was inclined to be scathing.

'Of course, Slade's by far and away the coolest band around,' said Gardar, biting into a *kleina*, or doughnut twist.

'Glam-rock rubbish,' sneered Marteinn. 'They won't last – you won't even remember their name in a few years. Why don't you listen to Procol Harum or something halfway decent like the Stones? They're a serious band. I bet they'll still be rocking when they're fifty!'

'Nah, Slade's the business, man.'

'Isn't Pelican doing the same kind of thing?' asked Erlendur, who took little interest in the music scene but recalled seeing an article in the paper.

'Well, of course, they're way cooler,' said Marteinn. '"Jenny Darling" is pure genius.'

They ended their shift down by the harbour, not far from the slipway, where a man had fallen in the sea. He had been saved in the nick of time by a passer-by who had jumped in after him, and he had now been taken to hospital. His rescuer made light of his own condition as he sat in the police van, soaked to the skin, wrapped in a couple of blankets. He was able to give a clear account of the incident and was far more concerned for the man he had fished out of the harbour than for himself.

'What'll happen to him?' he asked.

'I expect they'll send him home after a check-up,' said Erlendur.

'He's in a bad way.'

'Don't worry, they'll take a look at him.'

'No, I mean mentally. They'd better keep an eye on him.'

'What do you mean?'

'He didn't fall.'

'Oh?'

'No, it wasn't like that. He did it on purpose. He jumped.'

'Are you sure?'

'Sure! He was fighting me the whole time, begging me to let him go. Pleading with me to leave him to die.'

10

During their rare encounters Hannibal hadn't mentioned any relatives, and when Erlendur started asking around about the tramp, he learned that Hannibal never used to talk about his family or his former life. If anyone tried to draw him out he would get angry and accuse them of interfering.

Erlendur discovered in a roundabout way that Hannibal's sister was a married mother of three. She had gone back to work once her children had left home and was now a doctor's receptionist in Reykjavík. There was a brother too who was a building contractor up north in Akureyri, married, with no children. Both were sober, respectable citizens, from what Erlendur could ascertain; in fact the brother was an active member of his local temperance movement, perhaps in an attempt to compensate for Hannibal's lifestyle.

After giving it some thought, Erlendur decided to try to find out more about Hannibal's background from his sister. He rang the surgery, was put through, and, having introduced himself as an acquaintance of her brother's, asked if he could have a word.

'What about?' she asked. He could hear a phone ringing in the background. Reception was obviously busy.

'Your brother Hannibal.'

'What about him?'

'I –'

'Why do you want to discuss him?' She sounded a little flustered. 'Why are you asking me about Hannibal?'

'I knew him slightly. Perhaps I could explain better if you'd spare a minute to meet me.'

'No, you know what, I really don't have time.'

'I'd be grateful if –'

'Look, I'm afraid I don't have time, I've got to take this call.'

'But –'

'Sorry, but I'll have to hang up now. Thank you, goodbye.'

She cut him off.

Erlendur was surprised at this reaction but on reflection he guessed that she had taken him for one of her brother's homeless friends and wanted nothing to do with him. Perhaps he should have been more specific, explained who he was and the nature of his business, put more pressure on her to meet him. It dawned on him that he didn't actually know what his business was, or why he had this urge to learn Hannibal's backstory.

Why was he fixated on the fate of some poor tramp, whom he had, let's face it, only met a handful of times? Was it because he had been first on the scene and personally fished him out of the water that the image was etched on his brain? He had been shocked when he saw who it was, but he shouldn't have been all that surprised to come across Hannibal's body. It was bound to happen sooner or later. The man was in poor shape; after all, he had been living rough, in desperate straits, for years. And his mental state had not been much better. The last time they met, in a cell at the station, Hannibal had spoken of his misery and how he lacked the guts to end to it all.

Was it guilt pushing Erlendur to unearth everything he could about the man? Could he have done more for him, despite Hannibal's rejection of any help or sympathy? No one cared if a vagrant, who was on his last legs anyway, wound up dead. It just meant one less bum on the streets. No one else was asking questions about this man who had drowned like a stray dog. Even the tramp at the Fever Hospital, who had seemed sure that Hannibal's death was no accident, had been fairly flippant about his death.

Or could it be that Hannibal had touched a nerve when he exploded, accusing Erlendur of interfering, and demanded to know why he wouldn't leave him alone?

Whatever it was, something about Hannibal's sad story had captured Erlendur's imagination. His fate, yes, but also his dogged determination to withdraw from human society. Where had this need come from? What had caused it? Erlendur sympathised with his loneliness and mental anguish, and yet there was some element of his character – the uncompromising fact of his existence – that was also strangely alluring. The way he had set himself against life and stood, alone and untouchable, beyond all help.

Still lost in this reverie, Erlendur found himself at the doctor's surgery. It was nearly closing time and there were no more patients in the waiting room. A woman of about forty, with backcombed blonde hair, dressed in a green blouse, a tight skirt and a pretty pearl necklace, was tidying up in reception.

'Rebekka?' he said

'Yes?' The woman glanced up.

'Sorry to bother you, but I rang earlier –'

'Do you have an appointment?'

'No, my name's Erlendur and –'

'We're closed,' she said, 'but I can make an appointment for you if you like. Who's your doctor?'

'I'm not here to see a doctor,' said Erlendur. 'I rang earlier about your brother, Hannibal.'

The woman hesitated. 'Oh,' she said, then carried on putting things away.

'Sorry to be so persistent. But, as I mentioned on the phone, I was acquainted with your brother and wanted to know if you had time for a chat.'

'Were you on the streets with him?' she asked in a low voice.

'Good Lord, no,' said Erlendur. 'I've never been on the streets. In fact, I'm with the police. We had to pick him up from time to time. That's how I knew him.'

'You're a policeman?'

'Yes.'

'I'd rather not discuss him with you, if you don't mind,' she said. 'He's dead. It was a sad story, but it's over now and I don't wish to go over it all again with a stranger.'

'I completely understand,' said Erlendur. 'That was my impression when we spoke on the phone but I just wanted to be sure. My intentions are good, if that's what's worrying you. I'd like to have got to know him better, but he died so suddenly. I was first on the scene and pulled him out. Perhaps that's why I can't get him out of my mind.'

The woman switched off a large electric typewriter. She

52

emerged from the office, locked the door carefully behind her and accompanied Erlendur out onto the pavement.

'Hannibal wasn't a bad man,' she said in parting.

'No, I know that.'

The surgery was on Lækjargata, in the centre of Reykjavík, and the traffic was heavy. Horns blared and people hurried past on their way to the shops or to a cafe or just home after work.

'Can you think of anyone who might have wanted to harm him?' asked Erlendur.

'You didn't know him very well, did you?'

'No, sadly, I –'

'There was only one man who wanted to harm him, and that was Hannibal himself.'

11

Erlendur was about to take a nap before going on duty when the silence was shattered by his phone.

Home for him was a small basement flat in Hlídar. When he'd joined the police he was told he could be called out any time, day or night, so he would need to install a telephone. He hadn't felt the need for one before, but he acquired a clunky black model with a metal dial. In the end, the phone rarely rang in connection with work, unless it was the duty sergeant calling to arrange his shifts, but from time to time some of the other officers would call to invite him along to a film or a night out. Neither really appealed to him, but he sometimes let himself be talked into joining them. He took no pleasure in drinking; at most he might sip at a small glass of green Chartreuse. Occasionally they would stop by his place on their way to a nightclub and try to drag him along, but he was usually reluctant. Staying in to read, listen to the radio or play records was more to his taste. He had purchased a decent hi-fi and built up quite a collection of albums, mostly European and American jazz. He also enjoyed Icelandic folk songs and works by his favourite poets, Tómas Guðmundsson, Davíð Stefánsson and Steinn Steinarr, set to music.

Similarly, when it came to eating, his preference was for plain, traditional fare: boiled fish – haddock or cod – with potatoes. Or roast lamb on special occasions. In the evenings he usually dined at Skúlakaffi, a cafeteria popular with workmen and lorry drivers, which served Icelandic home cooking. Lamb chops in breadcrumbs had been a staple of the menu ever since the place opened.

From Erlendur's flat one could enter the garden via the communal laundry, and there, just outside the door, he preserved traditional delicacies – brisket, liver sausage and whale blubber, supplied by a local shopkeeper – in a small bucket of sour whey. Erlendur topped up the bucket on a regular basis. He often got into arguments about eating habits with Gardar, who was a big fan of American fast food. To Erlendur, all Gardar's impassioned talk of pizzas and hamburgers was gibberish.

He answered the phone and was taken aback to hear Rebekka's voice. Given that she had said a rather curt goodbye before walking off, he had not been expecting to hear from her again.

'I got your number from the police station,' she said. 'I hope you don't mind.'

'No, of course not,' Erlendur replied. 'I'm ex-directory.'

'So they told me. They were a bit reluctant to pass it on.'

'Thanks for ringing, anyway.'

'I've been thinking about what you said.'

'Oh?'

'Why did you ask if I knew of anyone who might have wanted to harm my brother? What did you mean by that?'

'Just wondering if he had any enemies that you were aware of.'

'Well, I know his life wasn't easy,' said Rebekka, 'but my brother wasn't one to make trouble. That would have been out of character. Were you implying that it wasn't an accident? His death, I mean?'

'Oh, no, it seems more than likely that it was, but the world he was living in can be pretty unforgiving. He may not have made trouble, as you put it, but I get the feeling he wasn't afraid to speak his mind to people. And I know he never wanted to be beholden to anyone.'

'No, he was always like that. He could be incredibly bloody-minded.'

'Yes.'

'I hadn't had any contact with him over the last few years,' she said, 'so I don't know exactly what he was doing with himself or who he was mixing with. You'd probably know more about that.'

'Not really. He kept himself to himself. Hung out with a few other people in similar circumstances, but I don't think he saw anyone else. He didn't stay in touch with his family, then?'

'He just disappeared from our lives,' said Rebekka. 'I don't know how else to describe it. It happened so suddenly. Vanished from our lives and lost himself in some kind of no-man's-land.'

She fell silent.

'We tried to help, but he wasn't having any of it. My other brother, the older one, quickly gave up on him. Said he was a lost cause. I . . . Hannibal didn't want to hear from us. We belonged to a world he'd turned his back on – that he was doing his best to avoid.'

'That sort of thing can be hard to cope with,' said Erlendur.

'Well, I refuse to feel guilty about it,' she said. 'I tried everything I could think of to help him get his act together. But he said he wasn't interested. Said I didn't understand. The last time I managed to get through to him he sobered up for two or three months. That was eight, nine years ago. Then he hit the bottle again and after that he really was a lost cause.'

'So your other brother wasn't in contact with him either?'

'No.'

'They didn't have any unfinished business?'

'What are you suggesting?'

'No, I simply –'

'Are you insinuating that he might have attacked Hannibal?'

'No, of course not. I'm simply trying to work out what happened.'

'My brother lives up north. In Akureyri. He wasn't even in Reykjavík when Hannibal died.'

'I see. Look, I really didn't mean to insinuate anything.'

There was an awkward pause.

'You're the only person who's ever asked about Hannibal,' Rebekka said at last. 'Ever shown the slightest interest in him. I should have been more polite, but you took me by surprise. I was a bit thrown, to be honest. If you like, I could meet you one day after work.'

'That would be great.'

They said goodbye and a few minutes later the phone rang again. This time it was Halldóra.

'I just wanted to hear your voice,' she said.

'Yes, sorry, I've been meaning to get in touch.'

'Busy?'

'Yes, you lose track of time on night duty. How are you?'

'Fine. I wanted to tell you . . . I've applied for a new job.'

'Oh?'

'At the telephone company.'

'That'd be good, wouldn't it?'

'I think so. As an operator on the international switchboard.'

'Think you'll get it?'

'I reckon I'm in with a chance,' said Halldóra. 'Why don't we meet up? Go into town?'

'Yes, let's.'

'I'll give you a call.'

'All right.'

After they had rung off, Erlendur took a book from the shelf and, hoping to manage a quick snooze before work, settled himself on the sofa. When he was in his teens, and bored with life in the city, he had taken to browsing in antiquarian bookshops. One day he had chanced upon a series of volumes recently acquired from a house clearance, a collection of true stories about people going missing or getting lost on their travels in Iceland. Some had survived to tell of their own ordeals, but there were also second-hand accounts of incredible feats of endurance or of tragic surrender to the forces of nature. Erlendur had not realised that such tales existed in print. He devoured the entire series and ever since then he had been collecting books, and anything else he could find, about human suffering in shipwrecks, avalanches or on the old roads that crossed the Icelandic wilderness. He either tracked these works down in bookshops or was tipped off by dealers when they received books, papers, even private correspondence, reports or eyewitness accounts on the subject. He bought them all without haggling and had built up an impressive library of material from around the country, though he still kept an eye out for new publications. The sheer amount published on the subject surprised him. The stories belonged to an older way of life, before the city began its sprawl and the villages grew at the expense of isolated farming communities; yet clearly they still resonated with Icelanders. The traditional farming society had not vanished entirely, merely found a new home.

Many of the accounts were of people who lost their way in violent storms and whose remains were not found for months, years, decades even. Some were never found. Rebekka's words about her brother still echoed in Erlendur's ears: *he just disappeared from our lives.* Erlendur understood what she meant. As he thought about Hannibal he reflected that people could just as easily lose themselves on Reykjavík's busy streets as on remote mountain paths in winter storms.

Feeling drowsy, he laid aside the book. His thoughts shifted to the Reykjavík nights, so strangely sunny and bright, yet in another sense so dark and desperate. Night after night he and his fellow officers patrolled the city in the lumbering police van, witnessing human dramas that were hidden from others. Some the night provoked and seduced; others it wounded and terrified. As he was far from nocturnal himself, it had been an adjustment to leave the world of day and enter that of night, but once he was there, he found he did not mind it. In those hours, more than at any other time, he became reconciled to the city, when its streets were finally empty and quiet, with no sound but the wind and the low chugging of the engine.

12

When Erlendur arrived, the owner of the house was standing by the cellar steps, smoking a battered pipe. A large trailer, hooked to an ancient, beaten-up Soviet jeep, had been reversed up to the door. It was half full of rubbish. The man was sixtyish, red-faced, with small eyes and a sizeable paunch, clad in a grey jumper and threadbare jeans, a grubby flat cap on his head. His pipe was clamped between strong teeth, giving his lips a pale, bluish hue. He looked like a manual labourer. His name, Erlendur knew since Hannibal had mentioned it, was Frímann. Landlord was perhaps too grand a title, since Hannibal had paid no rent in return for dossing in the cellar. On the other hand, benefactor would be putting it too strongly, as the basement was barely habitable, though Hannibal had made himself as comfortable as he could down there. Erlendur greeted the man.

'Come to look round the house?' asked Frímann, knocking the pipe out in his hand.

'No. Is it for sale?'

'For the right price,' said Frímann, as if he held the keys to a palace. In fact, his house was little more than a wooden shack, clad with corrugated iron that had once been painted blue. Above the basement were the main living area and a tiny attic, and the whole place was in need of drastic renovation.

'Is the cellar included?'

'Of course. It's a good size. I just need to clear out this damn rubbish. Lord knows where it all comes from.'

'I'm not looking for a house,' said Erlendur, surveying the trailer. 'I'm here to ask about a tramp who used to live in your cellar. Name of Hannibal.'

'Hannibal?'

'That's the one.'

'What's Hannibal to you?'

'I used to know him,' explained Erlendur.

'Then you'll be aware that he's dead,' said Frímann, shoving the pipe in the pocket of his shirt under his jumper.

'Yes. He came to a sad end, I know. You let him sleep in your cellar?'

'He wasn't in anyone's way.'

'How did you know each other?'

'Used to work on a boat together donkey's years ago.' Frímann prepared to descend the steps for another load of junk.

'Can I help with that?' asked Erlendur.

Frímann regarded him in surprise.

'Are you really offering?'

'If you like.'

Frímann hesitated a moment, trying to get the measure of this young stranger.

'If you wouldn't mind.'

'I came by with Hannibal while he was living here,' said Erlendur, 'so I know you've got quite a job on your hands.'

'I've made three trips to the tip already,' said Frímann, 'but you can hardly see any difference. It's not all my stuff, mind. I've been storing a load of useless junk for people who never came back for it. And some was left by the previous owners – worthless rubbish. Other bits have ended up here; I've no idea where from, though I suspect Hannibal hoarded some of it.'

The cellar was marginally tidier than the last time Erlendur had visited. Hannibal's mattress was gone, along with the ragged blanket he had used to cover himself; the *brennivín* and methylated spirits bottles had been cleared away; even the stench had dissipated somewhat, although it still lingered. Beside the entrance, the ceiling beams and part of the door jamb were black with soot.

Erlendur rolled up his sleeves and started helping to cart things outside. In no time they had filled the trailer.

'He lived in such damn squalor,' said Frímann when Erlendur brought the conversation back round to Hannibal. 'That was one of the reasons why I wanted rid of him. Apart from that you'd hardly have known he was there. Not that I came by often.'

'So you don't live in the house yourself?'

'No.'

'Did the tenants complain about him?'

'Never heard a peep from them. But then they used to hit the bottle fairly hard themselves. A couple, from down south. They didn't look after the place either, so in the end I chucked them out and decided to sell while I could still get something for it. Haven't been able to do it up. Can't afford to.'

Frímann lit his pipe again, looked over at the trailer and said he'd shifted enough bloody rubbish for one day. He would continue tomorrow and hopefully finish it off then.

'Thanks for your help, young man.'

'You're welcome,' said Erlendur. 'The fishing boat you both worked on – was it harboured here in Reykjavík?'

'No, Grindavík.'

'But Hannibal was from Reykjavík, wasn't he?'

'Yes, he was.'

'Do you know anything about his family?'

'No. He used to talk about his mother from time to time, but I don't know if he had any brothers or sisters.'

'One brother, one sister. His parents died years ago.'

'Well, he never mentioned any brother or sister.'

'Any idea why he ended up like that?' asked Erlendur.

'You mean, why he drowned?'

'No, I meant –'

'Wasn't he just plastered as usual?'

'Probably,' conceded Erlendur. 'I suppose what I'm really asking is if you know why he ended up on the streets?'

'Is there any simple reason why people go off the rails?' asked Frímann. 'Obviously, he was an alcoholic. And he could be . . . Hannibal was a strange mixture. He could be as nice as pie, but his temper often landed him in trouble. I remember when we were on the boat, he drank so heavily he lost his job in the end. He couldn't be trusted. Got into fights. Missed departures. Gave too much lip. Why are men the way they are? Search me.'

'I see there was a fire.' Erlendur indicated the scorched beams.

'That's why I sent him packing in the end,' said Frímann. 'I was always scared to death something like that would happen. Told him to take his stuff and get lost. Next thing I heard, he was dead.'

'Know if he had any enemies?'

'The police asked me that at the time and I told them I hadn't a clue. Surely he was drunk, fell in and couldn't get out again?'

'Suppose so.'

'Well, better be off to the tip,' said Frímann, knocking out his pipe again.

'How did the fire start?' asked Erlendur, refusing to give up. 'Hannibal alleged it was arson, aimed at him.'

'Typical,' said Frímann, opening the door of the jeep. 'He claimed he was asleep and woke up all of a sudden to see flames over by the door, so he went and put them out. Swore he'd single-handedly saved the house from burning down. But it wasn't quite like that. The couple upstairs were out but the brothers next door saw smoke pouring from the cellar window and ran over. They found Hannibal out for the count. It's mainly thanks to them things didn't turn out worse. They woke him up and got him out. Said he was smashed out of his skull. They found the remains of a candle stub by the door. He must have kicked it over into some rubbish.'

'Didn't they call the fire brigade?'

'No.'

'So there was no inquiry into what happened?'

'No. Inquiry? What for? The brothers called me. There was no point in making a big deal out of it. But I didn't want Hannibal living here any more in case he sent the whole place up in smoke, so I threw him out.'

'How did he take it?'

'Badly,' said Frímann. 'Swore blind he wasn't to blame. That someone had done it deliberately – tried to bump him off.'

'And who's it supposed to have been?'

'Who what?'

'Started it.'

'No one,' said Frímann. 'It was bullshit. The ravings of a drunk. He was trying to lie his way out of trouble, as usual. That's all.'

Their shift was uneventful; a quiet Wednesday night in the city. As they drove west along Miklabraut, Gardar started on about food – or the lack of it – as he usually did when he was hungry.

'For example, why are there no decent pizza places in Reykjavík?' he asked in an aggrieved tone, as if it were the most ridiculous situation he'd ever heard of. An already thickening waistline testified to the amount of time he devoted to thinking about his stomach. Recently he had spent two weeks in the States with his parents, which had only intensified his obsession with fast food.

'Isn't there anywhere in town that sells them?' asked Marteinn.

'A "pisser" place?' said Erlendur. 'Do you mean those Italian pies?'

'Pies . . .? No, seriously,' said Gardar. 'It's hard enough even to find somewhere that does burgers and fries. There are only maybe a couple of places. I'm telling you, it's so backward.'

'There used to be an all-night truckstop at Geitháls,' pointed out Marteinn.

'They did pretty good sheep's heads,' said Erlendur.

'With mashed swede,' added Marteinn.

'This is exactly what I'm talking about. What kind of takeaway is that? Mashed swede! Anyway, Geitháls is miles away. Why don't they get their act together here in town?'

'I quite liked Geitháls,' said Erlendur with a smile.

'Who buys sheep's heads at a drive-in?' asked Gardar indignantly. 'We need burger joints and proper pizza places. A bit of culture! If I had the money I'd open one myself. God, I'd make a killing.'

'On "pissers"?' said Erlendur. 'I don't know . . .'

'*Pizzas*, Erlendur! At least try to say it right. Fast food tastes great and it's incredibly convenient. Cheap too. Saves you the bother of having to cook haddock and boiled potatoes all the time. And you don't have to go to a smart restaurant like Naustid. The Yanks have got it sorted. They get their pizzas delivered to them at home. You don't even need to go to the restaurant. You just ring and order everything you want and they send it round.'

An alert came over the radio: a man had been found lying beside the road near Nauthólsvík cove. They responded that they were in the area, and Gardar switched on the flashing lights. They arrived to find a patrol car already there and an ambulance just pulling up. A middle-aged couple walking to Nauthólsvík had spotted the man lying face down in the grass about three metres from the roadside. He had not reacted when they called out to him and, on taking a closer look, they had realised he must be dead, so they had hurried over to Hótel Loftleidir and reported their discovery.

The ambulance turned out to be unnecessary as the man was indeed dead and had been for some time. A hearse was sent for instead. All the evidence suggested that he had collapsed where he was found. There were no signs of a fight, no visible injuries; the grass nearby had not been flattened. The man had simply clutched at his chest with both hands and crumpled where he stood. The doctor who was called to the scene gave a provisional verdict of heart attack.

The body was that of a homeless man who had found

temporary refuge in a dilapidated Second World War Nissen hut in Nauthólsvík. Erlendur recognised him straight away, though he couldn't remember his name. A few days earlier they had spoken briefly outside the Fever Hospital. This was the man who had claimed that Hannibal was deliberately drowned in Kringlumýri.

Erlendur identified him by the thick winter coat and hat, the filthy hands, and, when they turned him over to carry him to the hearse, the lines chiselled in his face, deep as the crevasses in an ice cap.

The cellar door had been fitted with a new padlock. No lights showed on the floor above. A small notice stuck in the window read: *For sale*. Erlendur took hold of the padlock: it had been snapped shut. Abandoning it, he went in search of a gap to squeeze through and eventually managed to force open a small window round the back of the house. It was dark inside but Erlendur had brought along a little torch and its feeble glow lit up the walls.

Frímann had done a thorough job of clearing out the rubbish. The cellar was nearly empty and the floor had been swept: it looked almost presentable.

Erlendur directed the torch beam at the area by the door and hunted for clues as to how the fire could have started. There was no mains supply or fuse box down there, only the wire to the overhead light by the entrance, so it was unlikely that an electrical fault had been the cause. Judging by the soot on the walls and ceiling beams, there must have been quite a blaze by the time the brothers from next door had arrived to put it out.

Erlendur ran his hand over the soot marks and tapped the tinder-dry wood. Presumably it was too late now to establish how the fire had started and spread to the beams. Although Hannibal had denied all responsibility, he may not have been sober enough to remember.

But if Hannibal were to be believed, some other person had been at work, had lifted the latch, pushed open the cellar door, tiptoed a foot or two inside and held a candle flame to the litter on the floor. It would have taken no time at all to ignite the rubbish then slip away.

But what would have been the point? Did the perpetrator know Hannibal was in there? Was the intention to kill him? Or did the arson have nothing whatsoever to do with Hannibal? The cellar was an easy target with its timber partitions and thick wooden beams. If the neighbours had not spotted the blaze straight away, the house would have been reduced to ashes in the blink of an eye.

The brothers had assumed that the candle stub must have rolled into the doorway from Hannibal's lair. But Erlendur hadn't noticed any candles there on his previous visits.

The second time he had escorted Hannibal back to his cellar, Erlendur had been on the beat in town and had run into the tramp on Hafnarstræti, not far from his home. Hannibal had looked rougher than ever, limping and battered, so Erlendur went over and asked if he was all right.

'I'm fine.' Clearly Hannibal wanted nothing to do with the cops.

'You're limping,' Erlendur pointed out. 'Let me help you.'

The other man stared at him bemused, as if unused to such kindness.

'We've met before, haven't we?'

'I accompanied you home from Arnarhóll the other day. You were lying under the Tin.'

'Oh, that was you, was it, mate?' said Hannibal. 'Did I ever thank you properly?'

'Yes, you did. Are you on your way home now?' asked Erlendur.

'Give us a hand then, would you?' said Hannibal. 'There's something wrong with my leg. You haven't by any chance got any booze on you?'

'No. Come on, I'll take you. It's not far.'

'A few krónur, then?'

Erlendur took his arm, walked him home and saw him safely inside to his mattress. Hannibal kept pestering him for a drink or some spare change, and eventually Erlendur slipped him a few coins. Feeling the tramp's frozen fingers, he asked if he had any means of warming himself down there – a candle even.

'No,' Hannibal had answered flatly.

'Why not?'

'I'm scared to death I'll burn the bloody house down.'

13

The name of the tramp found in Nauthólsvík turned out to be Ólafur. The post-mortem had confirmed the cause of death as a heart attack and the police saw no reason to treat the circumstances as suspicious. His closest relative was an elder sister who lived in the countryside and had not been in touch with him for years. She had requested that his body be sent to her for burial in the family plot.

During his conversation with Erlendur outside the Fever Hospital, Ólafur had mentioned one of Hannibal's acquaintances, Bergmundur, who had recently fallen off the wagon and could usually be found hanging out in Austurvöllur Square. Not having come across this Bergmundur before, Erlendur wasn't having much luck as he wandered round town in search of him. The weather was perfect, sunny and still, and the streets were teeming with shoppers. On fine days like this boozers and vagrants gathered to lounge on the benches in the square, knocking back meths, illegally distilled spirits with a variety of mixers, or cardamom extract, basking in the warmth and bickering among themselves or shouting insults at passers-by. If there was a woman among their ranks, she would generally be forced to defend her virtue with foul-mouthed vitriol.

Erlendur raised his eyes to the statue of the independence hero Jón Sigurðsson, who stood in the middle of the square, back turned to the outcasts. He wondered if that's how Jón really would have felt about them and smiled at the thought, though in fact he did not believe the man had been a snob. In the grassy hollow behind the statue sat a disreputable-looking young man with a downy beard, wearing a peasant smock, Jesus sandals and a huge pair of what Erlendur took to be women's sunglasses.

'Seen Bergmundur around?' Erlendur asked casually, as if he were well acquainted with this crowd.

'Bergmundur?' repeated the young man, turning the outsize shades towards him.

'Yes, he's back on the booze.' It was all Erlendur knew about the man.

'Bergmundur, you mean? He was in town yesterday.'

'Seen him today at all?'

'Nope.'

'Was he dry for long?'

'No, not long; didn't last,' said the young man, as if it had been a foregone conclusion.

'Know where I can find him?'

'He lives with a couple of other guys in a condemned house on Hverfisgata.'

Out of the corner of his eye Erlendur spotted an old friend of the law, a thug and small-time crook called Ellidi. He was mixed up in alcohol smuggling and other minor-league stuff, including burglary, and had also served time at Litla-Hraun for grievous bodily harm. With him was a man Erlendur didn't recognise. He watched them walking from bench to bench as if searching for someone. Ellidi took a swig from a bottle that he kept inside his jacket, then passed it round. He made a comment and brayed with raucous laughter at his own joke.

'He hangs out on Arnarhóll too sometimes, under the Tin,' added the young man with the sunglasses.

Ellidi, catching sight of Erlendur, stopped dead and stared at him. They had already crossed paths twice since Erlendur had joined the police. On the first occasion a fight had been reported at a house in the Breidholt district. Ellidi had put a man in hospital, but the victim had refused to press charges on the grounds that it was his own fault. Ellidi had merely been detained overnight at Hverfisgata. Later Erlendur learned that the victim had owed Ellidi money for a consignment of alcohol. On the second occasion, he and his fellow officers had picked Ellidi up for speeding in the vicinity of the container harbour at Sundahöfn. He had tried to make a break for it but they had pulled him over and found a hundred and fifty cartons of American cigarettes and several gallons of American vodka in his car. Ellidi, who was drunk and high at the time, had first threatened to kill them all, then decked Marteinn. At that point reinforcements had arrived, and they overpowered Ellidi, but only after a considerable struggle.

'Well, if it isn't the country bumpkin,' Ellidi said now with a smirk as he approached. He was big and brawny; his lower lip was swollen and he had a plaster over one eye. 'What are you doing here?'

Erlendur could smell the spirits on his breath. Ellidi brandished the bottle in his face.

'Looking for a drink, are you?' he sneered. 'There's more where this comes from, if you're interested.'

'He was asking questions about Bergmundur,' said the man with the sunglasses, rising to his feet, his gaze fixed on the bottle.

'Bergmundur? What do you want with him? Has he been a bad boy?'

'No,' said Erlendur.

'Wasn't he on the wagon?' asked Ellidi.

'Just fallen off,' said the young man with the shades.

Ellidi handed him the bottle. 'Seen Holberg around?'

'No,' said the young man, taking a long pull.

'Grétar?'

'No, haven't seen him either.' He took another large gulp.

Ellidi snatched the bottle back.

'Hey, don't hold back, shithead.' He gave the young man a violent shove.

'I was supposed to meet them here,' Ellidi announced to Erlendur. 'If you think I'm a fucking head-case, you should meet Holberg. Grétar and him . . . they make a lovely couple.'

This last comment was accompanied by a low, rasping laugh. Erlendur moved on and, watching his progress, Ellidi cackled again.

'Country bumpkin!' he shouted. 'Sheep shagger!'

Erlendur finally found Bergmundur up by the Swedish fish factory. A group of men were sitting with their backs to the perimeter fence, soaking up the sunshine, sharing a bottle they had managed to get hold of and puffing away. One had stripped off his shirt, his corpse-like pallor blindingly white in the sun.

Erlendur asked if they knew where Bergmundur was. At this,

one of them spoke up, saying he was Bergmundur and wanting to know who was asking. He was middle-aged, fairly robust, and looked marginally less disreputable than his companions. Erlendur shook his hand and asked if they could have a word in private. The man had no objection, so he walked with Erlendur to the benches by the statue of Ingólfur Arnarson, Iceland's first settler. They took a seat overlooking the centre of town. Bergmundur pulled out a bottle of meths and took a slug.

'That was the last of them,' he remarked. 'They're reluctant to sell it to us at the chemist's nowadays. They'd only let me buy one bottle at the shop on Laugavegur. One per chemist, that's the new rule. You have to traipse all over town to get enough.'

'Did you know Ólafur – the bloke who died the other day?' asked Erlendur. 'He used to bunk down in an old Nissen hut in Nauthólsvík.'

'Óli a friend of yours, was he?' Bergmundur screwed the cap back on the meths and returned it to his pocket. 'Didn't think he had any.'

'I ran into him recently and he told me you used to know Hannibal.'

'Sure, I knew Hannibal. He drowned last year. But maybe you already knew that?'

'Yes, I did. Do you remember when his cellar caught fire? It was shortly before he died.'

'Got him kicked out.'

'Yes, the owner thought it was his fault.'

'Maybe he was right,' said Bergmundur. 'I wouldn't know.'

'What did Hannibal think happened?'

'That someone else started it – he was clear about that. Whether it was true, I don't know.'

'Who's supposed to have done it?'

'They'd sell more to you,' Bergmundur said, digressing.

'More what?'

'Bottles.' He dug out the methylated spirits again.

'You mean you want me to buy you meths?'

'You can buy five at a time if you want. You're no alky.'

'Do you have the money?'

'Thought you might shell out for a few bottles. Five would do the trick.'

'Did Hannibal tell you who started the fire?'

'He had his suspicions.'

'But did he know the culprit? Was it someone he hung around with? Another tramp, for example?'

'Culprits, you mean. And they weren't tramps.'

'So there was more than one person?'

'He reckoned it was the brothers next door.'

'The brothers next door . . .?'

'Don't know their names or anything,' said Bergmundur. 'All I know is that there were two brothers who lived next door. He insisted they'd started the fire and then blamed it on him.'

Erlendur thought of the couple who had lived upstairs from Hannibal. They had heard the same story: that the brothers were behind the arson.

'Reckon you could go to the chemist for me?' Bergmundur persevered.

'Why would they have wanted to burn down the cellar? Did Hannibal have any idea?'

'A few bottles and we'll be quits. Five'll do.'

'Quits? I don't owe you anything.'

'Yeah, well, have it your way.' Bergmundur made as if to leave.

'I can't be doing with this. You'll just have to find some other sucker to answer your questions.'

'All right, all right,' said Erlendur impatiently. 'I'll go to the chemist for you. Keep your hair on.'

'They wanted to get rid of him. Used to complain about him to the owner, who was a friend of Hannibal's and let him sleep there. The brothers wanted him gone. According to Hannibal, anyway. He said he never even dared keep matches down there. Too scared. The brothers set fire to some junk by the door while he was asleep, then pretended they'd saved the day. They wanted Hannibal thrown out there and then, so the owner gave him his marching orders.'

'Did he have any proof of this?'

'Proof! What are you talking about? Proof?'

'I mean –'

'Hannibal was sure,' said Bergmundur firmly. 'There was no one else in the picture. You think he went out and bought a magnifying glass? Hunted for clues like a bloody detective?'

'When did he tell you this?'

'Shortly before he died. We were sat up here by the Tin. Hannibal was positive. I reckon they were out to get him and succeeded in the end. Wouldn't surprise me.'

'Drowned him, you mean?'

'Wouldn't surprise me. He said they were ugly customers.'

'Ólafur believed Hannibal had been deliberately drowned.'

'There you are, then.'

'But that's all he knew. Why would they have wanted Hannibal dead?'

'Because he knew they were behind the fire?' Bergmundur suggested. 'Search me. Maybe he had something else on them.'

'You mean they wanted to silence him?'

'Of course, why not? It's not unheard of. Hannibal had something on them, so they bumped him off.'

The rumble of traffic carried to them from below. Erlendur gazed out over the harbour and beyond to Faxaflói Bay, where the Akranes ferry was coming in to shore.

'Wouldn't you rather I just bought you some *brennivín*?' he asked, reluctant to go to the chemist for the man.

'No,' said Bergmundur after a moment's consideration. 'Make it meths.'

A few minutes later Erlendur found himself on Laugavegur in Bergmundur's company, headed for the nearest chemist's. On the way he tried to come up with an excuse for purchasing a bulk order of methylated spirits that would not arouse suspicion. While Bergmundur waited outside, he hurried in and asked for five bottles of the stuff. The sales assistant hesitated before fetching them, and watched with a censorious expression as he counted out the coins. Erlendur was sure she had him down as recently lapsed.

14

The brothers who used to live next door to Hannibal had found themselves more salubrious accommodation on Fálkagata. Erlendur had obtained their names from Frímann. He decided to pay them a visit the day after his meeting with Bergmundur, combining it with a stroll along Ægisída, on the city's western shore, to enjoy the salty evening air. Since his plan was to drop by unannounced, he thought he stood the best chance of catching them directly after supper. He was right. When he arrived they had just settled down to watch the news. Ellert and Vignir were both around forty, born no more than two years apart, though they looked nothing like each other. One was stocky and ungainly with coarse features; the other tall and lean with finer features, yet it seemed they were inseparable. Frímann thought they both worked as carpenters or builders. As far as he knew, in the seven years they had been his neighbours no woman had ever darkened their door.

Vignir, the stocky one, answered Erlendur's knock. He did not appear unduly surprised to receive an unexpected visit, as if the brothers were used to having their evenings disturbed. Erlendur introduced himself as an acquaintance of Hannibal, their old neighbour – if that was the right word – who had died suddenly about a year ago, and wondered if he could ask them a few questions about him.

By the time Erlendur had finished Ellert had joined his brother in the doorway. They exchanged glances.

'Will it take long?' asked Ellert.

'No, not long, I only have a couple of questions.'

'We were just about to watch *Ironside*.' Vignir ushered him in. 'Never miss it.'

'Oh no, shouldn't be a problem,' said Erlendur, unsure what he was referring to. 'I won't stay long.'

The television set in the sitting room looked brand new. The news had finished and a nature programme was starting. The entire time the brothers were talking to Erlendur they kept one eye on the box, as if resenting every minute they missed of the broadcast.

'We've just bought a new set,' said Vignir.

'Our old one was on its last legs,' added his brother.

It emerged that they'd barely interacted with Hannibal. Not that they had anything against a tramp living next door. He had rarely been home, except now and then to sleep. Frímann had asked them if they minded his taking refuge there, and the brothers had made no objection. Hannibal was no trouble; he never made any noise or had any guests, male or female, so, to cut a long story short, they'd had no reason to complain.

'He never brought any bums home with him,' said Vignir.

'No, not that I noticed,' agreed Ellert.

'Though there was no lock on the door,' Erlendur pointed out, 'so anyone could have walked in.'

'Actually there used to be a padlock,' said Vignir, 'but I gather Hannibal lost the key one night and had to break in.'

'We had nothing to do with the guy,' said Ellert.

'Frímann seems to have been very easygoing,' remarked Erlendur.

The brothers did not reply. They were watching, fascinated, as a lioness sank her claws into an antelope. They were seated in twin armchairs, parked directly in front of the television, their faces lit up by the glare.

'Bloody hell, look at that,' exclaimed Vignir as the pride began to rip the antelope apart.

Erlendur did not like to interrupt, so for several minutes the three of them sat there, intent on the events unfolding on screen. The sitting room was small and carpeted, furnished with book-shelves but few ornaments. The whole flat appeared to be very tidy. From where he was sitting, Erlendur could see into a compact kitchen. He wondered idly whether they took it in turns to cook or shared the housework. He might as well have been visiting a contented married couple.

'What was that?' asked Vignir when the lions had finally had their fill.

'Oh, I was asking about Frímann,' said Erlendur. 'Any idea why he's selling the house?'

'Obviously skint,' said Ellert.

'Probably needs the money,' agreed Vignir.

'But do you know why?'

'No,' said Ellert.

'What happened the night the house caught fire?'

'The guy nearly burnt it down,' said Vignir. 'If we'd gone to bed, there's no telling what would have happened. The whole place would have gone up in smoke. But luckily we were still up.'

'The broadcast went on quite late that evening,' said Ellert. 'Probably saved his life.' His eyes flickered back to the box.

'I smelt burning,' elaborated Vignir. 'Looked out of the window, only to see smoke coming from the basement. We ran out and by then flames were blazing up inside the door. Fortunately, though, the fire hadn't caught hold, so we were able to put it out Ellert burnt his hand.'

'It was nothing serious,' said Ellert. 'We pulled Hannibal out. He was coughing his guts up but was all right apart from that.'

'Did he know how it started?'

'We never got a chance to ask,' said Vignir. 'He just staggered away as if it had nothing to do with him. Don't know if he ever came back after that.'

'He was pissed,' said Ellert with conviction.

'Smashed out of his skull,' confirmed his brother.

'And you didn't call the fire brigade?'

'What for? The fire was out. And the damage wasn't that bad. We rang Frímann, and he came over but didn't call the police or anything. Just said it was an unfortunate accident. Immediately assumed it was Hannibal's fault. Must have banned him from ever coming back.'

'The couple who lived upstairs were out,' prompted Erlendur.

'Yes, apparently.'

'So you believe Hannibal somehow kicked a candle over and that's how the fire started.'

'Well, we found a stub by the door in a load of rubbish, card-board and so on' said Ellert. 'So it seemed a likely explanation.'

'Were you aware of Hannibal using candles down there?'

'How would I know?' said Ellert. 'I never went inside. Like I said, I didn't know the guy.'

'Neither did I,' said Vignir.

'Did it occur to you that someone might have started the fire deliberately – to harm Hannibal?'

'Well, if they did, they'd only have had to reach inside the door,' said Ellert, becoming restless now that the nature programme was finishing and *Ironside* was on next.

'Who knew he lived there?'

'Haven't a clue,' said Ellert. 'No one ever came to see him. At least, not that we were aware of.'

A popular furniture advertisement came on and the brothers were instantly transfixed. A woman's hand caressed a plastic tabletop. 'Is this marble?' the voiceover asked. 'No, Formica,' came the cooing reply. Cupboard doors were opened. 'Is this hardwood?' 'No, Formica.'

'But Hannibal was afraid of fire,' objected Erlendur. 'I know he was scared to use candles because he was terrified of exactly that kind of accident. I don't believe he'd have lit a candle, let alone knocked one over, drunk or sober.'

'Oh?' grunted Vignir distractedly.

'It's starting,' said Ellert, gesturing at the screen.

The brothers gave it their undivided attention.

'So you never fell out with Hannibal?'

'About what?'

'About anything he was up to. Or you were up to, for that matter.'

'No.' Vignir turned to look at him. 'What are you implying?'

Erlendur hesitated, uncertain how far he should go in making accusations based only on hearsay. Besides, he was there in a private capacity and needed to tread carefully; he didn't know how to play this, had no experience of detective work. To the brothers he was nothing more than an annoying bloke butting in on their quiet night at home.

'I've heard he blamed you for the fire,' he said at last.

'That's a lie,' retorted Ellert.

'Bollocks,' snorted his brother.

'That he had something on you that –'

'What do you mean? He had nothing on us,' said Ellert. 'Look, we didn't even know the man. Someone's been having you on, mate.'

'So you deny it?'

'It's total bullshit,' said Ellert. 'I hope you're not going around spreading this kind of shit.'

'No, I'm not.' Erlendur rose to his feet. 'Well, I'd better not take up any more of your time. Thanks, and sorry to bother you.'

'No problem,' said Vignir. 'Sorry we couldn't be any more help.'

'Is he in a wheelchair?' Erlendur blurted out as the credits rolled and the main character appeared. He was unfamiliar with the programme as he did not own a television himself.

'Yes, it really holds him back,' Vignir replied earnestly.

They did not see him out but remained riveted to the screen. Erlendur walked home in the light evening breeze, marvelling that the brothers were more interested in gawping at the fictitious crimes of an American TV series than discussing a mysterious incident in their own lives, an incident that had nearly resulted in the death of a man they knew.

15

Erlendur was sound asleep when the phone started ringing. Shrill and insistent, it echoed through the flat until finally he dragged himself to his feet and answered it. The man on the other end sounded distinctly agitated.

'Is that Erlendur Sveinsson?' he demanded brusquely.

'Yes, that's me.'

'I've just been talking to my sister Rebekka. She told me about your conversations and what you said about me and I wanted to tell you that it's outrageous! To imply . . . to imply I harmed my brother Hannibal is insane and if you keep spreading lies like that I'll be forced to take action. How dare you suggest that? How dare you!'

The brother, Erlendur thought.

'I won't have you poking your nose into something that's none of your business,' the man went on. 'And as for spreading lies about me, it's downright disgusting.'

'But I don't believe I have,' Erlendur objected.

'No? That's not what it sounds like to me.'

'Everything I discussed with your sister was in strict confidence. The thing is, I knew your brother a little and I want to find out how he ended up drowning like that.'

'You're interfering in a painful family matter that has nothing whatsoever to do with you and I want you to stop,' said the man. 'Right now! Rebekka told me you're a junior officer and have no involvement with the inquiry. I'll complain to your superiors if you don't stop.'

'Actually, Rebekka was keen to help,' said Erlendur.

'What do you mean?'

'We had a long talk which, let me stress, was in complete confidence. I don't know what she told you but if you're under the impression I was disrespectful then I must apologise. I'd very much like to meet you and discuss the matter in person. If you'd be interested.'

'Meet me? Out of the question! You can leave me alone. And leave my sister alone too. This is none of your business. I repeat, none!'

'Hannibal was –'

Before Erlendur could finish the man had slammed down the phone.

That night Erlendur was more taciturn than usual. It was one of their quieter shifts. They were on traffic duty and so far all they had done was pick up a man on suspicion of driving over the limit, a charge he stubbornly denied. He had hit a cyclist, a baker on his way to work, who claimed that the man had reeked of alcohol and had shoved a handful of liquorice sweets in his mouth while they were waiting for the police. The cyclist was understandably furious. Not only was he injured but his new bike was practically written off. They dropped him at Casualty on their way to take the driver for a blood test. The whole way there the driver ranted and blustered about the pointlessness of the exercise; it was all a big misunderstanding that he had been drinking; he would report them and make sure that they lost their jobs.

Threats like these were run of the mill and Erlendur turned a deaf ear to the man's remonstrations. All evening he had been distracted by thoughts of Hannibal and the phone call from his brother.

'You all right, Erlendur?' asked Marteinn after they had submitted their report and a specimen and were back in the police van, cruising down Laugavegur.

'Sure,' he said, his mind far away.

'You're very quiet,' said Gardar, who was driving.

When Erlendur did not respond, Marteinn shot a quizzical glance at Gardar. They let it drop. As they drove along Pósthússtræti they spotted a vagrant and Erlendur saw that it was Bergmundur. He must have long since finished the meths Erlendur had bought him in exchange for information. He was leaning against a building, not moving at all.

'Should we check on him?' asked Marteinn.

'I'll do it,' said Erlendur. 'I know him. You can drive around the block in the meantime.'

Gardar paused to let him out, then drove off along Austurstræti. Erlendur walked up to Bergmundur and said hello. Bergmundur stared back glassily; it took him a minute before he could place Erlendur. No doubt he was confused by the white cap, the baton hanging at his side. The tramp kept looking his uniform up and down. Finally he twigged.

'You're never . . . a bloody cop?' he slurred in a voice so thick it was almost incomprehensible.

''Fraid so.'

'But you bought me . . . that meths?'

'Yup.'

'What the . . . hell. Why didn't you tell me?'

'Why should I?' said Erlendur. 'Are you all right?'

'I'm . . . fine. Needn't . . . worry . . . 'bout me.'

He was utterly plastered, remaining upright only by propping himself against the wall. Since they last met his face had acquired a new graze, probably from a fall, and he stank to high heaven.

'Why don't you come with me and sleep it off at the station?' asked Erlendur. 'You can't stand here all night.'

'No, I'm going . . . going . . . see my girl, my Thurí. You needn't . . . bother 'bout me.'

'Thurí?'

'Wonderful . . . woman. My girl . . . she's . . .' The rest was unintelligible.

'Where does she live?'

'You know . . . up on . . . Atmanssígur . . . At . . . Amtsstíg . . .'

It took Bergmundur several attempts to articulate the street name. He waved a hand, nearly overbalanced, and Erlendur reached out and steadied him. There was a hostel for female alcoholics on Amtmannsstígur, run by Reykjavík Social Services. He had never been there himself but knew of its existence from the female drunks who occasionally spent a night in the cells.

'Is she staying at the hostel?' he asked.

'Thurí's honest . . . honest, a good woman,' said Bergmundur, assuming a pious expression.

'I don't doubt it,' said Erlendur. 'But are you sure she'll want to see you in this state?'

'State . . . what state?'

Marteinn and Gardar drew up beside them, their circuit complete, and Erlendur gestured for them to give him a minute. The police van rolled forward a few metres and stopped again.

'Maybe you should postpone your visit till tomorrow morning,' said Erlendur. 'Where are you living?'

'Where . . .?'

'I'll take you home.'

'I'm . . . see Thurí . . .'

'Maybe you should go another time.'

'If she . . . carry on with . . . Hannibal . . . good enough for me.'

'Hannibal?'

'Yeah.'

'What about him? Did he and Thurí know each other?'

'Of . . . course.'

'How?'

'I . . . I . . .'

But by now Bergmundur was beyond speech.

'Were they lovers?'

Bergmundur slid slowly down the wall until he was sitting on the road with one leg folded beneath him. Erlendur made a sign to his colleagues and the police van reversed towards them. They decided to take Bergmundur to the station to sleep it off and he made no protest as they lifted him into the back of the vehicle. Erlendur tried to talk to him but it was futile. The man had slipped into oblivion.

16

Although on the outside it was indistinguishable from the other houses in the old Thingholt neighbourhood, the hostel on Amtmannsstígur provided sanctuary for women with drink problems who had nowhere else to turn. There was a female warden who ensured that the house rules were observed and who kept an eye on the cleaning, but otherwise the women had the place to themselves. When Erlendur paid a visit, the hostel had no fewer than eight residents receiving food, lodging and a refuge from life on the street. All were alcoholics who had been reduced to vagrancy, like the men at the Fever Hospital. Some had been battling for many years with the 'bloody booze'.

Erlendur had intended to question Bergmundur more closely about Thurí, but by the time he made it down to the station, the man had woken from his stupor and gone on his way. So Erlendur had taken his time walking to Amtmannsstígur in the fine summer weather. He had a word with the warden, who knew Thurí and informed him that her proper name was Thurídur. Though formerly a resident, she was currently sober. Nevertheless, she often dropped in to share the wisdom of her experience, especially with the younger women. In fact, she had only just popped out and would be back soon. Declining the warden's invitation to wait for her inside, Erlendur decided to walk around town and try again later.

After an hour he returned to find that Thurí had still not shown up, so he took a seat in a spacious living room where three women of varying ages were engaged in a quiet game of Ludo. They looked up and said hello as he entered but otherwise ignored him. The last thing he wanted was to eavesdrop, but although their voices were listless, hardly rising above a murmur, he couldn't help hearing that their conversation revolved around nasty drinks.

'If you want the industrial stuff you need to know a barber.'

'But it's so disgusting. Bloody Portugal hair tonic.'

'If you ask me, cardamom extract's the worst. Can hardly get it down without gagging.'

'Tell you one thing, though. It's easy to smuggle into bars. You can stick it up your fanny. The bouncers won't look there.'

She stole a glance at Erlendur as she rolled the dice, then moved her counter.

'I couldn't swear to it but I reckon the craving's not as bad,' one remarked a little later.

She was the eldest, in her fifties perhaps; a fleshy woman with grizzled hair, a large mouth and coarse features. The second, clearly the youngest, looked to be in her twenties. She was thin, with long lank hair and a slight squint. The third was fortyish, Erlendur guessed, though most of her upper teeth were missing, which had made her cheeks cave in, and her hair was a colourless mess.

'You have to want to quit,' the eldest continued with conviction, moving her counter. 'Or it won't work. It'll never work. There's no point saying you're quitting, then constantly going back on the booze again.'

'The Antabuse helps,' put in the youngest.

'Antabuse is nothing but a crutch.'

Just then a woman appeared in the doorway.

'Were you asking for me?' she said to Erlendur.

'Are you Thurí?'

'Yes, I am. Who are you?'

Erlendur stood up and introduced himself, then asked if they could talk in private. The three women looked up from their game.

'What do you want?' asked Thurí.

'It's about an acquaintance of mine, who I believe you knew.'

'Bit young for you, isn't he, Thurí?' said the woman with the sunken jaw.

At this the three Ludo players perked up and started to laugh. The eldest, evidently out of practice, broke into a fit of coughing, accompanied by much wheezing and gasping. The toothless woman bared her gums. Ignoring them, Thurí beckoned Erlendur to follow her.

'Oi, leave some for us!' called the eldest, and they all howled with laughter again.

Erlendur and Thurí went outside and stood in front of the house. Thurí produced a small tin of roll-ups, lit one and sucked in the smoke.

'Stupid bitches,' she said, in a hoarse, inarticulate voice. 'They're only jealous because I've been dry for four months and they know I have the guts to drag myself out of this shitty life.'

She was short, dark and scrawny, and wore a threadbare jumper and jeans. Brown blotches disfigured her wizened, hollow face. Erlendur thought she couldn't be much under fifty. She was jittery; her beady eyes constantly searching, never still.

'I wanted to ask you about a man called Hannibal,' Erlendur began. 'I gather you used to know him.'

Thurí regarded him in astonishment. 'Hannibal?'

'Yes.'

'What about him?'

'Did you know him well?'

'Well enough,' she said guardedly. 'Why are you asking about him? You know he's dead?'

'Yes, I do. And I'm aware of the circumstances. But it occurred to me you might be able to fill me in a bit more.'

'About how he died, you mean? He drowned.'

'Were you surprised when you heard? Did it strike you as unexpected?'

'No, not particularly,' she said, thinking back. 'Every year a few of the homeless guys cop it. When I heard I just thought to myself that Hannibal's number was up. But then . . . I was in a mess back then, so everything's a bit of a blur.'

'Did you know he was sleeping up by the pipeline?'

'Yes. Went to see him there once. Not long before they found him in the pool. Wanted to talk him out of sleeping rough; make him come home with me. I had OK digs at the time. He didn't take it too badly. Was getting fed up with life in the pipeline. Feeling the cold at night, though he wouldn't admit it.'

'But nothing came of it?'

'No, he wanted to think it over. He could be such an awkward bugger. Couldn't hack it when I . . . couldn't hack some of the things I did. Then right after that I heard he was dead.'

'What couldn't he hack?'

'The things I did to get hold of booze and pills.'

'Things . . .?'

'Look, I sold myself, OK?' Thurí blurted out angrily. 'It happens. Go ahead and judge me, if you like. I don't give a shit.'

'I'm not judging you,' said Erlendur.

'That's what you think.'

'Were you close?'

'Me and Hannibal used to knock about together. But then I cleaned up my act and turned my back on that world. You have to if you want a real shot at life. Only saw him on and off for a while. Then I lapsed. Ended up in the same old rut. We started seeing each other again. Went on like that for years. Always ending up in the same old rut.'

'Did you live together?'

'Yes. Shared a dump of a room on Skipholt – for a whole year, I think. That was the longest. We used to get up to all sorts. Hannibal was a bit of a loner but he could be good company. He . . .'

She paused to inhale.

'He was a good man. Could be an awkward sod at times. Boring. Moody. But he had a good heart. Was always understanding. Treated me like an equal.'

She blew out a cloud of smoke.

'He was a dear friend to me. Terrible what happened to him.'

'Do you know of anyone who had it in for him? Did he ever mention being afraid of anyone? Like people he'd got on the wrong side of?'

'Hannibal used to get himself into a hell of a mess sometimes. He'd lose his rag with people and push them too far. Got into fights for all kinds of stupid reasons. But I can't think of anyone who'd have wanted to do him in.'

'Last time I spoke to him he'd been beaten up.'

'It wouldn't have been the first time,' said Thurí. 'When he was in good shape he could take the bastards on. But not by the end. By then he was no match for anyone.'

'So you can't think of anybody he was frightened of or –'

'He wasn't frightened of anyone; didn't hate anyone either,' Thurí answered quickly, then changed her mind. 'Except maybe those brothers.'

'The brothers from next door?'

'It's thanks to them he was chucked out of the cellar,' she said. 'They accused him of setting fire to the place but really they'd done it to get rid of him. The landlord didn't believe him. That's how he wound up sleeping by the hot-water pipes.'

'Did Hannibal have any dealings with them after that?'

'Haven't a clue. But he didn't have a good word to say about them. Out-and-out criminals, he called them.'

'Any idea what he meant by that?'

'No, he never explained. But he was scared of them. Shit-scared, I reckon. Look, can we call it a day? I need to get going.'

'Of course. Thanks for your help.'

'I went to fetch his stuff from the pipeline,' Thurí added, opening the front door of the hostel. 'A few days after they found his body. But the police had taken the best bits – sent them to his family, probably. At least I hope so. Hope they weren't stolen.'

'Surely not.'

'Wouldn't have been worth much.' She paused in the doorway.

'He wasn't one for hoarding stuff. Though he did have a little suitcase with a few books and other odds and ends he'd picked up. That'd gone.'

'I'm sure the police passed his possessions on to his family.'

'Wanted something to remind me of him,' Thurí said. 'Something that . . . Anyway, it had all gone. Only thing I found was the earring.'

'Earring?'

'Yes, lying under the pipe.'

'You found an earring where he used to sleep?'

'Yes.'

'What . . . what kind of earring?'

'Looked newish. Quite big. Nice too. Gold. Hannibal must have picked it up somewhere, then dropped it in the tunnel.'

17

That weekend Erlendur was busy at work. It was mid July, summer was at its height, the nights were light and sunny, and the warm weather brought people out in droves. The bars were packed. At closing time, crowds poured out into the streets to mill around in the mild air. The party continued in Austurvöllur Square or Hljómskálagardur, the park by the lake. Bottles were produced and passed round. Scraps broke out in alleyways, maybe over a girl. Then there were the habitual troublemakers, brainless thugs who roved around town in various stages of inebriation, provoking fights, looking to get even. If apprehended, they were thrown in the cells, but it could take as many as three officers to subdue them. Break-ins were all too common as thieves took advantage of the holiday period to clean out empty homes. It was up to vigilant neighbours to raise the alert.

Erlendur attended two such incidents that weekend. On Friday night, in the new suburb of Fossvogur, a neighbour had noticed figures sneaking round the back of a detached house at the bottom of the valley. Erlendur, who was driving, let the van roll noiselessly down the hill in neutral and parked by the house. They took care not to slam the doors. Marteinn went round the front; Erlendur and Gardar took the garden. There was a broken pane of glass in the back door, which was standing ajar. They crept closer but could see no movement inside. On entering, they found themselves in a smart sitting room where a middle-aged woman was slumped fast asleep on the sofa, cradling a brandy bottle. They heard a noise from the hallway. Gardar stayed with the woman while Erlendur tiptoed towards the master bedroom. When he peered inside he saw a man stooping over a handsome chest of drawers. He had found a jewellery box and was turning out its clinking contents into his hand, before stuffing them into his trouser pocket.

Erlendur watched him for a minute or two, then barked sternly: 'What do you think you're doing?'

The thief was so shocked that he jumped and emitted a high-pitched shriek. Then he whipped round and, before Erlendur could react, charged straight at him. Erlendur lost his balance and tried to grab at the burglar who shot out of the bedroom, cast a glance into the sitting room where Gardar was standing guard over his sleeping girlfriend, then made a beeline for the front door. He flung it open, only to run straight into Marteinn, who forced him onto the ground. Erlendur came to his aid and between them they handcuffed the man and loaded him into the van. He was not one of the usual suspects and remained obstinately silent when asked for his name.

Nor did they recognise his accomplice, who was still sleeping like a baby. She must have been either dead drunk or completely exhausted to have nodded off on the job and slept right through her partner's arrest. In low voices they discussed what to do. Gardar thought it a pity to disturb her but it couldn't be helped. Tapping her knee he commanded her to wake up, and after several tries she began to stir and finally opened her eyes. Blinking, she peered at the three police officers.

'What are you doing here?' she asked.

'What are we doing?' said Marteinn. 'What about you?'

'No, I mean –'

'I'm afraid you'll have to come with us,' said Gardar.

'I . . . no, I mean . . . eh, you what? Where's Dúddi?' She sat up.

They exchanged glances. The cuddly nickname seemed singularly inappropriate for the thug they had just loaded into the van.

'Dúddi?' said Marteinn, trying not to laugh.

'What the . . .? Where is he?'

'*Dúddi's* waiting for you outside in the van,' Gardar told her. 'Care to join him?' He offered her his hand.

They couldn't work out whether she was still plastered or merely woozy from her nap. She sized up these three men in their black uniforms, before eventually accepting Gardar's hand and tottering out of the house on his arm. She was still clutching the brandy bottle and took a long swig, then held it out to Gardar.

'Want some?'

'No, you hang on to it,' he said. 'You can share it with Dúddi.'

Erlendur avoided Marteinn's eye. His colleague was shaking with silent laughter. Dúddi subjected the woman to a torrent of abuse when they put her in the van with him. He was not impressed with her failure as a lookout.

'You drunken bitch,' he snarled, unsurprisingly incensed.

'Oh, why don't you shut up?' the woman snapped back, hanging her head as if used to bearing the brunt of his rages.

18

Erlendur had to psych himself up to pay a second visit to the brothers. He wanted to question them further about the fire in the cellar. Out-and-out criminals, Hannibal had called them. The more details Erlendur uncovered about Hannibal's case, the more his curiosity grew.

On the way there his thoughts returned to the gold earring Thurí had found in Hannibal's camp. She had told Erlendur he was welcome to come round and see it. How on earth had it ended up in the heating conduit? Rebekka could hardly have lost it there. As far as Erlendur could recall, she wasn't wearing earrings, nor had she mentioned visiting the pipeline, either before or after her brother's death. It couldn't have belonged to a police-woman, either, because although women had long been employed on the force in other capacities, the first female officers had gone out on the beat only this summer. That ruled out their presence at the scene last year.

On the other hand, Hannibal might well have chanced upon it, wandering around town, as Thurí suggested. He had a magpie's eye for valuables lying in the gutter. Thurí had the same training, which is how she had spotted the earring under the pipes.

Before saying goodbye on the steps of the hostel, Erlendur had put another question to her: how do women lose earrings? It was the only time during their conversation that she had cracked a smile. It didn't take much, she said. This one was a clip-on. Clip-ons slipped off so easily that women were always losing them.

'So it wouldn't require a struggle?'

'Not necessarily. Though obviously they'd be more likely to come loose in a struggle. But they just fall off anyway. For no reason. All the time.'

'Could the woman who owned it have got into a fight with Hannibal?'

'Listen,' said Thurí, 'Hannibal would never have come to blows with a woman. I knew him from way back. He'd never in a million years have laid hands on a woman.'

Erlendur walked along Sudurgata past the old graveyard. He sometimes came this way on his evening rambles, drawn by the fact that an author he admired lived on the street. He had twice spied him walking round the lake, though he hadn't wanted to bother him. Years ago the author had written a book – one of the funniest Erlendur had ever read – about a young man who moved from the countryside to Reykjavík during the war and became a journalist. Whenever he walked this way Erlendur would look up at the writer's window and send him a silent greeting. Another writer he liked to pause briefly beside, a poet this time, was no longer of this world but lay in his grave in the old cemetery.

Erlendur used to peer over the black wall that separated the living from the dead, and hail Benedikt Gröndal.

By now he could hear the sound of a match in progress at Melavellir football ground. He crossed Hringbraut and followed the long, yellow perimeter fence, listening to the shouts of the spectators. He took no interest in sport so didn't know who was playing. Back in his early twenties he had boxed for a while after a friend from the building site he was working on took him along. He had trained with him for two years, mainly out of curiosity. Erlendur was powerfully built, with a strong pair of fists, and the man who owned the gym and lent him his gloves had said he had promise. Pity, he had added, that like the rest of the men who trained there he couldn't put it to use. Boxing was banned in Iceland and the sessions were not widely advertised. Since then, Erlendur had not been tempted by any other sports.

Little by little he had become better acquainted with the city to which he had moved when he was twelve, learning about the buildings, the streets and their inhabitants, both living and dead. They had moved into a small house on the outskirts, which had once been a bathhouse for British soldiers. Later, after his father died, he and his mother had rented a basement flat in the west of town, not far from the harbour, and his route had often led him past the graveyard. Soon he had taken to lingering there, exploring its narrow paths and deciphering the inscriptions on the headstones. The dead held no fear for him. Nor did the cemetery, though it could be eerie in winter when the trees reached up their twisted branches into the blackness. Rather he found peace and solace among the sleeping souls of the departed.

Beyond Melavellir, there was a view across Sudurgata to the recently completed Arnamagnæan Institute where Iceland's medieval manuscripts were housed. He had visited once to see the most precious treasure in the collection, the Codex Regius of Eddic poetry, and was principally struck by the fact that the manuscript containing these cultural gems was so small, grubby, dog-eared and generally unimpressive.

The brothers gave him a cool reception. They invited him in, but only as far as the hall this time. Having no wish to stay, Erlendur did not beat about the bush. He asked them again about the fire, reminding them of what he had said before about a rumour doing the rounds that they had started it themselves to get rid of Hannibal.

'What's this rumour you keep going on about?' demanded Vignir. 'Are you spreading this bullshit yourself?'

'Hannibal was adamant,' Erlendur replied, undeterred. 'He said so to his friends.'

'Well, it wasn't us,' said Ellert, with a glance at his brother. 'Is that what he claimed, the old sod?'

'Did you want him out of the cellar?'

The brothers' eyes met. The day's programming had not yet begun and the television stood dark and silent in the sitting room.

'That was none of our business,' said Vignir. 'And we had nothing to do with the fire either. The tramp started it himself. It was us who put it out. Not that he thanked us.'

'But he was afraid of fire,' said Erlendur. 'Didn't even dare light a candle down there. You said you found one by the door where the blaze started, but I don't believe it was his.'

'Well, it wasn't ours,' said Vignir. 'Have you asked Frímann if he did it himself?'

'Frímann?'

'Maybe he had his own reasons for torching the place.'

'Like what?'

'An insurance scam.'

'Insurance scam?'

'He's always trying to make money from that dump, isn't he?'

'You think Frímann . . .?'

'I really wouldn't know,' answered Vignir. 'Ask him. But we sure as hell didn't light a fire. We put it out, for Christ's sake!'

'If we weren't responsible,' added his brother, 'and the tramp wasn't either, maybe Frímann's the man you're after.'

'Did you have any contact with Hannibal after he was kicked out?'

'No,' said Ellert.

'None at all,' confirmed Vignir.

'Remember hearing about his death?'

'Saw his name in the papers,' said Ellert. 'Wasn't the poor bastard drunk as usual?'

'Were you in Reykjavík at the time?'

'What the hell's that got to do with you?'

'Did you know where he was sleeping?'

'No.'

'You don't seriously believe we hurt him?' said Vignir. 'Why are you asking us all these stupid questions?'

'Did you hurt him?' asked Erlendur bluntly. 'Did he have something on you?'

'What do you mean? Are you implying we killed him?' exclaimed Vignir.

'On us?' spluttered Ellert. 'How the hell do you work that out?'

The brothers' eyes met again.

'Were you selling alcohol? From your own still? Or smuggled stuff?'

Erlendur scrutinised them each in turn, waiting for their reactions. They were not long in coming.

'What is all this bollocks?' said Vignir.

'You get out right now, you hear me?' said Ellert. 'I don't want to see your face round here again.' He hustled Erlendur out and slammed the door behind him.

19

Shortly before midday Erlendur was woken, as so often lately, by the phone. He heaved himself out of bed.

'Hello, it's Halldóra.'

'Oh, hello.'

'Did I wake you?'

'No, that's all right.'

'You sound so far away.'

'Is that better?' He raised his voice. 'I was working over the weekend.'

'You're always working.'

'Yes. Been on night duty for weeks.'

'Were you working last night?'

'Yes.'

'Anything interesting happen?'

'Oh, the usual,' said Erlendur, beginning to wake up properly. 'Nothing special.'

'I don't think I could stand working nights. Doesn't it mess up your sleep patterns – staying awake all night like that?'

'It can be a bit wearing,' Erlendur admitted. 'But it's not too bad.'

She was silent for a moment, then said: 'I hardly ever hear from you.'

'I've been busy.'

'I'm always the one who gets in touch. It makes me feel . . . like I'm bothering you.'

'That's rubbish.'

'Perhaps you want to end it.'

'I . . . Oh, please,' said Erlendur. 'You're not bothering me at all. It's just . . . I've been working so much.'

They lapsed into awkward silence, neither knowing what to say. It lasted so long he thought she'd hung up.

'Hello?' he said.

'I thought maybe we could meet up, do something fun,' said Halldóra. 'I'm free this afternoon.'

'Sure, great, all right.' Erlendur scratched his head.

'Want to go to a film or . . .?'

'Or into town maybe?' he suggested. 'To a cafe?'

'The weather's nice. Perhaps we could buy an ice cream and go for a wander. Then see.'

'Sure, I'm up for that.'

They agreed to meet in town at four, then rang off. Erlendur hastily showered, put on some coffee and ate a light breakfast. Halldóra was right. He was bad at getting in touch with her; she was usually the one who rang to suggest they see each other, go on dates; she kept their relationship going. There was much about her that he found appealing: her smile when she was speaking from the heart; her wariness when they made love; the interest that she alone took in him. His life was stagnating; perhaps it was time for a change. To try something new. Break the monotony of routine. Perhaps Halldóra was the answer.

Just then Erlendur remembered that he had been meaning to call Rebekka ever since Thurí told him about the earring. Rebekka had given him her number, saying he could phone her any time. They had also talked about meeting up again but nothing had come of it.

She answered after three rings, and once they'd exchanged pleasantries he got straight to the point.

'Did you ever visit the pipeline where Hannibal was sleeping?'

'You mean while he was alive?'

'Or after he died. Either.'

'No, never.'

'Did he leave any personal effects? Were any of his belongings passed on to you?'

'No, nothing really, apart from a few rags, a handful of books and a tatty suitcase. The police handed them over to me. They'd been looking after them. Didn't want anyone to steal them. As if they would. Why do you ask?'

'It's just that I was talking to a woman, an old drinking pal of Hannibal's, and she did go up there. Right after he died. She found a big gold earring where he used to sleep.'

'Oh?'

'It occurred to me that you might know about it. Haven't seen it yet myself. This woman still has it. But it sounds like it's a nice piece of jewellery – could be expensive – so . . .'

'You thought it might be mine?'

'Seemed only right to ask.'

'But I never went there.'

'Any idea whose it might have been, then?'

'No, I can't think of any woman who'd have visited Hannibal in that awful place. In fact, I don't know anyone who was in touch with him in the past few years. I'm afraid I can't help you there. Though I assure you it's not mine.'

'We probably shouldn't read too much into it,' said Erlendur. 'There are various ways it could have ended up there. It may have no connection to Hannibal. I just wanted to check.'

'I wonder . . .'

'What?'

'No, nothing . . . I'm not into jewellery, but some women wear so much you can hear them jangling a mile off. Though what a woman like that could have wanted with Hannibal is beyond me.'

'That's what I thought,' said Erlendur. 'Anyway, I'll let you know if I get hold of it.'

'Yes, please do. I'd like to see it.'

Before ringing off, they arranged to meet again later in the week. Next, Erlendur headed into town for his date with Halldóra. He kept racking his brains as to how the earring could have wound up in Hannibal's camp but couldn't come up with anything useful.

His conversation with Rebekka continued to preoccupy him too: something she'd said was niggling at the back of his mind, but he couldn't work out what it was. He hurried down Laugavegur, so engrossed in his thoughts that he paid no attention to the shop displays. He glanced at a large jeweller's as he strode by, then stopped, turned and took a second look in the window. Behind the glass lay an array of gleaming watches, gold and silver rings – some embellished with diamonds – necklaces, bracelets and earrings, all in handsome presentation boxes stamped with the name of the jeweller.

As Erlendur examined the jewellery, he finally worked out what it was that had been nagging at him ever since he spoke to Rebekka. It came to him as his gaze fell on a box containing a pair of beautiful earrings.

You can hear them jangling a mile off . . .

'*Mad about jewellery,*' he murmured to the glass. 'It can't be.'

He stared at the earrings.

'It can't be, can it?'

Not until he was standing in front of that glittering display did he remember the detail from the police file about the woman who had vanished on her way home from Thórskaffi. She was mad about jewellery, loved to wear all kinds: rings, bracelets, necklaces, earrings . . .

He stared at the box, unable to imagine what possible connection Hannibal could have had to her disappearance.

20

They reached the scene of a major accident on Skúlagata before the ambulance did. It was four o'clock on Sunday morning, and it was raining. There was little traffic, yet it was the third crash they had dealt with that night. The most serious too. A man driving a jeep had dropped a glowing cigarette ember on his seat and in trying to sweep it onto the floor had lost control of his vehicle, swerved into the left-hand lane and collided with an oncoming car. Both occupants of the car were badly injured: a woman was trapped, unconscious, behind the steering wheel; her daughter was moaning beside her in the passenger seat. The driver of the jeep, his face bleeding, wandered, shocked and bewildered, around the crash site. Erlendur led him to the police van.

'I didn't see what happened,' the man said. 'Didn't see a thing. They'll be all right, won't they? You do think they'll be all right?'

'The ambulances are on their way.'

'I tried to avoid them but it was too late and I smashed straight into them,' the man said. 'I tried to open her door but it's jammed. They're trapped inside. You've got to get them out.'

Though he did not appear drunk, Erlendur assumed they would test him at the hospital anyway.

Marteinn and Gardar managed to force open the rear door of the car and Marteinn crawled inside in a vain attempt to free the girl in the front seat. There was blood on her face and hands, and her legs were crushed under the dashboard. She had already lost a lot of blood. Her mother was showing signs of coming round. She had smacked into the steering wheel so hard that she had broken it, then cracked her head on the windscreen, knocking herself out. Her face was bleeding too and Marteinn didn't want to move her. He reassured them that a team was on the way to get them out as quickly as possible so they could be taken to hospital.

The woman reached over to the girl and took her hand.

'It'll be all right,' she said soothingly. 'It'll be all right. They'll be here any minute to get us out and then everything'll be all right.'

The girl squeezed her hand.

They heard the ambulances approaching, and in no time at all a fire crew arrived to release the mother and daughter from the wreckage. Marteinn and Gardar began to sketch out the scene of the accident, measuring distances and tyre marks. Gardar pushed a small measuring wheel in front of him and scribbled in his notebook. Erlendur took charge of directing what little traffic there was around the crash site. He watched as the women were freed and carried on stretchers to the ambulance, which sped off with flashing lights and loud sirens. The driver of the jeep left in the second ambulance. Tow trucks were brought in to drag away the wrecked cars and soon it looked as though nothing had happened there. Having swept up the broken glass, Erlendur and the others climbed back into the police van and resumed their patrol.

Next they arrested two men suspected of drink driving, which involved taking samples and preparing reports. Paperwork bored Erlendur, though he understood why it was necessary. It took up too much of their time; everything had to be accounted for and carefully recorded. Names had to be taken, incident reports written up, one form after another meticulously filled in and filed. Nothing must be neglected. Accuracy was paramount.

Gardar and Marteinn were now discussing their chances of taking any leave that summer. Erlendur was only half listening.

'Maybe after the anniversary celebrations at Thingvellir,' said Gardar.

'I suppose we'll all have to be there for that?' asked Marteinn.

Preparations were in full swing for the national holiday at the end of July when Icelanders were to celebrate the eleven hundredth anniversary of the settlement of their island. There had been meetings about extra policing and overtime. A huge crowd was expected to attend the festival at the ancient assembly site of Thingvellir, and the police would have a vital role to play in ensuring that everything went smoothly.

'It's incredible really,' said Gardar.

'What is?'

'That we've bothered to scrape a living on this rock for eleven hundred years.'

A little while later they were summoned to a basement flat in the centre of town. Someone had complained about noise, but by the time they arrived all was quiet. They climbed out of the van and Erlendur checked they had the right address. The neighbour who had phoned the police emerged from one of the houses, clothes hastily pulled on over his pyjamas.

'They've been making a hell of a racket,' he said as he approached. 'Then suddenly just before you arrived everything went silent.'

'Who lives there?' asked Erlendur.

'A pack of dope fiends. They've taken over the basement and cause nothing but trouble. Music on full blast, yelling and shouting. And their friends come round here revving their motorbikes and roaring up and down the street. It goes on all the time, but especially at night. Wakes you up with a jerk. Disturbs the children. We've complained repeatedly to the tenants, a couple of idiot boys. Tried talking to the landlord too but he doesn't do a thing.'

'Why do you say they're dope fiends?' asked Marteinn.

'Because it's a drug den. There are all kinds of undesirables hanging about, so it's obvious they're selling dope. Earlier today one of them threatened to beat me up. He was standing here smoking and I had the audacity to ask him not to chuck his cigarette stubs on the pavement. He almost went for me. Told me to eat shit. You can see the stubs everywhere.'

'I'm afraid there's not much we can –'

They jumped when heavy rock music started blasting out of the flat. It was cranked right up.

'There you go! They carry on like that till the early hours,' the neighbour exclaimed. 'Can you imagine what it's like putting up with that?'

'Does anyone else live there apart from the two boys?'

'I have no idea,' said the neighbour. 'People are coming and going all the time. It's impossible to tell.'

They knocked on the door. Nobody answered, so they hammered long and hard. When there was still no answer, they saw no alternative but to enter. Erlendur opened the door and found himself in a hall with a bare bulb hanging from the ceiling. He could see into the sitting room where the source of the disturbance, a brand-new stereo, was set up on a table. Gardar and Marteinn followed him inside. They discovered two young men lounging on a squashy sofa, sharing a pipe. Billows of blue smoke curled around the flat. The men were so spaced out that they didn't even bat an eyelid when they saw three police officers enter the room.

Gardar walked over to the turntable and lifted the needle. In the sudden peace that followed, one of the men on the sofa finally noticed that something was wrong.

'Hey, quit that, man,' he cried. 'Don't turn off the record.'

'We've received a complaint about noise from this address,' Gardar informed him. 'We have to ask you to turn off your music so your neighbours can get some sleep.'

'Why are you hassling us? Leave us alone, man,' his friend said. Neither made any effort to stand up; they were far too stoned, their eyes swimming with incomprehension.

On the table in front of them, amid all the other mess, Erlendur could see three flat brown cakes the size of wallets, one of which had several chunks cut out of it. There were also three small plastic bags containing white powder; three pipes; a stash of matchboxes and lighters; several bottles of alcohol and packets of cigarettes; and various jars of pills.

The neighbour had not been exaggerating when he called it a drug den. Erlendur couldn't help thinking the two boys must be exceptionally stupid to draw attention to themselves by making that much noise in the middle of the night. They appeared to be celebrating the arrival of a new shipment – another successful smuggling job. They had obviously wanted to check it was pure first. But they could have been a lot less conspicuous about it.

While Marteinn went out to the car to radio for back-up, Gardar watched over the two boys, leaving Erlendur to explore the rest of the flat. Just off the sitting room he found a bedroom, its floor piled high with rubbish and clothes. In the gloom he could see a dirty duvet on the large bed and under it a shape he thought he should investigate. Presumably the third occupant of the flat.

Walking up to the bed, he whisked off the duvet, revealing a young girl, peacefully asleep. She was fully dressed and it only took Erlendur a moment to register that her clothes fitted the description of the girl who had recently been reported missing: jeans, pink peasant blouse, even the trainers. The camouflage jacket could not be far away. The word at the police station was that she came from a good home. Her parents, who were divorced, had explained how, without their realising, she had spiralled out of control. Nowadays she would hardly communicate with them, so they rarely knew where she was hanging out; yet she was quick to blame them for the state she was in.

Erlendur prodded the girl and she woke up, rolled onto her back and opened her eyes. She couldn't make out his face in the semi-darkness.

'What . . . who are you?'

'My name's Erlendur.'

'Erlendur . . . what . . .?'

'Are you all right?'

'Are you . . . are you a cop?'

'Your mother's worried about you.'

Just then he heard a commotion in the sitting room; the two men had finally grasped the situation and had launched themselves at Gardar.

Later that grey morning the car crash on Skúlagata was the lead story on the radio news. The announcer, in a sombre yet dispassionate tone, as if he had delivered too many such reports, read that a jeep had veered into oncoming traffic and collided with an approaching car. An eighteen-year-old girl, who had been in the passenger seat, had died on the way to hospital. Her name could not be released at present.

A couple of items later the newsreader announced that the girl who had recently been reported missing had now been found alive and well.

21

Erlendur slept until late the following afternoon, then went out to Skúlakaffi for a meal. As he ate, his thoughts turned to Thurí. He was anxious to take a look at the earring, so he kept an eye out for her on his way to meet Rebekka outside the doctor's surgery. The day was hot and still; the sun rode high in the sky and people were making the most of the weather as they wandered through the streets and squares in summery clothes. While he waited outside the surgery, Erlendur looked up the slope to Bakarabrekka where a huddle of old wooden houses had fallen into ruin. A debate was raging as to whether they should be demolished to make way for new buildings or renovated and preserved for their historical interest.

'You came,' said a voice behind him. It was Rebekka.

'Yes, hello.'

'I was wondering, would you like to take a walk round the lake? The weather's so good, and I've been stuck inside all day.'

They strolled south along Lækjargata, rounded the corner by the old Idnó Theatre and saw a group of parents and small children feeding the ducks. The birds quacked and splashed, squabbling over the pieces of bread, while the children tried to throw scraps to the ones that hung back.

They walked on with the sun in their eyes, along the lake to the park. Arctic terns swarmed above the little island in the lake, fighting a losing battle with the black-headed gulls.

'There are fewer and fewer of them every year,' remarked Rebekka. 'The gulls are so aggressive.'

'There are plenty of terns out on Seltjarnarnes,' said Erlendur. 'Perhaps they can take refuge there.'

'Anything new on Hannibal?' asked Rebekka after a pause.

'Not much,' Erlendur admitted. 'Did you hear about the fire?'

'What fire?'

'Not long before your brother died the cellar he was sleeping in caught fire. He was thrown out because the owner thought he was to blame.'

'Was he?'

'It seems unlikely. He told me he was afraid of fire – actively afraid of setting the place alight. And I learned recently that the men who lived next door might have had their own reasons for wanting to get rid of him. You didn't know about any of that?'

'No, as I said, I hadn't been in touch with Hannibal for years. Until the police told me, I had no idea he'd been living in the pipeline.'

'He moved there after losing his room in the cellar.'

'I did go looking for him once – about three years ago – down at the Fever Hospital. They told me he turned up from time to time, but he was almost always drunk so there was nothing they could do for him.'

'Did you want to find him for any special reason?'

'No, not really. I used to try and look him up every now and then, even after I finally gave up on him. Wanted to know how he was doing. But they couldn't tell me where he was living.'

They reached the park. Rebekka perched on a bench and Erlendur sat down beside her.

'I'm ashamed to say it, but I wasn't particularly surprised when I heard Hannibal was dead. Even if the circumstances weren't what I expected, I knew sooner or later he'd die somewhere, homeless and destitute. When the police rang, I sensed it was about him, that it was all over. I'd been expecting the call for years. So, like I say, it didn't come as a complete surprise.'

'When did you last see him?'

'I bumped into him in Austurvöllur Square. Completely by chance. He was with a group of other men in the same boat. He seemed all right then. At least, as far as I could tell he wasn't that drunk or under the influence of drugs or whatever it was he was on.'

'What did you talk about?'

'Nothing,' said Rebekka. 'We had nothing to say to each other. It was all over. Finished. Nothing left. Like two strangers trying to make polite conversation. It was a relief to both of us when we abandoned the attempt. He knew where I lived. I asked him to get in touch if ever he felt the urge, but . . .'

She gazed across the lake.

'What?'

'I felt . . . Thinking about it later I felt so sorry for him. No one had ever been allowed to pity him or show any sympathy.

But that day . . . he seemed different, embarrassed, as if he was ashamed of himself. As if he didn't want me to know how he was living. I'd never seen him behave that way before.'

'How did he end up like that? What made him go off the rails?'

'Our brother used to say it was gutlessness. It didn't take him long to give up on Hannibal. He couldn't handle what happened to him. The way he wasted his life.'

'It must have been hard to watch.'

'Do you believe Hannibal was murdered?'

'I don't know. There's no reason to think so. What do you think made him end up like that?'

'He never told you?'

'What?'

'About the accident?'

'No, what accident?'

'He had a weakness for alcohol – from the beginning, I think,' she said. 'Always had a problem with drink, but after that . . .' She grimaced. 'After that it was as if he couldn't bear to be sober.'

'What do you mean? After what?'

'They let me go with them,' said Rebekka. 'He asked if I'd like to come. He was like that. Always thinking about other people. About me. If I hadn't been with them it would almost certainly have turned out differently, so I suppose it was my fault.'

'What was?'

'What happened to her. I keep asking myself – was it because of me?' Rebekka's voice had dropped to a whisper. 'I've never been able to answer that question.'

Erlendur waited for her to go on. Two swans swam past, eyeing them, then continued on their way.

'My brother says Hannibal was weak,' she said, picking up

the thread at last. 'He was always very hard on him. Before the accident too. His wife was Helena's sister, you know. They married sisters. No doubt that had a lot to do with it. His wife never forgave Hannibal. You see, one day – it was a Saturday evening – nearly thirty years ago . . . he borrowed the car . . .'

22

Hannibal and his brother had kept busy throughout the war, working first for the British, then the American occupying forces. They made a decent living building army camps and laying the foundations for Reykjavík's airport and new road system. Hannibal wasn't good with money. He was lively and fun, generous; he lived for the moment. His elder brother couldn't have been more different: clean-living, careful with money to the point of being tight-fisted, already setting cash aside for the future. He was forever lecturing Hannibal about taking better care of his earnings but his words fell on deaf ears.

Rebekka, considerably younger than her brothers, was still at primary school. Hannibal was her favourite. He took more of an interest in her, spoke to her like an equal, invited her along to the cinema, bought her presents and treats, helped with her homework. She had little to do with her older brother. Their relationship was very different; he never really concerned himself with her at all.

Her elder brother had left home and was taking a carpentry course with an eye to starting up a building firm with two of his friends. Not only that, he had acquired a flashy American car through his army contacts and was engaged to a girl from Hafnarfjördur. They had met after the war when he was working on a new processing plant for her father, who owned a fishery in the town. She had a younger sister called Helena, and they were very close. One evening the brothers took the sisters on a double date to the cinema. It was the first time Hannibal had set eyes on Helena. From then on they were inseparable.

Helena was attracted to everything about Hannibal that Rebekka knew and loved: his generosity, his helpfulness, the kindness he always showed his sister, the happy-go-lucky nature that at times bordered on recklessness, yet made him carefree and sunny. He was never bad-tempered or disagreeable; he would tackle problems with a smile instead of getting angry. Not that he was by any means a pushover. On the contrary, he was tough and knew his own mind; he had the kind of self-confidence that inspired respect and attracted friends.

Helena and Hannibal. Soon they were only ever mentioned in the same breath. She shared his vitality and the admirable quality of never getting worked up over small things, always looking on the bright side. At the time they met she was studying to be a nurse. They had been together only six months when they heard that their brother and sister were planning to hold their wedding that summer. Hannibal, who had been thinking along the same lines, needed no further encouragement. He went straight out and purchased a plain gold ring on credit from the jeweller's in Hafnarfjördur, persuaded Helena to accompany him on a long walk out to the Álftanes peninsula, and proposed as the sun was sinking below the mountains in the west. A large double wedding was held, with speeches, good-luck songs and dancing until dawn.

Their honeymoon was brief. Helena had just finished her course and started work at St Jósef's Hospital when the accident occurred.

From time to time Hannibal used to borrow his brother's car. He had learned to drive a lorry during the war and later passed his test, though he had never bought his own vehicle. His brother was somewhat reluctant to lend him his car, but on this occasion he was out of town and his wife was happy to let Hannibal take it. It was a beautiful summer evening and Hannibal wanted to go for a drive with Helena. They stopped off at his parents' house in Laugarnes to help his father with a small job first. When they got back in the car, Rebekka was standing in the drive, looking a little forlorn in her summer dress, so he asked if she'd like to go with them. Beaming, she jumped into the car. Hannibal was always so nice to her.

They drove down to Hafnarfjördur where they bought chocolate and vanilla ice creams and enjoyed them while chatting and giggling about some story Hannibal had heard at work. Helena was in the front seat, smiling, quick to laugh. Rebekka was in the back, savouring her treat as she listened to them talk about their dream of buying a place in Hafnarfjördur. At the time they were renting a small flat in the oldest part of town, but it was rumoured that work would soon begin on a new residential estate out here at Kinnar.

They cruised down to the harbour. Though he enjoyed being behind the wheel, Hannibal was not a very experienced driver. He was inclined to get carried away, and more than once Helena had to ask him to slow down. Now, his mind on other things, he drove out onto one of the jetties and realised belatedly that he was going too fast. He slammed on the brakes but the docks were slippery from the recent catch and the car skidded on fish slurry. Hannibal was unable to regain control and before they knew it they were plunging over the edge into the harbour.

The car sank straight to the bottom of the cold sea. They had been driving with the front windows rolled down and the icy water poured in. When they hit the surface, Rebekka had banged her head violently, first on the side window, then on the roof, and blacked out. Hannibal could see her floating, unconscious, in the back. Helena had cut her head open on the windscreen. Stunned by the blow, she had slid under the dashboard and was now jammed against the seat.

Hannibal knew he had to act fast, but it dawned on him he could only take one of them up to the surface at a time. The other would have to wait. He lost precious seconds coming to terms with this horrific dilemma, taking in his wife trapped under the dashboard, Rebekka motionless in the back seat. Helena tried to free herself and reached out for his hand.

The seconds ticked by.

Finally, Hannibal grabbed his sister and kicked his way out through the side window, pulling her after him. Her summer dress caught on the door and he tugged in a frenzy until the fabric tore and she was free.

More precious seconds had gone to waste.

He gasped as he broke the surface. There was no one around. No one had witnessed the accident. He trod water, holding Rebekka's limp body in his arms, yelling for help, then in desperation he struggled over to one of the struts supporting the jetty. There was a thin rope hanging there which he worked under his sister's arms; then he hastily lashed her to the piling with her head above water.

Having paused to check she was still breathing, he left her suspended there, took a gasp and dived down to the car again. He was uninjured, apart from a cut on his head and a sharp pain in his side. He swam with every ounce of his strength back down to the window, slid inside and saw that Helena was still caught between the dashboard and seat. The hand that had reached out to him in despair was now floating lifeless. He yanked it, but Helena did not stir. He grasped her shoulders, straining with all his might to lift her. At last he succeeded in freeing one of her legs and soon the other followed. He shoved her out of the window before him.

By then he had been under too long himself and started gulping seawater; yet he never lost his grip on Helena. Just as he thought he would never make it, he surfaced, coughing, spluttering, his chest heaving. Holding Helena's head above water, he swam with her to where Rebekka was dangling unconscious from the post.

Out of his mind with terror, he screamed for help. Screamed at Helena in his arms. Screamed at Rebekka. Screamed in despair to God, but nobody heard his cries.

In the end, he swam with Helena to a narrow iron ladder, heaved her over his shoulder and began to climb. Every step was sheer torment. There was no time. His immersion in the numbing cold had taken its toll and he was shivering uncontrollably when he finally made it up onto the jetty, laid Helena on the ground and started pumping the seawater out of her. He pressed down on her chest again and again, calling out her name, talking to her, telling her everything would be all right, comforting her, shouting at her to wake up. In between he yelled repeatedly for help, but nobody heard.

Despite the water spurting from her mouth he knew he was too late, though he didn't want to admit it to himself.

He knew she couldn't be saved.

Eventually, unable to leave Rebekka in the sea any longer, he dived back into the harbour, swam over and released her from the rope. She was beginning to come round as he carried her up the ladder and laid her beside his wife.

He resumed his battle to revive Helena. Then, finally accepting defeat, he knelt exhausted at her side, hid his face in her lifeless breast and wept.

23

The two swans swam by again, slowing to see if there was any hope of breadcrumbs from the humans on the bench. Disappointed, they moved on, then abruptly took fright, flapped their wings and ran noisily along the surface of the water, before soaring gracefully into the air and heading north towards Mount Esja. Rebekka watched until they vanished.

'Hannibal was never the same again,' she said. 'It goes without saying. A tragedy like that can change a person, alter the whole course of their life.'

'Yes, I suppose it can,' said Erlendur.

'His happy side disappeared,' Rebekka continued. 'Like so much else. So much went out of him after Helena died. He wasn't the same person. He refused to talk about the accident, never mentioned Helena's name. Started drinking heavily. Kept changing jobs. Tried moving to the countryside for a while. Over the next ten years or so he changed into the vagrant you met. We did what we could but it was impossible to save him from himself. On the rare occasions when we got him to talk about the accident he was full of anger and self-recrimination – self-hatred really. If we tried to help he would accuse us of interference. He couldn't tolerate that.'

'So he blamed himself for what happened.'

'Yes.'

'What about you? It must have been a traumatic experience for you too.'

'Even after all this time, I can hardly bear to think about the way I imposed myself on them,' she said. 'And what happened to Hannibal made me feel worse. It was like a constant reminder of the accident – the way his life fell apart, the way he isolated himself, the way he lived. And . . . Oh, I don't know . . .'

'What?'

'The way he died. That he should have drowned too, so long afterwards. Talk about irony.'

'But it must have been some comfort to him that you, at least, survived,' said Erlendur.

Rebekka made no reply.

'Wasn't it?'

'I don't know,' she said. 'Honestly, I don't know. Maybe, in a sense. Yes, of course. It must have been. But clearly it wasn't enough. All he could think of was Helena.'

'I'm guessing your older brother did nothing to ease the pain.'

'No, that was another thing. He and his wife – Helena's sister – said a lot of things they shouldn't have. Things I know they regretted later – or at least my brother did. Asked him straight out if he'd been drinking, because they knew he could be reckless and couldn't really handle alcohol. But he hadn't touched a drop.

Of course, I could testify to that, but there was an inquest too which removed all doubt. In spite of that, they couldn't get over their anger, and my brothers hardly ever spoke again. Mind you, I'm convinced Helena's sister had a say in that. I never liked the woman.'

'When you heard Hannibal was dead did you think of them at all?' asked Erlendur.

'Them?'

'Your older brother.'

'No. How do you mean?'

'That they might have had an argument?'

'That's what you said the other day.'

'Yes.'

Rebekka thought.

'You don't seriously believe he could have killed Hannibal? After all these years? No, it's utterly absurd. I don't understand . . . don't know how it could even cross your mind. Nothing I've said has given you any reason to make allegations like that.'

'No, of course not,' said Erlendur. 'By the way, he rang me after you and I talked the other day. He was none too happy.'

'No, I . . . I told him the gist of our conversation. He and Hannibal hadn't had any contact. None at all. Not for decades.'

'Did they turn up to the funeral?'

'Yes. Well, he did. She stayed behind up north. Which is typical of her. Not an ounce of forgiveness in her heart. But you mustn't think that about my brother. Seriously. He'd never have been capable of hurting Hannibal.'

'But he did, didn't he? Indirectly?'

Rebekka stared at Erlendur, startled and indignant. He immediately regretted it.

'How can you imagine . . . how can you talk like that? How dare you?'

'I'm sorry, I –'

'Why are you so curious about Hannibal anyway?'

'Because I'd got to know him a bit. There was something about him – the way he chose to live. Perhaps more than anything it was what he said the last time I saw him. He'd been beaten up and we took him down to the station where he and I had a chat. He talked about his misery, said it didn't matter if he lived or died. I wondered what it would take to make a man talk like that.'

'He said that?'

'Yes. Honestly, I didn't mean to accuse anyone. Please forgive me if it came across that way.'

Rebekka studied Erlendur; the resolute mouth, the deeply entrenched lines of sadness around his eyes.

'This isn't just about Hannibal,' she said. 'There's more to it.'

Erlendur did not respond.

'Did something happen?' she asked.

'What do you mean?'

'What exactly was it about my brother that caught your imagination?'

'I told you.'

'No, you haven't told me anything. Whereas I've been open with you and told you all about my family. I feel you owe me an explanation for your curiosity. For why we're sitting here discussing my brother. I don't think you're being straight with me.'

She waited for an answer.

'Well?'

Erlendur remained silent.

'Then we've nothing more to discuss.' Rebekka stood up.

'Goodbye. I hope you'll honour my request to treat what I've told you about my family in strictest confidence.'

She walked off towards town, leaving him staring across the lake. Eventually he rose to his feet.

'I . . . I had a brother once, like you,' he called after her.

She halted and turned.

'A brother?'

'He went missing,' Erlendur said. 'In the mountains out east, where we grew up. We got lost in a blizzard. I was found; he never was. When you say you can hardly bear to remember how you went with them on that outing . . . I know the feeling. When Hannibal talked of his misery, it struck a chord with me.'

He sat down again and Rebekka came back.

'And you're still suffering?' she asked, after a while.

'I think about it almost every day.'

'I've tortured myself over the years, constantly brooding about what happened,' Rebekka said. 'If only I hadn't gone with them, hadn't been standing in the drive when they set out. If only I'd been playing with my friends instead . . . I used to brood like that endlessly when I was younger. What if he hadn't had to worry about his sister in the back seat? Surely then he'd have had time to save her? Was it my fault she died? Was it all my fault?'

'I'm familiar with those thoughts,' Erlendur admitted quietly.

'Then one day I realised I was being too hard on myself,' she went on. 'Using the incident to torture myself unnecessarily. I've stopped now. There's no point. He saved my life and his own life fell apart. I struggled with that knowledge for years but I've learned not to connect the two things.'

'I don't suppose Hannibal ever stopped,' said Erlendur. 'Torturing himself with thoughts like that.'

'No. They were his constant companions.'

'And destroyed him in the end.'

'Yes,' Rebekka said, her eyes on Erlendur. 'And destroyed him in the end.'

24

After meeting Rebekka, Erlendur headed towards the hostel on Amtmannsstígur. Thurí was not in, nor did he see the three women who had been playing Ludo last time. It turned out that Thurí had not been by for several days, but as far as the warden was aware she was still sober.

Erlendur asked two residents if they knew Thurí or had any news of her. Neither could help. One remembered something about her renting a room with another woman in the west end, but didn't know the address.

Erlendur walked down to Austurvöllur. A few drinkers had congregated on the benches in the square, screwing up their eyes against the afternoon sun. They varied in age, shabbiness and degrees of intoxication. The youngest was about twenty; long hair, muscular build, the rolled-up sleeves of his shirt revealing tattoos running up his arms. The eldest, clad in a thick, traditional Icelandic jumper, was a frail, bearded, toothless old man.

The rest were somewhere on the spectrum between youth and decrepitude. When Erlendur turned up to disturb the peace, they were variously baking in the sun, talking with their neighbours or quietly watching the world go by with knowing expressions.

'Any of you seen Thurí?' he asked on the off chance that they might be familiar with the name.

The men appeared for the most part indifferent. But a couple looked up and squinted at him.

'Who are you?'

'I need to find her,' said Erlendur. 'Any chance you might know where she is?'

'Thurí who?' said the young man with the tattoos.

'She was staying at the hostel on Amtmannsstígur,' said Erlendur. 'But she's gone.'

'You shagging her then?' asked the tattooed man.

His companions sniggered. Their interest roused, they watched Erlendur intently.

Erlendur smiled. A troublemaker, he thought.

'Nope, I just need to get in touch with her.'

'To shag her?' the young man persisted.

He was in his element. The older men sitting around him laughed.

'Do you know where she is?' asked Erlendur, addressing them instead.

'Hey, talk to me,' said the young man, rising to his feet. 'Why are you asking them? What's with you and this Thurí anyway? You together or what? She cheating on you? Doesn't want to shag you any more?'

Erlendur looked him up and down and concluded that he must be high. His eyes were bulging.

'Reckon I saw her earlier,' the young man said. 'She was screwing Stebbi here.' He pointed at the toothless old man.

There was a chorus of guffawing. The young man jabbed a finger at Erlendur.

'Why don't you fuck off?' he said. 'And leave us alone. Before I deck you.'

'You're not going to deck anyone.'

'Oh, yeah? Want to bet? Eh?'

'Take it easy.'

'Take it easy yourself.' The man lunged at him. If Erlendur hadn't been ready, the blow would have caught him right on the jaw. But he danced on his toes and dodged the punch as his training came into play. The young man's fist met thin air. Fear of losing face in front of his comrades made him even angrier, but as he was bracing himself to take another swing at Erlendur, the man gasped from a heavy blow to his stomach, followed immediately by a second. Two powerful strikes in a row, just as Erlendur had learned to aim at the punch bag, and the man collapsed to his knees, doubled up, gripping his stomach and gasping helplessly. Erlendur steadied him to make sure he didn't fall flat on his face.

'So none of you know her?' he said calmly to the men who had been watching the abrupt end to the hostilities.

'I do,' announced the toothless man, eyeing his friend, who was still struggling for breath. 'Haven't seen her for ages though. Reckon she must have dried out. Friend of hers runs Póllinn. Name's Svana. You could try asking after Thurí there.'

'I'll do that.'

The others came forward to tend to the winded man, but he shoved them away, watching resentfully as Erlendur walked off down Pósthússtræti.

Erlendur was familiar with Póllinn, 'The Pole'. It was a pub for hardened drinkers, run by a buxom woman who had once lived in Copenhagen's notorious Christiania district. She liked to side with her regulars, calling them customers when others labelled them scum. They included homeless men like Hannibal, the women from the hostel and the men who lined the benches of Austurvöllur Square.

The place was empty when Erlendur put his head round the door. He wasn't even sure it was open, but he caught sight of the owner bending down behind the bar, shifting crates of clinking bottles.

'Svana?'

The woman looked up from her task.

'Yeah.'

'I'm told you know Thurí and might be able to tell me where to find her.'

'And you are?'

'I spoke to her at the hostel on Amtmannsstígur a couple of days ago and need to get a message to her.'

'It's a while since she's been in.' Svana returned to shifting crates. 'She's on the wagon. Doesn't show her face in here when she's off the booze.'

'I heard she rented a place on Brádrædisholt. Would you happen to know it?'

'Why do you need to see her?'

'It's personal.'

'Are you a relative?'

Erlendur thought quickly. Lying would be the simplest option given that the excuse had been handed to him on a plate. The alternative would be sharing information that was none of Svana's business.

'Yes.'

'Poor Thurí. She's a nice girl but a hopeless alky. I was so pleased when I heard she was trying to quit. She's tried so often but always ends up back on the bottle. It's like some demon just takes over. She lives near the fishery. On Brádrædisholt, by the football ground. Tell her I said hi. Hope things are working out for her. Hope she hasn't lapsed again.'

Having got the house number from Svana, Erlendur tracked Thurí down to a basement room in a two-storey building with bare concrete walls. The room had its own entrance, facing a garden that had completely gone to seed. When Erlendur tapped on the door he was surprised to find it open a crack. Muffled groans were coming from inside. Worried that Thurí might be in trouble, he pushed the door open.

It was more of a broom cupboard than a room, full of rubbish Thurí had accumulated. Old clothes, food containers and plastic bags cluttered the floor. There was a shopping trolley in one corner. The only pieces of furniture were an old armchair and a stained divan bed on which Thurí was now lying, trying to neck a bottle of meths, while Bergmundur, still wearing his filthy coat, was pounding away on top of her, raising loud groans of protest from the springs.

25

Neither of them noticed Erlendur. He crept out again, pushing the door to behind him, then walked round the house and out into the street. He would rather not have had that image burnt onto his retinas but it couldn't be helped. Two things were clear: Bergmundur had found his Thurí, and Thurí had lapsed again.

Twenty minutes later Bergmundur rounded the corner and swaggered off down the street towards town. He didn't observe Erlendur tucked between the buildings, watching him until he turned onto Hringbraut.

Erlendur loitered for another five minutes before going back into the garden and rapping on the door, much louder than before. This time it was shut and he had to knock three times before he heard a rustle and Thurí opened up.

'What's all this bloody racket?' she slurred.

'Remember me?' said Erlendur. 'We talked the other day down at the hostel.'

'No,' said Thurí. 'Who're you? Why should I remember you?'

She was dressed in a skimpy jumper and skirt, smoking a cigarette. The ash dropped onto the floor at her feet.

'I was asking you about a man called Hannibal.'

Thurí peered more closely at Erlendur, still none the wiser.

'I knew Hannibal.' She wandered back inside, leaving the door open. Erlendur followed. She bent down and picked up a clear glass bottle containing the dregs of some cloudy liquid and took a long drink. Then, wiping her mouth with the back of her hand, she sat down on the divan. There were several containers of methylated spirits on the floor. The wages of love, he supposed.

'You told me you went to visit him before he died,' Erlendur began, 'at the pipeline where he was sleeping. And you kept something you found there later on, after he drowned. I wondered if you'd let me see it. You did say I could come round and have a look.'

Thurí stared at him and eventually the fog seemed to lift a little.

'You?' she said. 'Hannibal's friend. It's coming back to me now. What did you say your name was?'

'Erlendur.'

'A mate of Hannibal's?'

'That's right. You picked up an earring under the hot-water pipe. A gold one. You offered to show it to me.'

Thurí raised the bottle to her lips again. She seemed in low spirits.

'I lapsed,' she said, full of self-hatred. 'Was dry for months but now I've lapsed. I'm pathetic. Totally bloody pathetic. That's the worst thing. That I'm such a pathetic piece of shit. Back in the day, I didn't drink with just anyone, you know. Used to associate with nice people. With a good crowd. Used to have fun, drank classy stuff. Now I'm like a dog drinking out of a ditch.'

She brandished the bottle for emphasis.

'Nothing but sodding piss.'

Erlendur didn't know what to say so thought it best to keep his mouth shut. He surveyed the dingy little room. Her situation was grim. She had tried to claw her way out of the mire but kept falling back into it.

'Do you remember the earring?' he asked, eager to cut short his visit. There was an unpleasant smell that he associated inescapably with the image of Thurí and Bergmundur on the bed.

''Course I do,' said Thurí. 'I found it, didn't I? Think I'd forget? No way. It's my lucky charm.'

'Could I possibly see it?' asked Erlendur. 'Do you have it here?'

'What's it to you?'

'You do still have it?'

'I lent . . . pawned it.'

'You what?'

Thurí waved the bottle again.

'Got to drink something.'

'You sold it for booze?'

'Home-made spirits,' she clarified. 'Anyway, I didn't sell it. I pawned it. I'll get it back when I have the cash. Then you can see it. Why the hell do you want to see it anyhow? It's none of your business. I'm the one who found it. It's mine. If I want to sell it, I will and I don't need your permission.'

Erlendur could tell she wanted to pick a fight, so he tried the conciliatory approach. It took him a while to win her over, but in the end, he persuaded her to reveal the address of her supplier.

'Did you know Hannibal was married once?' he asked when she had calmed down.

'Yeah.'

'Did he ever tell you about the accident that happened when he was young?'

'I know how he lost Helena,' Thurí said. 'Though he didn't like to talk about it. Not to just anyone. He did tell me, but it wasn't easy for him. He wasn't one to open up about himself.'

'No, I don't suppose he was,' said Erlendur. 'Did he ever mention his elder brother? Or his sister-in-law?'

'No. Were they in contact? Hannibal never mentioned them.'

'So you don't know if his brother was in town when Hannibal died?'

'How would I know that? What the hell are you on about?'

'It doesn't matter,' Erlendur said. 'I heard from him, that's all. He wasn't exactly friendly.'

'Well, I don't know a bloody thing about him.'

Thurí slouched on the bed, bottle in hand, fumbling with a crumpled cigarette packet. She was not having much luck. Erlendur took the packet, extracted one and lit it for her.

'Maybe you should go down to Amtmannsstígur,' he said in parting.

'Yeah, yeah, yeah,' she said. 'Just leave me alone.'

Thurí's supplier had a place in Skerjafjördur, near the domestic airport. If Thurí was to be believed, he had an illegal still in a small garage, from which he was emerging when Erlendur arrived. They exchanged greetings, the man a little warily. He was short, with an impressive gut.

'What can I do for you?' he asked, locking the garage door.

'Thurí sent me,' Erlendur explained, working on the assumption that she was one of his regulars.

'Thurí, eh? How's she doing?'

'Bad. Your poison's put her in a foul mood. Have you got the earring she sold you?'

'Earring?'

'The gold earring she gave you in exchange for booze. She told me you had it.'

'So what if I do?'

'I'd like to buy it off you,' Erlendur said. 'For the same price you paid for it. What does a bottle of your home-made spirits cost?'

'Hey, I'm not –'

'Cut the crap.' Erlendur didn't want to waste time arguing. He was tired; he had been traipsing round all day, and the people he'd met and the things he'd seen had only exacerbated his fatigue. 'I'm with the police,' he continued. 'I'm confident that if we entered your garage we'd find distilling apparatus and a store of illegal alcohol. And I'm sure you do a tidy line in smuggled booze – expensive stuff from abroad.'

'The police?' the man repeated.

'Look, all I want is the earring,' said Erlendur. 'I know you've got it. Give it to me and I'll leave you alone.'

The man hesitated.

'There's no point in hanging on to one earring,' he said at last.

'Exactly,' Erlendur agreed.

'And it's not gold. No way. It's a piece of crap. I had it valued. It's plate.'

'You mean you gave Thurí too much for it?'

'No. Not really. It's just not worth much so . . . you . . . you can have it if you like.'

The man's eyes strayed to the garage door. Erlendur understood that he was trying to make the best of a bad situation.

26

The jeweller inspected the earring intently, thought for a while, then finally announced that he had never stocked it or anything like it.

'Not a bad piece,' he added. 'The gold plate's fairly thick and it's a nice bit of work.'

'What about the pearl?' asked Erlendur.

'That's genuine. But I didn't make this and I didn't sell it either.'

In his professional opinion, the earring was unlikely to be very old as the style was still in fashion. It was fairly large, made of two quite substantial linked hoops. Suspended from the lower, slightly smaller, hoop was a tiny, white pearl. Altogether it was an attractive piece, possibly bespoke; good quality, though the jeweller did not recognise the handiwork. It could have been purchased in Reykjavík or elsewhere in Iceland, but just as easily from somewhere abroad.

The earring looked none the worse for its spell under the

hot-water pipe. It couldn't have been lying there for long before Thurí spotted it glinting in the darkness of the tunnel. Her lucky charm, she had called it. It hadn't brought her much luck so far.

Two days had passed since Erlendur acquired the earring from Thurí's supplier. He had been carrying it around with him ever since. He had studied it minutely under his office lamp but had no idea what secrets it might hold, nor if it had any bearing on Hannibal's story. He'd most likely come across it by chance. But it was the only piece of the jigsaw that didn't fit; the only piece that had arrived there without explanation. The only gleam of light in Hannibal's squalid shelter.

The jeweller handed the earring back. He was the second expert Erlendur had consulted in the hope of tracing its owner. Erlendur was employing the only strategy he could think of: to take the earring to every jeweller in Reykjavík.

'Nice Christmas present,' commented the man. He was wearing a white coat and had a powerful magnifying glass hanging from a cord round his neck. 'Not too expensive, but pretty. Or the sort of thing you might give your wife for a wedding anniversary. Or a birthday. I could make another to match it, if you like.'

'Thanks, but there's no need,' said Erlendur. 'I just happened to find it and was hoping I might be able to return it to its owner.'

'Very conscientious of you,' the man said with surprise.

'No harm in trying.'

'The clip's all right,' the jeweller continued, inspecting it carefully. 'Nothing wrong with it. Though clip-ons like these can easily come off. Real earrings are less likely to get lost, but lots of women don't like the idea of having their ears pierced.'

'How do they come loose? Would they have to be knocked in some way? Or do they just slip off?'

'They slip off,' said the jeweller, confirming what Thurí had told him. 'The clips vary in quality. What did you mean by knocked?'

'If the owner was involved in a tussle, say.'

'Well, yes, of course. It goes without saying.'

In the third shop a young woman examined the earring carefully before announcing that she did not recognise it. But she added that she had worked there less than two years – she was training to be a silversmith – so it might have been sold before her time. The manager had popped out for a minute but Erlendur was welcome to wait. She too was impressed by his attempt to trace the owner; she had never heard of anyone being so considerate. She wasn't busy, so seemed keen to chat, but soon realised she was wasting her time.

Erlendur was weighing up his options – whether to come back later, or wait and see if the manager turned up soon – when the door opened. A tall man marched in, ignoring both of them, and closed the door of the workshop smartly behind him.

'That's him,' the young woman whispered to Erlendur. 'He's getting a divorce,' she added, as if embarrassed by the man's behaviour.

'Oh,' said Erlendur discouragingly, finding this information quite unnecessary.

The assistant pursued the manager and a minute or two later he emerged from his workshop, having put on a white coat. It struck Erlendur as odd that jewellers dressed like doctors or scientists, but then again perhaps their work required the same precision as an operation or an experiment.

'Can I see it?' the man asked without preamble.

Erlendur handed it over. The jeweller recognised it immediately.

'It's one of mine,' he said. 'I made two pairs, if I remember rightly. A couple of years back. They sold almost at once. I gather you've lost the other one. Want me to make a replacement?'

'No, he didn't lose it,' put in the young woman. 'He found this one and wants to return it to the owner, if he can.'

'That's right,' Erlendur said. 'I was wondering if you could help me trace her.'

'I don't keep a record of small sales like this,' the man said. He really was unusually tall and towered over the counter. 'I didn't charge much for them.'

'But could you –?'

'Though, now I come to think of it, I do remember one of them being sent back for repairs. They come with a warranty. Everything I sell comes with a warranty.'

He clamped a loupe in his eye and took a closer look.

'I can't tell if it was this one. There's no sign of the pearl having worked loose. But I do remember the job. It wasn't very complicated, so it's hardly surprising if the repair's invisible.'

'You couldn't find the owner's name for me, could you?'

The man laid the earring on the counter.

'Hang on a tick,' he said.

The young woman gave Erlendur an encouraging smile. The jeweller reappeared from his office carrying a large file and began to leaf through it.

'I make a record of repairs,' he said, flicking through invoices, receipts, sums and notes, until he found what he was looking for.

'Here we are.' He removed a receipt from the file. 'Repair under warranty. That rings a bell.'

'What was the woman's name?' asked Erlendur.

'It's not on the invoice,' the jeweller said. 'It's coming back to me now. It was a man who bought this set. I took down his name because of the repair. It's here on the receipt. You should be able to track him down. I never met his wife, so I don't know if they suited her. I have a feeling he said something about a birthday present, though I may be wrong.'

He passed over the receipt.

Erlendur committed the name to memory. Then, picking up the earring, he returned it to his pocket and thanked them both.

'Very thoughtful of you,' said the tall jeweller in parting.

'I do my best.'

That evening, having unobtrusively obtained the necessary information from police records, he headed over to Fossvogur. It was only about half an hour's walk, and before long he was standing by a small flat-roofed house, located on a quiet street. The husband now lived here alone. No movement was visible inside and the curtains were drawn. Perhaps he was out.

It had been his name on the jeweller's receipt. None other than the man who had reported his wife missing the previous year. She had gone for a night out with colleagues at Thórskaffi and never come home. The police file had described her as mad about jewellery. Her husband had bought her a beautiful pair of earrings a year or so before she went missing, and now Erlendur knew beyond a doubt that Thurí had found one of them in Hannibal's old camp.

27

The night was unusually hectic. They were called out to an altercation at a residential address, followed by another in front of a
bar; then they stopped three motorists for speeding. One turned
out to be a teenager without a licence, who was driving a stolen
car and drunk into the bargain. They had noticed the car's erratic
progress along Miklabraut and sped off after him, lights flashing.
The teenager had tried to make a break for it, skidding onto the
Breidholt road, where he floored the accelerator. The car, however,
was an ageing Cortina with a tiny engine, so they had no trouble
overtaking and forcing him to pull over. The boy leapt out and
raced south towards Kópavogur. Marteinn was the fastest. With
a resigned sigh, he set off after the boy and eventually caught up
with him. The boy swore at them as they drove him to the City
Hospital for a blood test. With that, the incident was considered
closed. As it was a first offence, there were no grounds for keeping
him in custody overnight. The owner of the car had been informed

but did not wish to press charges against the 'young fool'. After all, his vehicle wasn't damaged and he hadn't even been aware it was missing until the police woke him with the news.

The boy's father, on the other hand, was so apoplectic that they had to pacify him before releasing the boy into his care.

'You're nothing but bloody trouble,' the father said, shoving his son out of the police station ahead of him.

Erlendur had been even more taciturn than usual that night and as they came off duty Gardar asked if he was all right. Erlendur had not confided in them, or indeed anyone else apart from Rebekka, about his private investigation.

'All right? Of course.' All night long he had been puzzling over the fate of the woman from Thórskaffi.

'There's something on your mind,' insisted Gardar.

'No, there isn't.'

'Are Marteinn and I really so boring?'

'Well, you're not exactly scintillating company.'

His companions chuckled. They parted outside the station and Erlendur made his way home in the morning sunshine, his mind still preoccupied with a succession of images: Hannibal, the earring, the house in Fossvogur that the missing woman had shared with her husband, her route home from Thórskaffi and what had happened on the way. He couldn't begin to fathom the implications of her earring turning up in Hannibal's camp just before he died. The woman had disappeared and Hannibal had drowned the same weekend, yet no one had thought to connect the two incidents, least of all Erlendur himself. They were two completely unrelated events. In fact, so much emphasis had been placed on finding the woman that the inquiry into Hannibal's death had been brushed aside, as it appeared to be straightforward and not at all urgent.

Erlendur knew he shouldn't read too much into the coincidence. Not as things stood. It was more likely that the husband had bought the earring for his wife than for another woman, such as his mother or sister – or even a mistress, if he had one. But that didn't mean his wife had lost it the night she vanished. Living as she did within walking distance of the pipeline, she may well have passed it on a regular basis. There was every chance she'd dropped the earring another time and Hannibal had picked it up.

Alternatively, the woman might have walked along the pipeline one last time before deciding to take her own life. It was not far to Fossvogur or Skerjafjördur, where she could have waded into the sea. The earring could have slipped off without her noticing and fallen into a gap in the casing before she even set off on her final journey. In which case her disappearance and Hannibal's demise were completely unconnected.

A further possibility was that Hannibal, or a friend who visited him, had found the piece of jewellery somewhere else entirely and later dropped it in the tunnel.

Only after running through all the permutations he could think of did Erlendur permit himself to visualise what might have happened if, after leaving Thórskaffi, the woman had encountered Hannibal. As far as he knew, they were not acquainted; indeed it was hard to imagine any circumstances in which they could have got to know each other. She had mentioned wanting to walk home to clear her head. One route she might have taken passed the pipeline. Something could have happened which caused her earring to fall off. In this version of events, she would have needed to be near Hannibal's makeshift home, if not actually inside it.

Was it conceivable that he could have harmed her?

Erlendur was reluctant to pursue the thought to its logical conclusion. After all, the woman might have run into someone else and had an argument; perhaps it had turned violent and she had lost her earring and ultimately her life. Hannibal may never have seen the woman, let alone witnessed her fate.

Erlendur wrestled with the problem, repeatedly contradicting himself, until in the end he decided there was nothing for it but to go up to the pipeline again. First, however, he went home to pick up a powerful torch. Then he walked up to Öskjuhlíd, where he clambered onto the conduit and followed it east.

He saw no sign of Vilhelm, the previous occupant. No doubt he had found somewhere better to sleep. His litter remained, though: empty plastic bags, bottles and meths containers. The grass was still flattened around the entrance but the place was clearly deserted. Even the feral cats had gone.

Erlendur lowered himself to the ground, switched on the torch and eased his way inside. A faint warmth emanated from the pipes. The daylight did not extend much beyond the opening: the dark tunnel stretched out on either side, winding its way through miles of countryside. The rough concrete walls were at least a metre high and topped with a series of convex slabs, each three metres long, their joins sealed with mortar. Even a man of Erlendur's size could fit between the pipes and the wall, and lie there with his back to the warmth if he so desired.

He shone the torch into the gloom to his left, the section that originated in the Mosfell valley, but could see nothing but pipes. The same went for the right-hand side, which ran back towards Öskjuhlíd. It was here, close to the entrance, that Hannibal had set up camp and where Vilhelm too had been sleeping when Erlendur encountered him. Thurí had found the earring under one of the pipes. Trying to master his sense of dread, Erlendur forced himself to crawl what felt like an interminable distance into the tunnel, first on one side, then on the other, looking for further traces of the woman from Thórskaffi.

It was a relief to emerge into the open air: he did not like narrow, enclosed spaces. Outside, he inspected the grass around the entrance, systematically widening the search area.

All he found was a golf ball, half buried in the turf. He doubted that it dated back to the time of the golf club. More likely it was recent; he recalled that the boy he met that evening in Kringlumýri had mentioned someone from Hvassaleiti practising there.

Pocketing the ball, he headed for home. It was mid morning and as so often that summer the sky was cloudless. He had done his best to reject the idea that Hannibal might have met the missing woman, but there was no getting away from the fact: Hannibal had been living in the pipeline when she vanished. And an earring, almost certainly hers, had turned up there.

It was not difficult to put two and two together.

Hard as it was to accept, Erlendur could not entirely dismiss the possibility that Hannibal was responsible for the woman's disappearance. He no longer knew how to proceed. Should he inform CID of his discoveries? Or would it be premature?

He hurried home wondering what on earth to do. In his mind's eye he saw Hannibal: on the bench in the square, propped half-frozen against the corrugated-iron fence on Arnarhóll, in the cellar. A crazy tramp. And there was the accident in Hafnarfjördur, the death of his wife. Could he have been blind drunk or off his head on drugs when the woman from Thórskaffi crossed his path?

Erlendur could not rule it out.

It was a relief that he had found no further evidence in the tunnel. The enormity of it was too horrible to contemplate: that Hannibal might have seen the woman passing and dragged her inside, never to escape.

At least he had not left her body in the tunnel: Erlendur had made certain of that.

His last conversation with Hannibal now came back to him: he had talked of his misery. Had Hannibal been on the edge? Should Erlendur have realised then that he might be a danger to himself and others?

He didn't know. He had no idea what to think any more.

28

The last time Erlendur saw Hannibal had been shortly before the boys found his body. He was coming to the end of his shift after a quiet night midweek. There had been few call-outs and Erlendur's only companion in the patrol car had been a veteran officer called Sigurgeir. They had stopped three motorists for speeding and, as usual, much of their time had been taken up with blood tests and forms. They had also followed up a report of an attempted break-in on Laugavegur, but the thieves had got away. A witness had spotted them trying to force open the back door of a watch shop, but they hadn't had much luck and had vanished before the police arrived.

As Sigurgeir swung into Hafnarstræti they heard over the radio that the thieves had been apprehended committing another burglary. Erlendur had found an old copy of the *Althýdubladid* newspaper left behind in the car and was immersed in a translated Swedish serial called *The Laughing Policeman*, about a shooting on a bus in Stockholm. He searched in vain for the author's name. Sigurgeir, who was familiar with the story, said it was written by two people – a couple, he thought.

'Who the hell's that?' he said a moment later, slowing down.

Erlendur looked up from the paper and saw a man lying in the gutter – a man wearing a green anorak.

'Is it Hannibal?'

'So you've already come across the poor sod,' said Sigurgeir.

'I've run into him a couple of times.'

They parked, stepped out of the car and went over to him. It was indeed Hannibal and he was in a bad state, with blood on his face from a cut to the head. Presumably he had either had a bad fall or been beaten up.

'Hannibal!' Sigurgeir poked him with his boot.

Erlendur knelt down beside the man and took his hand. It felt like ice. He tried to rouse him and heard him emit a low groan.

'Shouldn't we call an ambulance?' he asked.

'No need for that, is there?' said Sigurgeir. 'You're all right, aren't you, Hannibal?'

Hannibal opened his eyes and looked at Erlendur.

'Is it you?' he asked.

'Are you all right?'

'Have they gone?' Hannibal groaned again.

'Who?'

'Those bloody hooligans.'

'What happened?'

'They went for me.' Hannibal managed to ease himself into a sitting position against a lamppost with Erlendur's help. 'Three of them. Bloody hooligans!'

'Who were they?'

'How should I know? Never seen them before.'

'You're absolutely fine, aren't you, old boy?' interrupted Sigurgeir. 'You can walk, can't you?'

'I'm OK,' said Hannibal, gritting his teeth at the pain in his side. The cut, which was superficial, had stopped bleeding.

'Think you might have broken some ribs?' asked Erlendur.

'They kept kicking me in the side,' Hannibal said. 'Hit me over the head as well. But I'll be all right. It's not the first time I've been set on by thugs.'

'Can you stand?' asked Erlendur.

'Just leave me be, I'll sort myself out. I don't need any help. Least of all from the likes of you.'

This last comment was accompanied by a dirty look at Sigurgeir, who stood there smiling as if untouched by Hannibal's misfortunes.

'You should come with us,' said Erlendur. 'We'd better take you to Casualty – get you seen to.'

'I'm not going to any hospital. There's no need. I'm all right.'

'There's no way we're going to stink out the car with this sorry wretch,' said Sigurgeir. 'You heard what he said – he's absolutely fine.'

'The least we can do is give him a cell down at the station to recover in.' Erlendur helped Hannibal to his feet. 'So we can keep an eye on him, call a doctor if necessary.'

'I'm not going to the station,' said Hannibal, leaning against the lamppost.

'You heard him,' said Sigurgeir. 'If he's capable of arguing, there can't be much wrong with him.'

'Don't you call me a sorry wretch,' Hannibal snapped. He moved so quickly, despite his weakened condition, that Sigurgeir had no chance to dodge the punch aimed at his jaw.

'Think you can hit me, you son of a bitch?' Sigurgeir exclaimed, clutching his face. He was about to retaliate when Erlendur seized his arm.

'You don't want to do that.'

Sigurgeir gaped at him.

'Let me go,' he ordered.

'Only if you leave him alone.'

Sigurgeir's gaze swivelled between Erlendur and Hannibal; then abruptly his anger seemed to subside. Erlendur released him.

'I could bring charges against him for striking a police officer,' said Sigurgeir.

'What would that achieve?' asked Erlendur. 'You're coming with us,' he said to Hannibal, and helped him to the patrol car. Sigurgeir watched them, in two minds about what to do, then got behind the wheel. Having gently guided Hannibal into the back seat, Erlendur joined his colleague in the front.

'He can recover in one of the cells,' Erlendur said again.

'You leave me alone, boy!' said Hannibal angrily. 'Stop interfering.'

He tried to get out of the car again but Erlendur prevented him and eventually succeeded in calming him down.

'You're coming with us,' he insisted. 'Those wounds need attention.'

'Why the do-gooder all of a sudden?' asked Sigurgeir, annoyed. 'Why don't you just invite him home with you?'

Hannibal made no further objections, but emitted a low moan as Sigurgeir started the car with a jerk and drove at breakneck speed back to the station on Hverfisgata. All the cells were empty. Erlendur installed Hannibal in one of them, and the tramp lay down on the bed. Since Hannibal flatly refused all offers to take him to the City Hospital, Erlendur phoned a doctor who came over, examined him and tended to his injuries. In his opinion there were no broken ribs but he left Hannibal some strong painkillers.

Not long after the doctor's departure, Erlendur's shift ended and he experienced the customary relief at laying aside the cap, baton and belt, and dressing in his ordinary clothes again. He had never really been comfortable in his uniform and always felt a bit of an idiot strutting around town in his full regalia.

He went to Hannibal's cell, drew back the hatch and saw that the tramp was lying on his back, staring blankly at the ceiling. He opened the door and went inside.

'How are you?'

Hannibal did not answer. He gave off his usual stench: a pungent mixture of urine and other filth.

'I probably don't need to remind you to take the painkillers the doctor left,' Erlendur said, noticing the pills lying untouched on the table beside the bed.

Hannibal did not react.

'Of course, they'll chuck you out after midday,' Erlendur went on. 'But I asked them to give you some lunch first.'

Hannibal continued to contemplate the ceiling.

'Do you really have no idea who attacked you?'

Still no response.

'We can try to track them down. You can press charges. You're not completely without rights, whatever you may think. You can always turn to us if you need to.'

At this the other man shook his head.

'Well, I must be off,' said Erlendur. 'Take care. Hope you feel better soon.'

He was about to step out into the corridor again when Hannibal cleared his throat.

'Why are you doing this?'

'Doing what?' Erlendur paused in the doorway.

'Why are you helping me? What do you want from me?'

'Nothing.'

'Then why won't you leave me alone?'

'I could do.'

'You should.'

'All right,' said Erlendur. 'I'll remember that in future.'

'Yes, you remember that. You needn't bother about me.'

'All right then.'

Hannibal did not look at him, but Erlendur could sense the rage seething inside him. Perhaps it was a fresh, hot anger, flaring up now because he had been attacked and left lying in the gutter. Or because he had been brought to this cell against his will, even if it was for his own good. Or because Sigurgeir had called him a sorry wretch. But Erlendur guessed that it was a cold fury that had long lain dormant in Hannibal, fuelled by a life of hardship.

'What happened to you?' the tramp asked suddenly.

'Nothing's happened to me,' said Erlendur.

'Then what are you trying to make up for?'

'I have no idea what you're talking about.'

'Is that so?'

'Yes. What are you on about?'

'I'm talking about you,' said Hannibal.

'You don't know the first thing about me,' said Erlendur. 'So how can you be talking about me?'

'When did you screw up?' asked Hannibal, sitting up with an effort.

'What do you mean?'

'What are you trying to compensate for with all your do-gooding?'

'Nothing,' said Erlendur.

'Come on, what are you trying to make amends for? That's why you're helping me, isn't it? To atone for your sins? Is that it? Am I your penance?'

Glaring at Erlendur, who was standing in the doorway, Hannibal suddenly began to shout.

'Why are you doing this? Am I supposed to give you some kind of absolution?'

'You –'

'Tell me about it!'

Erlendur was completely wrong-footed.

'Is that why you can't leave me alone?' yelled Hannibal hoarsely, beside himself now with rage. 'Well, you needn't feel sorry for me. I don't need your pity. It's no use to me. You can go to hell, you and all your bloody family! I don't need anyone's pity. No one's! Just you remember that!'

29

Hannibal fell back on the bed with a grimace, clutched his side and groaned. Erlendur hesitated a moment before closing the door. He left it unlocked. He had no idea what had just happened, but he thought he had better respect the man's wishes and leave him alone. He walked away down the corridor, shaken by the tramp's sudden violent rage. Hannibal's words about penance and absolution rang in his ears as he left the station and he was barely aware of his surroundings until an officer caught up with him. By then Erlendur had already covered quite a distance.

'That alky wants a word with you,' the policeman said, panting.

'Alky?'

'That tramp you put in the cells. He wants to talk to you.'

'Oh?'

'Yes, he's calling for you. He was out in the corridor raising hell, demanding to see you. He stinks.'

'Tell him I've left.'

'He was very insistent,' said the officer. 'He wants to talk to you. Won't let it drop.'

Erlendur wavered. He had no desire to see Hannibal in that mood.

'He threatened us. We had to lock him in.'

'You mustn't do that,' said Erlendur. 'He's not under arrest. He was beaten up. He's free to go whenever he likes.'

'Well, he's not leaving till he's spoken to you.'

Erlendur shook his head.

'Right then,' said the policeman. 'We'll kick him out.'

'Don't do that – he needs a chance to recover.'

'Oh, for God's sake, why don't you just talk to him and calm him down, then everyone'll be happy. Wouldn't that be simplest?'

A few minutes later Erlendur went back into the cell. Hannibal was sitting, head bowed, on the bed, but as soon as he saw Erlendur he stood and, surprisingly, ran a hand through his hair in a futile attempt to smarten himself up. Erlendur sensed it was an old habit, a relic of his past life that lingered on with peculiar obstinacy. That world may have been irretrievably lost to him but the action was ingrained, a remnant of the self-respect he had once possessed. It sat oddly with his condition now. His green anorak, filthy from living rough, torn from beatings like the one last night, looked as if it was grafted to his flesh. It was cinched round the waist by a black leather belt, and a woollen hat poked out of one pocket. Around his neck Hannibal had knotted a thin, green scarf, and on his lower half he wore baggy, black trousers. His feet were clad in thick galoshes, minus their laces, with woollen socks peeping over the top. His trouser legs were tucked into the socks, which were secured with tough elastic bands. Under the grime his face had a corpse-like pallor and was criss-crossed with wrinkles, a testament to his daily battle for survival, waged in the darkest corners of the city. If his eyes had ever shone with joy, it had long since been extinguished. They were hard and grey as weathered stone.

'Thank you for coming back,' he began.

'What do you want from me?' asked Erlendur.

'I wanted to apologise for the way I spoke to you. It was uncalled for, and it matters a lot to me that you know I didn't mean anything by it. I hope you'll accept my apology and forgive my outburst.'

'There's nothing to forgive,' said Erlendur. 'We don't know each other. You can say what you like to me. I don't care.'

'All the same, I'd be grateful,' said Hannibal. 'You've been kind to me and I had no business attacking you like that. I know . . . I know you mean well and I should respect that. I suppose I'm a bit touchy about people meddling. Can't stand it when they try to push me about.'

'I wouldn't dream of pushing you about.'

'No, I know that.'

'Have you encountered them before?' asked Erlendur.

'Who?'

'The men who beat you up.'

'No, not them. Others, though.'

'So you don't know who they were?'

'No.'

'Or what sort of age?'

'Young. They were young. And they were wearing good shoes. I noticed that when they started kicking me. Sometimes these boys . . . boys like them try to get a rise out of me. Usually I ignore them but every now and then I'm stupid enough to fly off the handle and almost always come off worst.'

He sat down on the bed again with a stifled moan, pressing a hand to his ribs.

'They won't finish me off. Any more than the bastards who tried to set fire to my cellar.'

'What do you mean? Did someone start a fire?'

'Frímann blames me – he won't listen. But it wasn't me, I swear.'

'Do you know who it was?'

'I have my suspicions,' said Hannibal. 'Anyhow, I'd better take those pills.' He reached out for the painkillers. 'You're not from Reykjavík, are you?'

'Why do you say that?'

'You from the country?'

'I moved here when I was twelve,' said Erlendur.

'Where are you from?'

'The East Fjords. Eskifjördur.'

'Went there once. Beautiful place. How do you like Reykjavík?'

'It's not too bad.'

'Like that, is it?' said Hannibal. 'Why did you move?'

'I came here with my parents.'

'I was born here in the city,' said Hannibal. 'In Laugarnes. Lived here all my life, wouldn't want to be anywhere else.'

'In spite of everything.'

'I've no one to blame but myself,' said Hannibal. 'You do what you can with the hand you're dealt, and I'll be the first to admit I've ballsed up.'

'What did you mean before, about penance?' asked Erlendur.

'That was just nonsense. I come out with a load of crap sometimes. Don't take any notice.'

'Are you sure?'

'Yes, I'd rather not go into it, if you don't mind.'

'Do you feel you haven't done enough penance yourself?' asked Erlendur.

'I said I'd rather not talk about it.'

'Is this some kind of punishment? This life on the streets?'

Hannibal would not answer, so Erlendur abandoned the subject.

'You're a bit of an outsider yourself,' the tramp said after a lengthy pause.

'I wouldn't say that.'

'Is that why you feel sorry for me?'

'I just don't want you to die of exposure.'

'Why should you care?'

'Why shouldn't I care?'

'No one else gives a toss if I live or die, so I don't see why you should. Why did your family move to town? Did something happen?'

'My parents wanted to move to the city.'

'Why?'

'Various reasons.'

'Don't you want to tell me?'

'I don't see that it has anything to do with you.'

'No, of course not,' said Hannibal in a quieter voice, suddenly ashamed. 'Sorry. It's none of my business. I'm a nosy bastard, I'm afraid. Terribly nosy. Always have been. Don't know where it comes from. Just a habit. A bad habit.'

He ran a hand over his hair again, tidying non-existent locks. He had lost his vehemence and sat now without speaking, eyes fixed on the cell wall, as if it were one of the walls he had erected around his own life, which had confined him in a self-imposed prison for longer than he cared to remember.

'Doesn't matter if I live or die,' he said absently, almost whispering now.

'What did you say?'

'I'd probably end it all if I wasn't such a coward.'

'End what?'

'This misery,' Hannibal whispered, gazing unseeing at the wall. 'This god-awful misery.'

30

The woman who had gone missing from Thórskaffi was called Oddný. She was thirty-four at the time. She was born in Reykjavík and had been brought up in the old Thingholt district. After finishing secondary school she had moved on to college but quit after a couple of years and took a job instead. Before becoming an estate agent she had worked in a variety of places, including the supermarket on Hafnarstræti where she met her future husband. He was studying business at the university but had taken a summer job there. They got married but didn't have any children. After graduating he had been offered a position at the People's Bank and later at a pension fund, and with their combined salaries they had been able to scrape together the money to build their own house in Fossvogur. They had moved in three years before Oddný vanished.

'They both worked very hard, no question' said the woman with a smile. 'Pity they never had children. She wanted them so badly. Often talked about it. From what she said I gather they'd been for all kinds of tests but, well, I don't know if I should be gossiping about this . . .'

'What?' asked Erlendur.

'It's just that she once hinted that the problem lay with him. At least that's what she said. I don't know if it's true.'

Erlendur nodded. Behind the woman hung a large poster of central London and three clocks showing the time in Moscow, Paris and New York respectively. The woman worked for a large travel agency and sold tours all over the world. She had known Oddný from way back and later worked with her at the estate agency, but had been offered better pay and conditions in the travel business.

'Actually, I got her the job at the estate agency,' said the woman. 'She was very good – had an amazing gift for talking to people and winning their trust.'

The woman, whose name was Ástríður, was one of the chief witnesses. She had met up with her old work mates at Thórskaffi and was one of the last people to see Oddný alive. Erlendur had reread the case file, noting down the names of several witnesses and other people with some connection to the case. The inquiry was still ongoing, so Erlendur's questions did not arouse suspicion; all he had to do was mention that he was from the police. There was no reason to treat it as a criminal investigation yet, but not everyone was satisfied with this.

Although Erlendur was not officially involved in the inquiry, he didn't see why this should stop him conducting his own private investigation. Nor was he particularly concerned about how his superiors would react when they learned what he'd been up to. Anyone was free to gather information if they wanted to. Besides, he believed he was acting in Hannibal's interests. If there was fallout, he would explain about the earring. Indeed, that was his plan, but first he wanted to try to establish whether Hannibal had played any part in the woman's disappearance.

He wanted to avoid a situation where the press heard that the tramp had probably been the last person to see Oddný alive, and then printed a story about Hannibal being responsible for her death. Erlendur hoped to dispel any rumours of that kind but knew it would be difficult. He would not be able to hush up the discovery of the earring much longer. The moment he informed CID who it belonged to and where it was found, the case would be promoted from a missing-person inquiry to a full-blown murder investigation.

'Did it affect their relationship?' he asked now.

'What?'

'The fact they couldn't have children.'

'No, well, actually only the other day at our sewing circle we were discussing whether she had found herself a new lover. You hear so many stories – that sort of gossip's always doing the rounds, you know what I mean? So I can't vouch for it. I knew her very well and wasn't aware of it, so . . . in my opinion it's rubbish. But we were discussing whether he might have been the man she met at Thórskaffi that evening.' Ástrídur lowered her voice. 'The man in the drawing.'

Erlendur nodded again. Oddný's family had commissioned an artist's impression of one of the men at the nightclub, based on a description by her childhood friend, and circulated it to the papers and the television station. The friend in question had seen Oddný talking to the man just before she left. The picture had resulted in a few leads from the public, among them customers from Thórskaffi, but none of these could be substantiated.

'It did emerge that she'd once been unfaithful to her husband,' said Erlendur. 'In connection with that drawing.'

'Yes, that came out in one of the papers,' said Ástrídur in disgust. 'It's terrible, printing something like that. Poor couple.'

'The circumstances were similar. It seemed significant.'

'Admittedly, she did meet that guy at a nightclub,' said Ástrídur, 'but it was the only time.'

Three years before her disappearance Oddný had slept with a man after meeting him at Rödull, a nightclub. After two or three more encounters she had decided to break it off, but the man didn't want to let her go. Then Oddný's husband had found out. He had gone berserk and threatened to leave her, but they had managed to sort it out and, as far as anyone knew, she had never met the man again.

'Why did she have a fling?' asked Erlendur.

'Your guess is as good as mine,' said Ástrídur. 'The first I heard about it was when I read it in the papers.'

'But you think she may have done it again — cheated on her husband?'

'Well, it's possible that the man she met in Thórskaffi wasn't just a casual acquaintance. Maybe there was something more between them and they really did leave together. The girls in my sewing circle think it's very strange that he's never come forward.'

'Was their marriage in trouble?'

'For all I know, it was fine. At any rate, she didn't complain to us. I get on all right with her husband. We sometimes take our partners along when we go out together, and he was always very nice. He doesn't come out any more, though. We've invited him

173

but he . . . naturally he's been going through a very tough time and . . .'

'What?'

'Oh, just, I think he's coped really well, considering.'

'Does he still live alone?'

'I believe so. As far as I know. For the moment, anyway. But life goes on.'

'Yes,' said Erlendur, looking up at the large poster of London behind her. 'I suppose it does.'

31

Rebekka was tidying up when Erlendur dropped by the surgery later that afternoon. All the patients had gone and the doctors were leaving, one after the other, calling out their goodbyes to her. She asked Erlendur to wait a minute while she finished up, then followed him out into the sunshine. They walked to the lake again, this time finding a bench at the near end, by the Idnó Theatre. He pulled the earring from his pocket and handed it to her.

'What's this?'

'It turned up in the pipeline where Hannibal was sleeping,' Erlendur explained.

'Oh, so you got managed to get hold of it?'

She examined it.

'Seen it before?' asked Erlendur.

'No, who –?'

'Quite sure?'

'Definitely,' she said firmly. 'Was it Hannibal's?'

'No, it wasn't his. But I think I know whose it was, and it's very odd that it turned up in his camp.'

'So whose was it?'

'Are you absolutely sure you've never seen it before?'

'Yes, I've never laid eyes on it,' said Rebekka. 'Did it belong to a girlfriend of Hannibal's? Someone who visited him there? Why did you say it's very odd? What's so odd about it?'

'The woman who owned this earring is almost certainly dead. There's a chance that the night she went missing she was in the pipeline with Hannibal at some point.'

'I don't understand. What do you mean? She went missing?'

'Her name was Oddný. Maybe you remember the news reports.' Rebekka thought.

'You mean the woman at Thórskaffi?'

He nodded.

'Was she at the pipeline?'

'Possibly.'

'How . . . what . . .?'

'It's a year since she vanished and the police still haven't worked out what happened to her. Either it was suicide or she was murdered. She disappeared around the same time – in fact the very same weekend – that Hannibal drowned in Kringlumýri. Nobody connected the incidents because there was nothing to link them. But recently I talked to a friend of Hannibal's who'd been on the streets with him. She claimed she'd gone to his camp shortly after he died, found the earring and took it away with her. I'm afraid there's no getting round the fact that Oddný may have been with Hannibal the night she went missing.'

Rebekka stared at Erlendur, stricken. Her gaze dropped to the earring and she jerked back her hand as if burnt. The earring fell on the ground. Erlendur bent over and retrieved it. Anticipating a reaction like this, he had tried to think of a way to mitigate the shock. Perhaps there wasn't one.

'Do . . . do the police know about this?' stammered Rebekka. 'Of course they must – you're a policeman yourself.'

'I've kept this to myself for the moment,' he said. 'But I can't cover it up for ever. The woman who found the earring saw no reason to report it, so for the time being it's just between us.'

'Are you saying that Hannibal . . . that Hannibal played some part in her disappearance? The woman from Thórskaffi?'

'Not necessarily. There's an outside chance that he came across the earring somewhere else and took it home with him. Or wasn't even aware it was in the pipeline and didn't lay a finger on her. Then again . . .'

'You think he might have harmed her!'

'I didn't say that.'

'But it's what you believe.'

'Is it possible?'

'For God's sake, no!' she exclaimed. 'There's absolutely no way. Hannibal could never have hurt her. I just can't . . . Anyway, what does that have to do with him dying the same weekend?'

'The earring was found in Hannibal's camp. It belonged to the woman. Those are the facts. How to interpret them is another matter.'

'She vanishes; he drowns. You really think there's a link?'

'It's hard not to connect them.'

'You'll have to report this.'

'Yes.'

'Can you find out?' Rebekka asked. 'If Hannibal harmed her? On the quiet? Before you do?'

'I'd really like to, but I can't hush it up for much longer.'

'Would you do it for me?' Rebekka asked. 'Please, Erlendur. Hannibal wasn't like that. He wouldn't have been capable of it. Under any circumstances.'

'I'll –'

'The minute you tell them about the earring everyone'll believe he killed that poor woman. Then the case will never be solved and we'll never find out what really happened. And people will believe that about Hannibal. For ever. You have to help me, please, Erlendur. He didn't hurt anyone. You have to believe me. He never hurt anyone!'

'I'll do my best. But I'm in an impossible position –'

'Of course, I understand, but . . .'

Her words petered out.

'You have to help me,' she repeated eventually. 'Please, for me, find out the truth before it's too late.'

32

It transpired that the police had seen no reason to interview a childhood friend of Oddný's called Ingunn. She was a housewife and mother of four, who lived in one of the new terraced houses in Breidholt, where the urban sprawl had spread with alarming speed in recent years. Whichever way you looked, everything was new – streets, buildings, gardens. Many of the sites had yet to be finished and wooden boards, some with mats on them, had been laid in front of entrances in an effort to keep the dirt from being trampled indoors. Only the cars parked outside were old, as many of those building new homes had been forced either to sell their vehicles to pay for the construction or to exchange them for rusty old wrecks that were reluctant to start in the mornings. One of these was puttering out of Ingunn's street as Erlendur arrived; it stalled, coughed into life again and disappeared round the corner in a cloud of blue smoke.

He had called ahead and Ingunn was waiting for him with

freshly made coffee and slices of home-made sponge cake. Her children were out playing on the construction sites and her husband was at work. Erlendur could see photos of them all in the sitting room.

'So you're still looking for Oddný,' she said, pouring coffee into cups. 'I suppose you've left no stone unturned.'

'That's right,' said Erlendur. 'The case isn't closed. But the police haven't interviewed you before, have they?'

'No, I . . . they haven't, and I really don't know if I can help you much. I've never actually spoken to the police before. My husband's been pushing me to get in touch with you but . . . there's been enough gossip about poor Oddný already.'

Erlendur had introduced himself as a police officer who was looking into the incident on his own initiative, making it clear that he had nothing to do with the formal investigation. Ingunn was satisfied and asked no further questions. In fact, she seemed completely devoid of curiosity. She had a quiet manner and spoke so softly that it was hard to hear her. She and Oddný had grown up on the same street and kept in touch all those years. They had attended the same sixth-form college, but unlike Oddný, Ingunn had completed her schooling and taken her final exams. But by then she was in a relationship and pregnant, so instead of going on to the university she had stayed at home and supported her husband during his further education. He was a doctor.

'I always wanted to study Icelandic,' she said, with a faint smile.

'Do you know why Oddný dropped out of college after two years?' asked Erlendur.

'I wasn't surprised,' said Ingunn. 'She wasn't really interested in studying, and she needed the money. She spent all her time at parties. Didn't revise. So she failed her exams, left college and never regretted it. She was very industrious – worked all the time – but studying just wasn't for her. She was still living with her parents too and wanted to make her contribution, which was only natural as her family was poor. They'd never had much money.'

'Then a few years later she got married.'

'That's right, to Gústaf.'

'Were there any other men before him?'

'Oh, yes, she'd been out with a few people, but nothing serious until Gústaf came on the scene. They quickly moved in together.'

'But had no children?'

'No, she was sad about that. She'd always dreamt of having children. But it didn't happen, unfortunately. She used to talk to me about it sometimes.'

'Do you know what the problem was?'

'No, not exactly. She was . . . he didn't like her discussing it. I remember she touched on the subject once when we were all out together, and he got incredibly angry. That wasn't like him, at least as far as we were aware. I suppose it's not really surprising – it must have been a sensitive issue for him.'

'She cheated on him once.'

'Yes, she did.'

'And was seen talking to an unknown man at Thórskaffi just before she vanished.'

'Yes, I read about that.'

'Do you know anything about the man?'

'No.'

'Or about any other similar incidents?'

'You mean other men in her life? No. She didn't necessarily know the man in Thórskaffi, did she?'

'No, that's true,' said Erlendur. 'He's never come forward and we know nothing about him. The artist's impression didn't help much. We can't even be sure he's connected to the case. When was the last time you saw Oddný?'

'The week before she disappeared, at the sewing circle she and I set up with some other friends. We've been meeting up for about ten years. She was her usual cheerful, lively self. She gave me a lift home and . . . that was the last time I saw her.'

'Why did your husband want you to talk to the police?'

'What?'

'You mentioned earlier that your husband had been encouraging you to contact us. Then you said there'd been enough gossip already.'

Ingunn frowned as if she did not like discussing her friend's affairs. So far she had answered tentatively, wary of his questions, careful to avoid being led into saying more than she intended.

'I don't know if it's relevant,' she said.

'What?'

'Just a comment she made. About six months before she disappeared. But she never referred to it again and the one time I raised it with her, she changed the subject. But . . . I don't know if it'll make any difference and, like I said, there's been more than enough gossip about her and Gústaf, and her affair. I had to promise never to tell. She was so ashamed; she couldn't bear for it to get around. I kept meaning to contact the detectives in charge of the inquiry and my husband has . . . I just couldn't bring myself to tell anyone. For her sake, you understand. She was so hurt and angry and crushed by the experience. Angry with him, and with herself for not having done anything about it.'

'What did she tell you?'

'I keep trying not to read too much into it. I don't know if it has any bearing on what happened but . . .'

'What?'

'Gústaf . . . he was violent. Used to abuse and humiliate her. Mostly it was verbal, but he raised his hand to her at least twice.'

'Oh?'

'Perhaps I should have come to you,' said Ingunn. 'My husband . . . I told him and he wanted me to get in contact. It's been preying on my mind . . .'

'You don't think there's any chance she took her own life?'

'That was my first thought. Horrible though that would be, it's worse to think she might have been murdered.'

'Her husband claimed he was at a Lions Club meeting when she was at Thórskaffi.'

'I haven't been in touch with him at all since it happened,' Ingunn said. 'He held a memorial service for her recently, to mark a year since she went missing, but I couldn't bring myself to go.'

'He hasn't altered his statement.'

'No, of course not, why would he?'

'But you believe she was frightened of him?'

'She didn't say that, but judging from the way she talked about him, the way he treated her, she probably had good reason to be. But I had to promise I wouldn't tell anyone. She was so afraid the news would get out. She couldn't bear it.'

'One more thing. Do you know if she was acquainted with a man called Hannibal?'

'Hannibal? No, not that I remember. Who's he?'

'Just one of the names that cropped up in the course of the investigation. Probably not important. Oddný never mentioned anyone by that name?'

'No.'

'Do you think her husband could have been involved in her disappearance?'

'I really couldn't say. Oddný confided in me, and I promised never to repeat it. Now I've broken my promise. She wanted to leave him, but he wouldn't let her. He told her so.'

'Do you think that's why she had the affair?'

Ingunn nodded.

'I think so. Oddný told me she should have left him as soon as it started.'

33

They had arranged to meet at Hressingarskálinn. She was already there, smiling at him, when he walked in the door. A fine drizzle was falling over the city. He shook the moisture from his coat, then went over and joined her. If she was expecting a kiss she was disappointed. He had never gone in for public displays of affection. She sometimes made him hold hands as they walked through town but he would find any excuse to let go, putting his hand in his pocket or running it over his hair. He seemed to have no need for physical contact.

'Miserable weather,' she said.

'It's supposed to clear up this evening. The forecast's good for tomorrow.'

He glanced around. Hressingarskálinn – or Hressó as it was familiarly known – was one of the few cafes in the centre of town. It attracted a crowd of artists, actors, poets and journalists who chatted and gossiped, perused the papers, had opinions on everything and spared no one. The poet Steinn Steinarr, who in Erlendur's opinion had no equal, used to hold court there. And he had spotted another luminary, Tómas Guðmundsson, in the midst of heated discussion once. Hressó did a decent lunch and Erlendur sometimes dropped in to eat, read the papers and watch the world go by.

'Shall we have waffles?' asked Halldóra. 'And hot chocolate with cream?'

'Yup, waffles and cream,' said Erlendur. 'That'll hit the spot.'

'Just the thing on a dreary day like this, isn't it?' She smiled.

'Yes.'

Once they had ordered, Halldóra took out a packet of cigarettes and offered him one. They smoked in silence until she began to tell him about a re-released film she had seen with her girlfriends. She gave a rundown of the plot and the actors. He had heard of Shirley MacLaine but not of the film, *Irma la Douce*. He very seldom went to the cinema.

They tucked into the waffles and sipped their hot chocolate. The place was quiet; only a few tables were occupied and the customers spoke in murmurs. Halldóra told him she had got the job at the telephone company. She was looking forward to learning the ropes, booking and connecting international calls. Then she asked him what it was like on night duty. He sketched a few of the incidents they dealt with, shorn of any excitement or romance. Instead, he emphasised the depressing side: the burglaries, the drunk drivers and car crashes. He had not told her about Hannibal or his unofficial investigation. Sooner or later he would have to report his unnerving discoveries to CID.

'Don't you get tired of being on night duty all the time?' she asked. 'Doesn't it mess up your body clock?'

'No, I like it fine,' he replied. 'I work with a couple of good guys, so the shifts pass surprisingly quickly.'

It was not the first time she had asked. He knew she cared about his welfare, but mostly she was just grasping at conversational straws.

'Gardar and Marteinn, you mean?'

'Yes. They're all right.'

'You don't have any of the new female officers on your shift?'

'No.' He smiled.

'Is it really a job for women? What if some crazy person attacked them? Isn't it too dangerous?'

'Not really. At least, not in my opinion,' said Erlendur. 'Not everyone's happy with women going out on the beat, but it was probably about time. There are plenty of situations where it's actually better to have a female officer.'

'Do you think I could be a cop?'

'Definitely.' Erlendur grinned.

She laughed and they sipped their hot chocolate again. He sensed that she was unsure of herself, as if she had something on her mind that she didn't know how to put into words. Or was too shy to tell him.

'I . . . I was wondering if . . .'

'What?'

'Oh, I . . . I wondered if you'd like to . . . if you wouldn't mind . . . I don't know . . . if I rented a place with you? If we moved in together? I just wanted to float the idea. It would save us having to pay for two places. And . . . well, it would save us a lot of money . . . so I was wondering if it might make sense, that's all.'

Erlendur took a mouthful of waffle. He had been to the small flat she rented in Breidholt a few times. It was in the basement of a detached house and Halldóra was always complaining about how it was so cramped and how inconvenient the location was. He imagined it would be even more inconvenient for her new job at the phone company headquarters in the centre of town.

'The thing is, they've given me my notice,' Halldóra continued. 'Their daughter's coming home. She's been studying abroad for two years but apparently doesn't want to stay, so they told me I have to move out by the end of the summer.'

Erlendur did not say anything to this.

'I just thought I'd run it by you,' she said. 'What do you think?'

'I –'

'We've known each other – been seeing each other or whatever you like to call it – for . . . I don't know how long, so perhaps it's time we did something about it. Took the next step. Made it serious. You know . . .'

He had given little thought to moving their relationship on to the next stage or even wondering where it was going. They met up fairly regularly, either at her flat or at his place in Hlídar, which was handier for a night out on the town. But they hadn't discussed any future plans. Admittedly, he had once given in and agreed to meet her parents. But as far as he knew Halldóra had been happy with the arrangement. At least she had never pushed him for more. Until now.

She noticed his hesitation.

'It was just an idea,' she said, immediately backing down. 'If you don't want to, that's fine. I can find myself a flat somewhere else. Of course it's cheapest to live way out in Breidholt, but it's quite a long journey to work. So . . . I need to weigh up the options.'

'No, what you're saying might make sense, I just need to think about it,' said Erlendur. 'I wasn't expecting it. Sorry if . . . I just haven't given it any thought. You've never brought this up before. We've never discussed it.'

'No, fair enough.'

'So . . . it's a bit out of the blue.'

'Yes, I know. It was just an idea,' Halldóra repeated, cheering up a little. 'Go away and think about it. It's all right. It's fine. You need time to mull it over. Of course. I should've warned you. Sorry to spring it on you like that.'

'No need to be sorry, Halldóra.'

'I could have handled it better.'

'It's fine.'

'Actually, I've been kind of dreading seeing you today.'

'Dreading? Because of that? Don't worry.'

He reached out and laid a hand on hers for emphasis.

'I just needed to know how you'd take it,' she said. 'It's important to me – in the circumstances.'

'Of course.'

'There's something else.'

Noticing that she still looked worried, Erlendur assumed he had failed to reassure her. The people at the neighbouring table stood up and went out into the drizzle. Their departure was accompanied by a cold gust of wind.

'I had to get that off my chest first – about us,' said Halldóra.

'Well, now you have.'

'Yes.'

'What is it? What's the other thing?'

'I think I'm pregnant.'

34

By evening the skies had cleared and the wind had dropped. The pools lay smooth and unruffled as Erlendur threaded his way among them, crossing Kringlumýri in the direction of Hvassaleiti. He had walked this way before after talking to the boy on the bicycle. Erlendur was keen to meet the man who practised his golf swing on Hvassaleiti. So far he had had no success in tracking him down.

He made his way through the neighbourhood, passing terraced houses and blocks of flats. The streets were full of children playing ball games or hide-and-seek – they had erupted from the houses as soon as the rain let up – but he couldn't see his friend on the bike. Neighbours stood around chatting about inflation or whether they planned to go to the Thingvellir celebrations. 'Depends on the weather,' Erlendur heard as he went by.

When he reached the edge of the development he caught

sight of a man standing in a dip not far from the corner of Hvassaleiti and Háaleitisbraut, where the National Broadcasting Company was planning to build its new headquarters. Next to the man was a small golf bag. He was extracting balls from a bucket lying on its side and hitting them a few metres at a time across the grass.

Erlendur walked over and said good evening. The man returned his greeting, hit a ball six metres or so, then hooked out another with his club. This time he messed up his stroke, sending a chunk of turf into the air; Erlendur had ruined his concentration. He turned.

'Can I do something for you?' he asked, a hint of impatience in his voice.

'Do you often practise here?'

'Sometimes.' The man was in his forties, tall and lean, dressed in golfing attire – cardigan, light checked trousers, a glove on his left hand. From his tan Erlendur guessed he had spent his summer on the handful of golf courses to be found near Reykjavík. It only confirmed his belief that the game had been invented for English and Scottish lords who had nothing better to do with their time.

'What's it to you?' asked the man.

'Oh, just curious,' said Erlendur. 'The local boys told me a golfer sometimes practised here in the evenings.'

He brought out the ball he had found and showed it to the man.

'This one of yours, by any chance? I found it up by the pipeline.'

The golfer looked from the ball to Erlendur, then took it and examined it more closely. He was surprised, not by the ball but by the fact that this young man should have come all this way to return it.

'Could be,' he said. 'I don't mark my balls specially so . . . and this one looks quite old. No, I'm fairly sure it's not mine.'

He handed it back.

'Don't you hit them towards the pipeline?' asked Erlendur, pointing to where the conduit crossed the waste-ground between Fossvogur and Kringlumýri.

'If I'm using the driver, they can travel up to two hundred and fifty metres. But mostly I work on my putting here. And I don't lose these balls so easily.'

'The driver?'

'The biggest club.'

'Oh, I see.'

'You're not a golfer, are you?'

'No.'

'Putting's the most important skill – those are the short shots. You can whack the balls as far as you like but the real knack lies in hitting them accurately over short distances.'

'I don't know the first thing about golf,' admitted Erlendur.

'No, not many Icelanders play.'

'Does anyone else practise here – that you're aware of?'

'Not that I've noticed.'

'Been coming here long?'

'I moved to this area four years ago.'

'Ever see any activity around the pipeline? People walking along it, for example?'

'Now and then.'

'Ever come out here late in the evenings?'

'Past midnight, sometimes, when it's light enough. Try to make

192

the most of these short summers. But I don't see why you're asking me all this. Can I help you with something specific?'

'I don't know if you remember, but a tramp drowned in Kringlumýri a year ago. He'd been sleeping inside the heating conduit. I found this ball nearby and wondered if you'd hit it over there and might perhaps have seen him.'

'I do remember them finding him,' said the golfer.

'Do you recall seeing him in the area? Or over by the pipeline?'

'Was he someone you knew?'

'We were acquainted.'

'No, I never saw him. Didn't even know he was sleeping there until I read about it in the papers. He must've been in a pretty bad way.'

'He was down on his luck, yes.'

'Actually, now you come to mention it . . . I was out here late one night last summer, working on my stroke, when I noticed someone bending over by the pipeline.'

'The tramp?'

'I don't know. He was just sort of bending over, like I said, and peering around, then he disappeared and popped up again. I've no idea if it was the person you're talking about. I couldn't see him that clearly. All I saw was a man busy with something over there.'

'Did you notice where he went afterwards?'

'No, I only spotted him briefly, then I went home. Though I do remember that the incident came back to me when those boys found the man's body a couple of days later and I heard he'd been living in the pipeline.'

'Did you tell the police?'

'The police?'

'Yes.'

'No, I didn't.'

'You didn't think it might have been important when they found the tramp?'

'No, it didn't even cross my mind.' The man hooked another ball from the bucket and positioned it on the grass. 'Not for a minute. After all, I didn't know if it was him. Why would I inform the police about some tramp hanging around in the old diggings?'

'Could you describe him in more detail – the man you saw?'

'No, not really.'

'And he was doing something by the pipeline?'

'I haven't a clue what he was up to but I do recall thinking he must have been searching for something. He was a long way off, though, and I wasn't paying attention. Just caught a momentary glimpse.'

'Could it have been a woman?'

'Not sure,' said the golfer. 'Maybe. Couldn't say.'

'And this was around the time the tramp was found in the pool? Do you remember when exactly?'

'Only about two days before. I'm fairly sure it was past midnight.'

'A figure bending over by the pipeline?'

'Yes, presumably that tramp. It was an accident, wasn't it?'

'What was?'

'His death. There was nothing suspicious about it?'

'No, I doubt it,' said Erlendur. 'I expect it was just an accident.'

When Halldóra told him she was pregnant, Erlendur didn't know what to think. The news was so unexpected that he was utterly thrown.

'Is it mine?' he blurted out as they sat in the cafe.

'Yours? Of course,' Halldóra answered.

'Are you . . .?'

'I haven't . . . there's no one else, if that's what you think. Is that what you think?'

'And you're sure?'

'Sure? What do you mean? Of course I'm sure. You're the only person it could be.'

'No, I mean that you're pregnant. You only said you thought you were.'

'No, I . . . I didn't know how best to put it, but . . . there's no doubt,' she said. 'I've seen a doctor.'

'But . . . when . . .?'

'In the spring. You'd been to the police party, remember? You don't seem terribly pleased.'

'It's just such a surprise. What –?'

'You should have realised how I'd feel,' said Halldóra.

Erlendur sat in silence while her words sank in. There was a loud crash from the kitchen as some plates fell on the floor, and everyone except Erlendur and Halldóra looked up.

'All that stuff about moving in together . . .?'

'I didn't know how to broach the subject,' said Halldóra. 'I don't know where I am with you. You were so reluctant to meet my parents. And I know almost nothing about you. About your family, for example. We've been seeing each other for two and a half years but I still don't know you at all and you know nothing about me. We meet at pubs, sleep together and go into town but . . .'

He thought she was going to burst into tears.

'Either we make it serious or we might as well end it,' she whispered across the table.

Erlendur had no idea what to say.

'What do you want to do?' she asked and he saw she was welling up. 'What do you want to do, Erlendur?'

35

The man had already gone over his story twice with the police but had no objection to repeating it yet again. He spoke calmly and deliberately, with a good memory for detail. Erlendur could see why she had fallen for him. Not only was he pleasant and polite, but he was handsome as well, with a dark complexion, a fine head of black hair, neat hands and a friendly smile. He was dressed in a suit and tie, his hair fell sleek to his shoulders and he had a good set of sideburns. Erlendur had found his name, Ísidór, in the police files. When Erlendur phoned, the man had immediately invited him to his office. He ran a small business importing goods from America and had a selection of samples by his desk: candy, potato chips and other unfamiliar treats.

He asked if there had been any progress in the inquiry and Erlendur said no, that he was looking into it unofficially at the request of a relative. The man asked no further questions but seemed keen to discuss the case.

When they first met, Ísidór didn't know Oddný was married. He had never seen her before that night at Rödull. They got talking and he bought her a drink. She explained that she had been out with work mates at another bar but had moved on to Rödull by herself. Before long she asked if he was married. He told her he was divorced and didn't have any children. She said she didn't have any children either, but he never thought to ask if she was married.

'She didn't look like she was,' Ísidór said, smoothing his tie. 'At least I didn't get that impression.'

They had shared a taxi to his place in Breidholt. At the time he was having a small house built on the northern side of the hill and it was still unfinished, with painted concrete floors and a makeshift kitchen. They had slept together and arranged to see each other again.

'As I explained to the police last year, it came as a nasty surprise when she told me she was married. It was our third date. She said we couldn't go on seeing each other; she'd have to break it off. Of course I demanded to know why and then it came out. You can imagine how shocked I was. It was totally unexpected.'

'Did she explain why she hadn't told you to begin with?'

'I think she was just using me to get back at him,' said Ísidór. 'Did he send you, by any chance?'

'No, definitely not,' said Erlendur. 'Why did she want to get back at him?'

'Unhappy marriage, I suppose.'

'Did she discuss it with you at all?'

'Yes, when she broke up with me. She said she was planning to leave him but couldn't do it yet. She needed more time. Said it was too soon. She couldn't just go from one man to the next.

I talked to her later, after her husband found out. She told me he'd gone completely mental.'

'That's understandable, isn't it?'

'Maybe. He threatened her.'

'Any idea how exactly?'

'No, but I had the feeling she was afraid of him. Of course I told the police but they saw no reason to take action.'

'You weren't happy when she broke up with you,' pointed out Erlendur.

'No, I wanted . . . I believed she was in real danger and –'

The phone rang and he answered it, took down an order, then explained he was in a meeting and hung up.

'Weren't you the one who told her husband about the affair?' asked Erlendur.

'I wanted to help her,' said Ísidór. 'I thought I was acting in her best interest. That's all.'

'But hadn't she asked you to keep the relationship secret?'

'Not in as many words.'

'Wouldn't it have been better to err on the side of caution, though?'

'Look, naturally I wasn't happy, and I rang her a few times. Once her husband answered and wanted to know who I was. I told him the truth, that Oddný and I were having an affair.'

'But she'd ended it by then. She'd stopped seeing you.'

'I happen to believe it was against her will,' said Ísidór.

'You must have known how much trouble it would cause, telling him.'

'Like I said, I thought I was helping her. She'd told me her marriage was on the rocks, but she didn't dare do anything about it.'

'She decided not to leave him.'

'It was a big disappointment,' said Ísidór.

'Were you aware that he used to beat her up?'

Ísidór nodded.

'That's why she wanted to leave him. Before our brief affair.'

'Do you think he could have harmed her?'

'That's for the police to find out,' said Ísidór. 'They have all this information but say they have no evidence against him. In my opinion they're dragging their feet.'

'A witness saw her speaking to an unknown man just before she left Thórskaffi. Any idea who it might have been?'

'No,' said Ísidór.

'It wasn't you?'

'No. I was at home that evening. Had an early night. I didn't hurt her; I tried to help her.'

'What do you think happened?'

'Ask her husband.'

'What's that supposed to mean?'

'I was shocked when I heard she'd disappeared. I'm not saying he killed her or anything. It's my belief the poor woman committed suicide and he was partly responsible. The police were quick to take that view, and I reckon they were right. But I gather there's not much they can do about it.'

'Did she seem suicidal?'

'Well, unsurprisingly she was depressed about her situation, but it never occurred to me she'd go that far. No, I never got that sense. Not when she was with me.'

'What about you? You weren't happy when Oddný dumped you.'

'That was three years before she disappeared,' said Ísidór. 'I had time to get over it. Let me point out that I've never been a suspect. You can check up on that for yourself.'

'Are you married now?'

'No,' said Ísidór, 'I'm not. I've . . . actually I'm living with someone, though I don't quite see what that has to do with it.'

'Did she give you an alibi? Your girlfriend?'

'Give me . . .? She didn't need to "give" me an alibi. We were together when Oddný went missing. I didn't do anything to hurt Oddný. Believe me. Not a thing. All I did was bring home to her how shit her life was.'

36

That evening Erlendur was on his way to work when he spotted Thurí at Hlemmur, near the police station. She was among a group of passengers stepping off a bus, the number three from Nes to Háaleiti. Hlemmur, a popular gathering place for the homeless, was the largest bus station in the city and had recently become the headquarters of Reykjavík Transport. Despite its new-found status, however, the station consisted of little more than a stretch of windswept tarmac, now covered in puddles from the rain that had fallen earlier that day. There was also a large, draughty, east-facing bus shelter, where people huddled in bad weather, praying that number 'Get Me Out of Here' would not be late.

He could see no sign of Thurí's boyfriend Bergmundur, and when he went over to say hello he thought she looked in pretty good shape. She recognised him immediately but was in a terrible mood. It turned out that she had been harassed on the bus and rather than put up with it had decided to get off early at Hlemmur and wait for the next one.

'Bastards!' She sniffed loudly.

'What happened?'

'There was a bunch of little wankers taking the piss out of me on the bus. I gave them what for. Bloody bastards!'

'Do you often have problems with . . . bastards like that?' asked Erlendur.

'What's it to you?' she countered, her hackles still up from her recent encounter.

'Oh, nothing, I just thought –'

'Yeah, well, think what you like.'

Erlendur was early; his shift did not start for another hour. He had intended to spend the time digging around in the police archives, but instead asked Thurí if she wanted a coffee. They could go and sit in a nearby cafe. He had been hoping to ask her a few more questions about how she found the earring, and this seemed like a good opportunity.

'Going to buy me a drink?' she fired back.

'I don't think they have a licence.'

'Then you can forget it.' Thurí stalked off towards the bus shelter. It was empty. She sat down on the bench and Erlendur joined her. The floor was studded with lumps of chewing gum and a drift of sweet papers whirled in the wind. In one corner an empty litter bin lay on its side, next to a broken bottle. Obscenities were scrawled over every inch of the walls.

'Seen anything of Bergmundur recently?' began Erlendur.

'That dickhead.'

'I thought you two were friends.'

'Bergmundur hasn't got any friends. What gave you that idea? He's a pathetic loser. A pathetic bloody loser.'

'Actually, I was on my way to visit you,' said Erlendur.

'Oh?'

'I wanted to ask you more about the earring you found.'

'Did you get it back from that crook?'

'I've got it, yes. It's at home.'

'I wouldn't mind having it back,' said Thurí.

'Any particular reason?'

'I wouldn't sell it again,' said Thurí touchily, 'if that's what you're implying. I didn't mean to sell it. I meant to keep it. But . . .'

A teenage girl with heavily made-up eyes entered the shelter and eyed them both carefully. Deciding neither looked like a soft touch, she went out again. She was wearing a miniskirt and platforms so high she could barely walk.

'I wanted to know where you found the earring,' said Erlendur.

'I already told you that – in the pipeline!'

'Yes, but where exactly? Do you remember?'

'Why the hell do you care?'

'I just want to know.'

'Not far from the opening.'

'Right- or left-hand side?'

'Right, left, what kind of question is that? What does it matter?'

'It probably doesn't,' admitted Erlendur, 'but it would be good if you could remember.'

'Left side,' said Thúri, 'under one of the pipes. It was dark and I'd never have spotted it if I hadn't banged my head on the bloody roof when I was crawling in. I saw something shiny and it turned out to be an earring. Have you discovered who it belonged to?'

'I'm working on it.'

'Or what it was doing there?'

'I'm not sure,' said Erlendur. 'If it fell off someone's ear, would it really have rolled all the way under the pipe? I had a look round the other day and no one could squeeze under there – it's too close to the ground. Do you have any idea how else it could have got there?'

'Maybe it was kicked under there,' suggested Thurí.

'It's possible.'

'Or . . .'

'What?'

'Or somebody put it there.'

'How do you mean? Who could have done that?'

'How the hell should I know?' Thurí was angry now, fed up with Erlendur's questions. 'I haven't given it any thought. That's your job. I haven't a clue how it ended up there. I just found it. I don't give a toss who put it there or how it got there or whose it was. I don't know why you're asking me. Who the hell are you, anyway?'

'All right, all right,' said Erlendur. 'I'm only trying to work out how Hannibal died.'

'Well, I can't help you there.'

'You've been helpful up to now.'

Thurí took out her tin of roll-ups, fished one out, lit it and inhaled.

'Has the earring got something to do with it?' she asked. 'With how Hannibal died?'

'Good question,' said Erlendur. 'The earring's the only piece that doesn't fit. The only piece you wouldn't expect to find among Hannibal's belongings.'

'Poor Hannibal,' said Thurí. 'They don't make many like him.'
Erlendur nodded.

'Did he ever mention his sister to you?'

'The one he pulled out of the sea?'

'Yes. Her name's Rebekka. She's devastated about what happened to her brother and feels partly responsible, which is absurd, obviously. I've got to know her a little and she told me about the accident. She wants to know what happened to Hannibal.'

'Is that why you're always pestering me?'

Erlendur smiled.

'Her name's Rebekka,' Thuri said. 'I didn't know. He didn't talk about her much. Or the rest of his family.'

'He couldn't save them both.'

'But why should she feel responsible?'

'She only joined them at the last minute,' explained Erlendur. 'It should have been just Hannibal and his wife in the car. She can't get over that. Even now it's still . . . hard for her to accept.'

Thurí took another drag on her cigarette. She had recovered from the confrontation on the bus; talking about Hannibal and the accident seemed to have calmed her down.

'Where were you going?' asked Erlendur, hoping this wouldn't wind her up again.

'Going?'

'Where were you taking the bus to?'

'Nowhere in particular. I just like riding the bus around the city, seeing the houses and streets, the new areas like Breidholt. Feels almost like I'm travelling. But I'm not going anywhere. Never do. Always end up back in the same place.'

She dropped the cigarette on the pavement and ground it under-foot. She had smoked it down until it burnt her fingertips.

'All I know is he missed his wife.'

'Helena?'

'Hannibal told me she'd waved him away.' Thurí gazed, unseeing, at the puddles on the tarmac. 'He went to save her but she pointed to the girl. He told me she'd sacrificed herself for his sister. She'd realised he couldn't save them both: it would take too much time and effort to free her, then rescue the girl. So she wanted him to concentrate on his sister. She pushed him away. That was the last time he saw her alive. She smiled at him, or so he claimed. But I get the feeling he invented that. It's what he said once when he was being gentle, but he never mentioned it again.'

After a while a bus arrived and Thurí stood up, saying a curt goodbye as if she wanted nothing more to do with Erlendur. The sky was leaden and it was raining again. He watched her climb aboard and select a window seat, ready to carry on circling the city with no destination, never leaving the vehicle, not caring where it went: her life a journey without purpose. As Erlendur followed the departing bus with his eyes, he pictured himself in her shoes, forever circling around life, alone, with no destination.

37

Erlendur was not personally acquainted with any of the detectives at CID, though he had visited their offices on Borgartún now and then on various errands, as well as encountering them at the scene of burglaries or cases of serious assault. Uniformed officers were sometimes called as witnesses in investigations but, as a junior officer on the beat, Erlendur had not yet been in that position.

The detective in charge of the inquiry was called Hrólfur; he was around thirty, easygoing, and with little apparent interest in his job. He was busy – Erlendur didn't know with what exactly – and hardly had a minute to spare, though Erlendur had dressed up in his full uniform in the hope of making an impression. Eventually he managed to corner Hrólfur by the department's new Xerox machine, which was as noisy as a tractor and shot out brilliant flashes of light in the dark copying room. He enquired if there had been any progress in the case of Oddný's disappearance.

'No, nothing new,' said Hrólfur, as he frantically copied a file. 'Why do you ask?'

The file seemed to relate to real estate: either Hrólfur was buying or selling a property himself or investigating a scam; Erlendur was unsure which. He had gone to CID with half a mind to report his discovery, since in spite of Rebekka's plea that he should keep it quiet a little longer, he was feeling guilty about failing to disclose what he knew. It was an awkward predicament, and he was keen to resolve it.

'Just curious,' he said. 'Do you still get tip-offs from the public?'

'Not many. What happened seems fairly clear.'

'Which was what?'

'Well, obviously the poor woman took her own life. Threw herself in the sea or something. It's the only explanation we can come up with.'

'Hadn't she been cheating on her husband?'

'Well, she'd had a brief fling several years ago.'

'And you've checked out the man in question?'

'Yes. He was at home with his girlfriend at the time.'

'So they weren't lying?'

'Lying? No, why would you think that?'

'What about the man she's supposed to have met at the nightclub?'

'Never traced him,' said Hrólfur, the flashes from the copier playing over his face. 'What did you say your interest in this case was?'

'So presumably you focused on the husband?'

'We don't have a shred of evidence against him.' Hrólfur lifted the lid of the copier. 'He may have knocked her about a bit but that doesn't prove anything.'

'Knocked her about?'

'There was a domestic issue. He used to give her the odd slap, nothing major, but enough to ensure that we grilled him about it. Interviewed the couple's closest friends too. But we never really got anywhere.'

'Were you tipped off?'

'Yes.'

'And her husband confessed?'

'He admitted it, yes. Who did you say you were?'

'I'm just interested in this case,' said Erlendur.

'Been in the police long?'

'No.'

'Acquainted with the people involved, then?'

'No, not at all. So, what now? Impasse?'

'We don't have a body,' said Hrólfur. 'Or a murder weapon. Or any real motive. Which makes suicide the most plausible explanation. Their marriage was on the rocks. She probably wanted to leave him. Maybe she found her own way of doing so.'

'Her husband was alone at home when she vanished?'

'It's not a crime, you know,' said Hrólfur. 'He'd been to a Lions Club meeting that evening. Look, I don't even know why I'm telling you this. It doesn't concern you. What did you say your name was?'

'Erlendur.'

'Well, Erlendur, why the curiosity? Seems like you know quite a bit about this case.'

'Only what I've read in the papers and heard the boys discussing down at the station.'

'We searched the husband's house,' Hrólfur said. 'And put him through a long, rigorous interrogation. Really got under his skin.

Talked to the neighbours too. No one saw him coming or going that night. In the end we had nothing the prosecution could work with. He didn't even hire a solicitor. The inquiry never got that far.'

'But he was a suspect?'

'Was. Still is, in fact. The ex-lover too. The case is unsolved, still open. We go over the file at regular intervals, make phone calls and try to come up with new angles. Follow up any new leads. But the fact remains . . . Her husband's sticking to his statement that she never came home from Thórskaffi; he never saw her the night she went missing. And that's how the matter stands.'

'So no new evidence has emerged?'

'No.'

'A man drowned in Kringlumýri the same weekend she vanished,' said Erlendur.

'So?'

'Are you familiar with the incident?'

'Yes, what was his name . . . oh, what was it again?'

'Hannibal.'

'Yes, that's it. A tramp.'

'You saw no reason to look into his death?'

'He drowned,' said Hrólfur. 'What were we supposed to look into? They did a post-mortem. There were no unexplained injuries, at least nothing related to his death. Does that sort of case interest you?'

'No, not particularly.'

'We concentrated all our resources on the woman.' Hrólfur gathered the copies together and switched off the Xerox machine. 'The tramp's death got sidelined. You know how it is.'

'What?'

'The first forty-eight hours are crucial in missing-persons cases,' said Hrólfur in an official tone.

'What about the fire in Hannibal's cellar? Were you aware of that?'

'Certainly. Our understanding was that he'd started it himself.'

'Or was it just that a bum like him didn't matter as much as a woman like Oddný?'

'What are you insinuating?' Hrólfur was angry now. 'We don't make that kind of distinction. The point is that Oddný could have been alive. We didn't know what had happened to her. There was a possibility we could still save her, so of course that took priority. The tramp fell in a pond and drowned. It was too late to help him. He was drunk. They found alcohol in his blood-stream. Why . . . what are you . . .? Did you by any chance know him?'

'Sort of,' said Erlendur. 'I used to run into him on night duty. He was a good bloke. Had a miserable life.'

'Yes, sleeping rough up at the pipeline, wasn't he?'

'That's right.'

'Anyway, was that all?' Hrólfur tucked the papers under his arm. 'I'm going to be late for a meeting.'

'Yes. Thanks for your help.'

Erlendur watched the detective hurry out of the room. He decided there was no particular urgency in reporting the discovery of the earring.

38

The man was busy in his garage when Erlendur arrived. The large door was drawn up and a new-looking car – a classy American model – was parked in the drive outside; its gleaming black paintwork was freshly polished. Inside the garage everything was neatly stowed away on shelves, in cupboards and in small boxes. The floor was so shiny you might have felt compelled to take off your shoes before entering. Gardening implements and other tools hung from nails on the walls, including two shovels, suspended by spotless blades.

As the owner of the house did not immediately notice his presence, Erlendur remained outside, studying him. He was not unlike Ísidór in appearance: dark hair and complexion, slim, neat, some years older than Erlendur himself, wearing a checked shirt and jeans. He was putting away a rag and a can of polish in their appointed places, ensuring that everything was just so. From the damp ground outside, Erlendur guessed the man had washed his car before polishing the paintwork. The hose had been painstakingly rolled up. He evidently took as much care of his vehicle as he did his garage.

The man was a manager at a large pension company. Erlendur had known he would have to speak to him eventually – there was no getting round it – but he had delayed the interview for as long as possible. He was nervous, unsure how to broach such a sensitive subject or predict how the man would react. One evening his wife had vanished into thin air, here in their home town, turning his whole life upside down; he had been a suspect ever since, and now Erlendur, a complete stranger, was about to stir it all up again.

Erlendur vacillated until the man, glancing up from his task, caught sight of him. He came out of the garage and said good evening. Erlendur returned his greeting.

'What . . . who . . . can I do something for you?' asked the man after an awkward pause.

'You're Gústaf, aren't you?'

'Yes, that's right.'

'My name's Erlendur. I'm a policeman.'

'A policeman?'

'A traffic officer, actually. I was hoping for a word with you – about your wife Oddný.'

'Oddný?'

'I'm aware that –'

'Why do you want to talk about Oddný?' asked the man. 'What concern is she of yours? Who did you say you were?'

'The name's Erlendur. I've been looking into your wife's case in my own time, in connection with a man who died the same weekend she went missing.'

'In your own time?'

'Yes. In connection with this man I knew. On his sister's behalf.'

'Who was the man?'

'His name was Hannibal. He was a tramp.'

'A tramp? What . . . Sorry, but what are you talking about?'

'He was living in the heating conduit to the south of Kringlumýri – not far from here. He drowned in one of the flooded workings, around the time your wife vanished. Maybe even exactly the same time.'

The man stood in the doorway, gaping at Erlendur. All around him was order, the only rogue element this stranger who had crept up on him in the quiet of evening and embarked on some bizarre story about a tramp.

'What's that got to do with Oddný?' Gústaf asked.

'That's what I wanted to ask you.'

'Ask me? I don't know any tramps. Nor do I know you, for that matter. You're not here on official business?'

Erlendur shook his head.

'Then I have nothing to say to you.' The man backed away into the garage.

'There's a chance that Hannibal and your wife ran into each other the night she disappeared,' said Erlendur, 'though I've no idea how or in what circumstances. I'm working on the assumption that your wife's dead. I know Hannibal is. I want to find out what happened. Hannibal's sister, Rebekka, wants some answers too.'

'Look, you'd better leave,' said Gústaf. 'You're talking to the wrong man. I can't give you any answers. I'm not even sure what you're talking about. I don't know these people. Never heard of them.'

'Fair enough. There's no reason why you should have –'

'And I don't understand who you are, so this all seems highly irregular. Highly irregular. I'd be grateful if you'd leave me alone. I have nothing further to say to you.'

'We don't believe Hannibal did your wife any harm,' said Erlendur. 'He had . . .'

He cast around for the right words.

'Let's just say there were things in his past that make it inconceivable that he could have hurt her. He had his problems, but he'd never have attacked your wife.'

'Yes, well, I'm not interested,' said Gústaf. 'I'm asking you to leave me alone. I have nothing to say to you. Are you listening to me?'

'The reason I'm telling you about Hannibal is because we believe that, at some point during the night she vanished, your wife may have been in the pipeline where he was camped.'

By now the man had a remote control in his hand and raised it to close the garage door. He hesitated.

'That's why I think their paths may have crossed,' Erlendur continued doggedly. 'At the pipeline. But I've no idea what happened to your wife after that. Or to Hannibal, for that matter. I thought you might be able to help.'

'Who is this Hannibal? I don't have a clue what you're talking about. I've never heard of him.'

'That's hardly surprising. No one's ever connected the two incidents before.'

'This all sounds extremely far-fetched . . . Look, what did you say your name was?'

'Erlendur.'

'Right, Erlendur. Thank you for taking an interest in the case but I'd be grateful if you'd back off and stop interfering in matters that are absolutely none of your business.'

The man pressed the remote control. Jerkily, with a motorised drone, the door began its descent, closing like a red wall in front of Erlendur's face. He dug into his pocket and pulled out the earring.

'Recognise this?'

The man regarded it blankly.

'Seen it before?'

The door continued its descent and Erlendur tossed the earring underneath just before it closed with a slight clang. He regretted it immediately. He had thrown the earring out of desperation, but now he had lost his only piece of evidence. He no longer had any proof to connect Oddný with the pipeline apart from his own observations and the word of Thurí – a hopeless alcoholic.

He stared at the garage door, his breath caught in his throat. He had no idea what to do. The seconds ticked by and he was on the verge of beating on the door when he heard the mechanism start up again and it began to open.

The man had picked up the earring and was examining it with a grave expression.

'Where on earth did you find this?' He raised his eyes to Erlendur, unable to disguise his astonishment.

39

Gústaf's house was as tidy as his garage, in marked contrast to the chaos that characterised Erlendur's own home. Nothing was extraneous. Tasteful pieces of furniture were arranged just so, porcelain figurines faced into the sitting room at precisely the right angle, the pictures on the walls hung perfectly level, the immaculate pale blue carpet still bore the marks of a vacuum cleaner. There was a pleasant smell too, a fragrance that was unfamiliar to Erlendur and whose source he could not identify. No reek of old fat from the kitchen. He had automatically made to remove his shoes on entering but the man had said there was no need. Erlendur was not sure he really meant it.

Having invited him to take a seat in the dining room, Gústaf drew up another chair facing him. He was still holding the earring, and Erlendur wondered how he was going to get it back. Gústaf's manner had undergone a transformation; he was suddenly eager to cooperate, had invited Erlendur inside and was apparently prepared to talk. He said he couldn't understand what had happened to his wife; her disappearance had left him a broken man. He had been attending a Lions Club meeting that evening.

'I've been a member for several years.'

'Was the earring Oddný's?'

'Yes.'

'Definitely?'

'I bought it myself,' said Gústaf. 'From a jeweller here in Reykjavík. I haven't . . .'

Emotion threatened to choke him.

'I haven't seen it since she vanished. It was a bit . . . a bit of a shock, to be honest. I don't quite know what to say, what to think.' He stared at the piece of jewellery in his palm.

Erlendur waited. He wanted to give the man time to recover his composure. He refrained from mentioning that he had already spoken to the jeweller, unsure how much he ought to reveal about his enquiries.

After a decent interval, he asked if Gústaf could confirm that his wife had been wearing the earrings on the evening she disappeared.

'Yes,' Gústaf replied. 'She was wearing them. I gave them to her once after we'd . . . when I was in a generous mood. She loved jewellery. This is hers. Definitely. But how did you . . . where did you find it? Are you trying to tell me that . . . you've found Oddný?'

'No,' said Erlendur emphatically. 'Absolutely not. Only the earring. Actually it wasn't me who found it but a woman called Thurí. She knew Hannibal, the man who was sleeping in the heating conduit in Kringlumýri. Not long after he drowned she went to his old camp and spotted the earring under one of the pipes. I got it from her.'

'How did you know it was Oddný's?'

'I didn't,' said Erlendur, unwilling to go into too much detail. 'It was just a hunch. Hannibal drowned the same weekend, not far from here, so it occurred to me to ask if you recognised the earring. I had a feeling there might be a link.'

'Sorry, but I'm still not clear where you fit in. What's your involvement?'

'Like I said, I knew Hannibal. I wanted, if possible, to find out how he drowned. I've been in touch with his sister and she asked me to look into it. Then the earring turned up. And now I'm here. I'm sorry, I know this can't be easy for you but I couldn't think what else to do.'

Gústaf couldn't tear his gaze from the earring.

'But how did it get there? How did it end up in the conduit?'

'It's possible Hannibal picked it up somewhere else,' said Erlendur. 'He was on the streets and had an eye for shiny objects, so he may well have spotted it on his travels and taken it back to his camp. We can't rule that out.'

Gústaf gave Erlendur a searching look.

'But you think differently,' he said at last.

'It's my belief that your wife was in the pipeline at some point,' said Erlendur. 'And conceivably died there.'

Gústaf was still staring at him.

'Have you found her?' he asked in a low voice.

'No.' It was the second time the man had asked this, and Erlendur was keen to remove all doubt. 'I haven't found her,' he said firmly. 'I've searched inside the pipeline but she's not there. It's a complete mystery to me. All I can say is that I believe she was in the conduit at some point the evening or night she vanished.'

'Was it this friend of yours, this Hannibal, who dragged her there?' asked Gústaf. 'Was he the one who attacked her? Is that what you're hinting at?'

'No, I very much doubt it,' answered Erlendur. 'In fact, I believe he suffered the same fate as your wife.'

'How do you mean?'

'I believe he was a victim too.'

'A victim?'

'Yes,' said Erlendur. 'I've been over and over this and it's the only plausible explanation I can come up with. I believe your wife was murdered and Hannibal saw what happened. The man who attacked your wife disposed of him to get rid of an inconvenient witness.'

A prolonged silence ensued. It was as if Erlendur's words had infiltrated that orderly home with its perfectly squared pictures, its neatly aligned porcelain figurines, and somehow knocked everything askew. Distracted, Gústaf put the earring on the table and Erlendur seized this chance to slip it into his pocket. Gústaf did not appear to notice.

'Of course, it's pure speculation at this stage,' Erlendur said. 'None of this necessarily happened. It's only one possible version of events. We know your wife's earring was found inside the pipeline. So chances are that she was there herself. What was she doing there? Hiding, most likely. Who from? That's where I thought you might be able to enlighten me.'

Unable to remain still while Erlendur was speaking, Gústaf had sprung to his feet and was pacing around the room.

'What are you insinuating?' he demanded, coming to a

standstill. 'How can I possibly enlighten you? What are you driving at?'

'I've spoken to various people about this case, and I'm told that –'

'People? What people?'

'People who knew Oddný, friends –'

'Which friends?' Gústaf interrupted. 'Surely you haven't . . . You haven't been talking to that nutter Ísidór?'

'I have, yes.'

'What, knowing that he tried to come between me and Oddný? Or didn't he tell you that?'

'Yes, he did, as a matter of fact.'

'He tried to destroy our marriage. Did his level best to ruin our relationship. He's . . . he's the biggest shit I've ever come across.'

'According to him, she wanted to leave you.'

'Yes, well, he would say that, wouldn't he? Actually, it was the other way round – she was trying to get shot of him. He was stifling her. I've always said he was dangerously unstable. If anyone's done away with Oddný, it's him. I told the police that but they were strangely reluctant to pursue the matter.'

'I gather he said the same about you.'

'He told the most appalling lies about me.'

'Why did she get involved with Ísidór if he's so unstable?' asked Erlendur.

'I don't know. A moment of madness. I never understood it.'

'But you forgave her?'

'I . . . I wanted to save our marriage. You know he had the temerity to ring here and ask to speak to her? That's how I found out about their affair. He had absolutely no qualms about making trouble for her. Can't you see that? That's what he's like. You must see that he's sick. It's obvious. I can't for the life of me imagine what Oddný was doing with him and, besides, it didn't work out. They met up a few times, she told me, before she realised – realised he was unhinged.'

'But I've heard it from other sources too,' said Erlendur. 'That you had marital problems.'

'Who? Who said that?'

'Just people I talked to. And not only problems. Oddný was having a very rough time, that's why she looked elsewhere. It's not only Ísidór who says that.'

'A very rough time?'

'I've heard rumours of violence,' said Erlendur.

Gústaf's eyes dropped to the hoovered carpet.

'Was that why you bought her jewellery?' asked Erlendur.

Gústaf did not reply.

'Was that why you bought her the earrings? To beg her forgiveness?'

'I've . . .' Gústaf drew a deep breath. 'I've gone out of my way to be polite to you, invited you into my house, listened to you, tried to reason with you. I'm glad you're interested in the case, in Oddný's case. No one's more desperate than me to find her. I've tried to talk to you man to man. About sensitive matters – extremely sensitive matters to do with my personal life – with our life together. But then you come out with this, this bloody slander! I've already been over this with the police. You'd better get out. I have nothing more to say to you.'

'Was that why she wanted to leave you?' Erlendur persisted.

Gústaf refused to rise to this.

'But you wouldn't allow it. Not only that but you forgave her for cheating on you and your marriage carried on as if nothing had ever happened?'

'You'd better get out,' repeated Gústaf in a controlled voice.

'How was your relationship after that?'

'We did our best to work it out. I don't see how it's relevant. I'm asking you to leave, please.'

'Did things improve?'

Gústaf strode into the hall and opened the front door.

'I can't see that it's any of your business.'

'Did you attack your wife?'

'No, I didn't. Now leave me alone. She never came home!' His voice sank to a whisper. 'Oddný never came home from Thórskaffi.' He shut the door on Erlendur.

40

Erlendur was off duty for the next four nights. It was always difficult to adjust. More experienced officers had told him it was best to tackle the problem head on and revert to a normal routine when off duty rather than remaining active at night and sleeping during the day. This was easier said than done. The trick was to stay awake all day after the last night shift, then go to bed at the usual time. When you woke up the next morning, so the theory went, your body clock would have reset itself.

Erlendur's attempts to follow this advice had not been particularly successful. He had dutifully stayed awake for twenty-four hours but the following night he tossed and turned, falling into a fitful doze only to wake again restless, sweating and confused. At two in the morning, sleep still eluding him, he went into the kitchen and sat at the table, alone in the silence, not knowing what to do. He stared into space, conscious that whatever ploys he used to try to switch off his churning thoughts, the problem of Oddný and Hannibal would prevent him from sleeping. And if not that, then Halldóra's announcement. And if not that, something else . . .

'What do you want to do, Erlendur?' she had asked, and he had suggested she move in with him for now; later they would find somewhere more suitable. She was not convinced. She wanted to be persuaded that he genuinely meant it and asked if he was serious about their relationship. He tried to reassure her, and even believed it himself. It was time to settle down, time to stop living a life that revolved entirely around himself, time to make changes and do something new, something different.

By now Halldóra was looking rather more cheerful and before long she was agreeing with him about finding more suitable accommodation. She had already been scanning the property ads in the papers and concluded that it would be better to buy a place than rent. Of course, they would need a second bedroom. One, for now. Her face broke into a smile and he realised she was happy again.

From there his thoughts roved on to Gústaf's reaction: had it been right to visit him and, if so, could he have handled the situation better? He felt a pang of regret now at how aggressive he had been, at the harsh accusations implicit in his questions. For all he knew, Gústaf might regard this as grounds for a formal complaint.

It seemed a reasonable assumption that Oddný was dead. Erlendur pondered the possibility he had put to Gústaf: that the same person had murdered Hannibal as well. Jealousy and revenge were the motives that sprang to mind, but he told himself he must not be too quick to point the finger. It was hard to work out the sequence of events at the pipeline and later at the diggings, but he thought perhaps Oddný had been assaulted and, in trying to come to her aid, Hannibal had been overpowered and killed. The perpetrator had then hidden Oddný's body but left Hannibal in the pool to make it look as if he'd drowned, gambling on the fact that no one would bother much about the death of a tramp.

He had assured Gústaf that Hannibal wouldn't have laid a finger on Oddný, and it was true: he simply couldn't imagine it. Couldn't picture him killing her, hiding her body, then drowning himself. That didn't add up. There must have been a third person, who was responsible for both their deaths. That was the conclusion staring Erlendur in the face.

His mind wandered back over the events of recent days and weeks, pausing at his meeting with Thurí at the bus station. At what she had said about the accident; how Helena had waved Hannibal away so that he would save his sister. Hannibal had confided in Thurí when his guard was down. When he was 'gentle', she had said. Hannibal had never been able to escape the memories of what had happened when they crashed into the harbour.

He pictured Thurí in the bus shelter, waiting for her next round trip, dreaming of travel. Remembered his first meeting with her when she had been perfectly sober, so different from the three alcoholics playing Ludo, who had been so coarse, cackling at them like three witches in a fairy tale. He tried to erase the image of Thurí and Bergmundur in her grotty little room in the west of town.

The west of town . . . where he sometimes took a detour past a certain house, when haunted by the story of the girl from the women's college who had vanished without trace. This fixation of his with disappearances – with the phenomenon itself, the fates of those who were never heard of again and the sufferings of those left behind to mourn. He knew his obsession had its roots in the tragedy he himself had endured on the moors out east, and that it had been intensified by all the books he had read on disappearances or terrible ordeals in this harsh land.

Perhaps that was the true origin of his insomnia. The compulsion that repeatedly interrupted his sleep, that kept him lying awake. An inexplicable tension in his body. A sense of anticipation he had not experienced before. A spark of life ignited by the investigation he had begun, on his own initiative, into a disappearance in the city.

Sooner or later he really would have to present his discoveries to CID. He would tell them all he knew, detail his conversations with everyone – from the brothers whom Hannibal had accused of trying to set fire to him, to Thurí who had found the earring.

The object in question was lying on the table in front of him. Erlendur picked it up and twiddled it between his fingers. According to Thurí it had been lying right under the pipe near the opening. If her account was correct, Oddný could not have lost the earring where it was found. Nobody could fit in such a narrow space. There was no telling how it had ended up there but presumably somebody had kicked it aside without realising. On the other hand, it might have been hidden under the pipes, and there was no getting away from the fact that Hannibal himself could have done that.

One further possibility occurred to him, but Erlendur could

hardly bear to think it through. Oddný herself might have secreted the earring there in the faint hope that it would one day come to light and the world would learn that she had met her death in that dark tunnel.

41

As was their custom, Erlendur met Rebekka after work, in front of the surgery on Lækjargata. While they were walking towards the lake, he told her about meeting Oddný's friends and about his conversations with Ísidór and Gústaf.

'Gústaf's reaction was the strangest,' he said. 'He used to hit Oddný, and it's obvious she was looking for a way out. He did confirm that the earring was hers but when I pressed him further, he refused to talk to me and kicked me out. Though that doesn't necessarily tell us anything. Maybe I went too far and made him angry. After all, he had a perfect right ask me to leave.'

Erlendur went on to describe his visit to CID and his discussion with the detective in charge of Oddný's case. How they'd had her husband in their sights but had been unable to find any evidence against him. For that they required a body, a murder weapon and a clear motive. Her former lover Ísidór had also been a suspect, but they had concluded that suicide was by far the most likely explanation.

They sat down on a bench on Tjarnargata, facing east across the lake to the church and school. The weather was warm, as it had been for most of the summer, one sunny day succeeding another. Rebekka listened without comment. She wore a pair of fashionably large sunglasses and was tastefully dressed, as always, in a pale summer jacket and fetching silk blouse.

'What about Hannibal?' she asked finally.

'They're not interested in him,' said Erlendur. 'They're treating them as two completely separate incidents.'

'Did you tell them about the earring?'

'I decided it wouldn't do any harm to wait a bit longer. A few days, no more. It's going to be increasingly difficult for me to come up with an excuse for not alerting CID straight away.'

'So they haven't linked Oddný and Hannibal at all?'

'No.'

'But they will do the moment you show them the earring.'

'Yes.'

Rebekka gave a quiet sigh.

'And Hannibal will be seen as the monster who murdered her.'

'They might well think that, but they'll still have to explain how and why he died. They'll have to realise that there's a chance he got mixed up in events that had nothing to do with him and lost his life as a result.'

They sat for a long while, warmed by the sun, listening to the rumble of the city and the honking of the birds on the water. People strolled along Tjarnargata in the sunshine. They could hear car horns in the distance above the roar of the traffic, and, further away, a police siren wailed. A crash, Erlendur thought, and hoped it was not serious.

'Tell me, how did Hannibal himself describe the accident in Hafnarfjördur?'

'Why do you ask?'

'It's just that I heard something he'd said to someone else. You said he didn't like to talk about it?'

'No,' said Rebekka. 'That's an understatement. He wouldn't discuss it at all. Not with anyone, as far as I know. What did you hear?'

'Stands to reason, with an experience that traumatic, that he wouldn't have talked about it to just anyone, only those closest to him.'

'I'm not quite sure what you're getting at,' said Rebekka.

'Have you ever heard of a woman called Thurí?'

'Thurí? No, I don't think so.'

'She was a friend of Hannibal's, another alcoholic.'

'Oh?'

'She's the woman I told you about, who found Oddný's earring in the conduit. After he died she went to pay a last visit to his camp and discovered the earring by chance under one of the pipes, but didn't tell anyone. Not until I met her. She hadn't stopped to wonder why it was there. It didn't bother her. She just kept it and later traded it for booze.'

'And she was a friend of Hannibal's?'

Nodding, Erlendur explained how he had tracked Thurí down to the hostel on Amtmannsstígur. He didn't know the precise nature of their relationship but it must have been intimate because Hannibal had apparently confided in her to some degree. Nor did he know how their friendship had developed in the first place.

232

Thurí had quite a temper on her and spent time with other drinkers. It was possible she used them to procure booze, pills or whatever she needed. But her heart seemed to be in the right place and she was clever. Beyond this, all Erlendur knew was that she dreamt of travelling and had devised a rather novel method of making her dream come true.

'It's the first I've heard of her,' said Rebekka.

'Once, when Hannibal was "gentle", as she put it, he started talking about the accident.'

'Gentle?'

'That's right.'

'If he was prepared to open up like that, they must have been close.'

'I get the impression they were good friends. It might help you to meet her, if she feels like talking to you.'

'But do you know what . . . what he told her? About the accident?'

Erlendur sensed she was apprehensive, unsure that she wanted to dwell any further on an event that had dogged her all her life and had shattered her family, her brother most of all. Erlendur phrased his answer with care, stressing his ignorance of what Thurí meant when she described Hannibal as gentle. Possibly he had been a little drunk, but the word might also have meant that he was in a tender mood. That he had opened up to Thurí when his guard was down. Whatever the circumstances, he had told her that he had intended to save them both. He had gone to free Helena but she had known they couldn't both survive and waved him away, gesturing to him to put his little sister first. So Helena had in all likelihood sacrificed herself for Rebekka.

'Apparently he claimed that Helena smiled at him, but for

some reason Thurí didn't set much store by that. She had the impression it was a detail Hannibal had invented for himself. She also stressed that this was the only time he spoke to her about the accident.'

Rebekka sat quietly beside him as he repeated Thurí's words.

'Did you know?' Erlendur asked, turning to her.

She sat deathly still on the bench. Observing her puckered lips and the tears pouring from under the outsize sunglasses, he realised he needn't have asked. It was the first time she had heard it. He was furious with himself for opening old wounds. He, of all people, should have understood.

'I expect he did,' Rebekka said at last, very quietly.

'Did what?'

'Invent it. The bit about her smiling.'

Erlendur could sense her pain.

'He loved his Helena,' she said. 'More than anything else in the world.'

42

The thief ran smack into him, realised his mistake, spun round, fled into Skólavördustígur, across the road and vanished down Smidjustígur. Reacting a split second too late, Erlendur charged after him and kept running even when his white police cap flew off into the road. The man sprinted straight down to Laugavegur with Erlendur hot on his heels. But the man was so fast Erlendur didn't think he'd be able to catch him.

It was after five in the morning when a passer-by had noticed suspicious movements in a jeweller's shop on Skólavördustígur. Since he was nearly home, the witness had run the last stretch to his house and phoned the police. There were two patrol cars in the area, one of which contained Erlendur, Gardar and Marteinn, and they were first on the scene. The thief had broken in through a window at the rear of the shop and was carrying a black sports bag over his shoulder. He didn't seem to be in any particular hurry, no doubt assuming he had plenty of time, and certainly hadn't thought the police would arrive that quickly. He escaped from the shop by the same route, only to find himself trapped in a courtyard. He took cover as Marteinn and Gardar came round the back and entered the shop by the broken window; then he darted out of his hiding place and into the street. He hadn't been expecting Erlendur to block his path, then chase him down to Laugavegur and down the hill to Hverfisgata.

The man suddenly swerved to the east, heading into Skuggahverfi with Erlendur close on his tail. He was still clutching the holdall, refusing to let go even if it slowed him down. He had planned the break-in carefully, as his black trousers, black jacket, black woollen hat and light plimsolls revealed, and had managed to disconnect the primitive burglar alarm, but he had not bargained for inquisitive passers-by that early in the morning.

Marteinn and Gardar were nowhere to be seen. They had missed their quarry in the shop and hadn't noticed Erlendur running after him. They stood outside the building, scanning the horizon. Marteinn called his name but there was no answer. Then they noticed the police cap lying in the road nearby and picked it up.

'Where the hell has he got to?' asked Gardar, as a second patrol car drew up noiselessly beside them.

The burglar showed no signs of flagging as he pounded rhythmically along Lindargata. Erlendur, beginning to fall behind, was afraid of losing sight of him. In spite of his aching legs and shortness of breath, he refused to give up and kept pushing himself on. His heavy boots might have been fine for forming a guard of honour but they were clearly not designed for marathons.

His heart skipped a beat when he saw the thief skid on a pile of sand and fall headlong into the road. Erlendur managed to cut down the man's lead before he leapt to his feet again and fled, limping slightly, in the direction of the abattoir buildings. By now Erlendur could hear his gasping breaths and the rattling of the jewellery in his holdall. It looked as if he was planning to jettison the bag after all. As the man glanced from side to side, Erlendur managed to tackle him in front of the abattoir gates.

They rolled over and over in the street until Erlendur got the upper hand. Straddling the thief's back, he pushed the man's face down on the paving stones while he tried to catch his breath. Then, with something of a struggle, he handcuffed the thief, dragged him to his feet and shoved him against a wall. An appetising aroma of dung-smoked meat wafted from the smoking ovens of the abattoir, reminding Erlendur how hungry he was. The night shift had been so busy he hadn't eaten a thing since coming on duty.

Erlendur had begun to hustle his prisoner back up the hill towards Skólavördustígur when it dawned on him that it would be quicker to take him straight down to the station on Hverfisgata and throw him in a cell. As he didn't have a walkie-talkie on him he couldn't pass on a message to Gardar and Marteinn but he didn't think it really mattered. He'd caught the culprit: their work was done.

He pushed the man ahead of him along Hverfisgata, the burglar objecting all the way, refusing to be hurried and complaining that this treatment was unreasonable since he was cooperating. Erlendur told him to shut up. He had never seen the man before. He was around twenty, slim, with long legs, built for running; his hands and face were covered in grazes from the fall. His hat had come off, revealing a thick mop of hair.

The sports bag, which Erlendur had slung over his own shoulder, clinked at every step with watches and jewellery.

'How did you lot know I was doing the shop?' asked the burglar.

'Keep walking,' snapped Erlendur.

'Did someone see me?'

Erlendur didn't answer.

'I nearly got away,' remarked the thief.

'If only you hadn't fallen flat on your face,' said Erlendur.

'I didn't think you'd chase me that far. Thought you'd give up. I've never run that fast in my life.'

Erlendur gave him a shove.

'Do you train?' asked the prisoner.

'Why don't you just shut up?' Erlendur pushed him on.

'Been a cop long?' continued the thief after a brief pause.

Again Erlendur ignored him.

'Or are you a summer temp?'

'Look, will you just shut it?' said Erlendur. 'I have no desire to talk to you. Why did you break into that shop, anyway? Can't you be bothered to work for a living? Think you're too good for that? Stop asking questions and get a move on.'

The thief took a few more steps, then baulked again.

'I need the money.'

'Who doesn't? Try working for it.'

'No, I need it right away. Lots of it. In a hurry. I can't go to prison.'

'Then you shouldn't steal.'

'Yes, but –'

'Take it up with someone else,' Erlendur interrupted him wearily. 'I'm not interested in your bullshit.'

They walked on, but the silence didn't last long.

'Just take it,' said the thief.

'Take what?'

'The bag. I won't spill the beans. You can say I got away. You lost me by the abattoir and I still had the bag. You'll get a good price for all that.'

'What, I keep the bag and you get away? Is that what you're suggesting?'

'You could say I'd made off with it. No one'll guess. I won't squeal. Honest. I won't say a word.'

'So I sell the goods and everyone's a winner?'

'I don't mind.'

'Cut the crap. Let's go.' Erlendur gave him another push. 'And no more nonsense or the report will look even worse.'

'Please, just take it and let me go. You can return the stuff to the shop. No harm done. A bit of broken glass, that's all. Anyway, shops like that are insured. The owner won't have to pay a króna.'

Erlendur couldn't be bothered to respond any more.

'What's the point in arresting me? I'm a complete nobody. Let me go.'

As they approached the police station the burglar was barely moving. Since pushing him was having no effect, Erlendur seized the man's shoulder and began to drag him along.

'They'll kill me,' the thief cried. 'You don't get it. I owe them. They ordered me to do it. Even told me which shop. Said I could repay my debt with the stuff I nicked.'

'What debt?'

'Drugs.'

'That's a new one on me,' said Erlendur.

'What?'

'Breaking in just to pay for drugs?'

'They said it was the only way. That's what they said. And

I . . . what was I supposed to do? They threatened to . . . they're totally mental.'

'Who?'

'The brothers.'

'What brothers?'

'I can't tell you.'

'I see.'

'I'll tell you if you let me go.'

They had reached the police station at last.

'Enough.'

'One of them's called Ellert,' said the thief. 'That's all I'm saying. I won't tell you any more unless you let me go.'

'Ellert?' repeated Erlendur. 'You don't mean Ellert and Vignir?'

It was the thief's turn to fall silent.

'Has he got a brother called Vignir?' asked Erlendur.

'Do you know them?' The thief had forgotten about withholding the other brother's name. 'You mean you know who they are? What they're up to? What was I supposed to do? They threatened me.'

Erlendur ignored him. He was trying to remember everything he knew about Ellert and Vignir, and think about what had happened on Kringlumýri.

What if there had been more than one person?

What if there had been more than one person at the pipeline the night Oddný went missing?

Erlendur froze on the steps of the police station; he was staring at the thief. What if he had it all backwards? Suppose it wasn't Hannibal who had seen Oddný's death but the other way round? What if she had witnessed Hannibal being attacked and drowned?

He had taken it for granted that Oddný had been the victim of an assault and that Hannibal had died because he had seen too much. But suppose she had seen Hannibal's murderers? Suppose she was the one who couldn't be allowed to get away?

Now he came to think of it, hadn't Bergmundur said something to that effect about the brothers? That he was sure they wanted to bump Hannibal off and had succeeded in the end.

What did Hannibal have on them?

Had they gone to the pipeline to look for him?

Were they the ones who attacked him?

Did they silence Oddný?

'So are you going to let me go then?' The thief sounded hopeful as he stood there on the steps in his handcuffs, having played his trump card in a bid for mercy. Erlendur looked so preoccupied that the young man thought he was seriously considering his offer.

'I can't let you go.' Erlendur gathered his wits.

He grabbed his companion and pushed him ahead of him into the station, announcing that the Skólavördustígur burglar had been detained and the stolen goods recovered.

43

The drug squad was extremely interested in the thief's account. It was still early morning when the detectives sat down with the young man, whose name was Fannar and who had no previous record. It didn't take them long to persuade him to cooperate. Fannar had never been arrested before, never needed a lawyer and was keen to avoid prison if he possibly could – as he said himself. They took advantage of his inexperience and almost childlike naivety. In fact, the interview went so smoothly that by the time the detectives paused for lunch he had told them all he knew about the brothers, Ellert and Vignir; how to go about scoring drugs from them and why he owed them money. They were particularly interested to hear that the brothers had ordered the robbery. The Reykjavík police had not encountered this method of debt collection before.

Fannar's life had been a sad mess since his early teens: he had started drinking heavily, had dropped out of school, then started taking drugs – dope, mainly – and had fallen in with a bad crowd who kept him supplied. His parents had done everything in their power to make him quit, but his habit had only grown worse and he had plunged ever deeper into the abyss. From time to time they had succeeded in locking him in the house, getting him to a doctor or into a home for delinquents, once even managed to get him admitted to Kleppur, the mental hospital, but it was all futile. Instead of coming to his senses, Fannar took harder, more expensive drugs, and was in serious trouble by the time Erlendur tackled him outside the abattoir.

CID immediately ordered close surveillance for the brothers and over the next few days gathered sufficient information for their arrest. They had been smuggling pills and powder, resin, amphetamines and the increasingly popular marijuana on cargo ships. They would bag them up and they'd be ready to sell. Originally the brothers had worked as crew members on the ships, smuggling small quantities of alcohol, but the drugs proved far more lucrative and took up less space on board. The brothers had established contacts in both Hamburg and Boston, and now had no fewer than five men working for them on various ships. The drugs were stashed either in an old baiting shed at Grandi, to the west of Reykjavík harbour, or at a property in the Vogar district, where they ran a carpentry workshop. Both premises were rented from landlords who had no involvement with smuggling or drug dealing and were stunned when the police knocked on their doors to inform them that their tenants were dealers. The brothers had covered their tracks so well that the police had been totally unaware of their existence.

Some of this they gleaned from Fannar's statement, the rest from police contacts in Reykjavík's rather half-baked underworld.

Among other things, the investigation revealed that the brothers had recently received a shipment from Boston. When the police arrived with back-up from Customs and Excise, the haul was found as yet untouched in the baiting shed. The brothers had been under surveillance for only three days before the arrests took place. They seemed to have become remarkably lax about security. The police decided their moment had come when the brothers went to check up on their goods. They did not resist arrest. They mostly seemed astonished at getting caught, though they did try to assert that the contents of the shed did not belong to them; they only rented it.

It would be an exaggeration to claim that the arrest of Ellert and Vignir uncovered a complex network of dealers and suppliers, since the brothers had worked more or less independently, apart from two or three other contacts in Iceland and the men on the ships. Although they had made a huge profit from their imports, they were careful to show no sign of it, continuing to work as carpenters, scrupulously filling in their tax returns, and avoiding buying new cars or anything else that might suggest they were wealthier than they appeared. Not one króna of their illegal earnings was paid into their bank accounts. This had caused them something of a headache. In the few years they had been in business, they had amassed a vast quantity of banknotes which they kept in plastic bags and boxes, some stored in the bait shed and workshop, the rest at home. Their profits had partly financed the house they moved into on Fálkagata.

As the police gathered more information about Ellert and Vignir, there was one thing that struck them. The men employed unusually brutal methods to call in their debts. Although they had never been charged, various cases of assault could be attributed to them now that their identity was known. They also had someone only too happy to do their dirty work. This individual was well known to the police; it was none other than Ellidi, the thug Erlendur had encountered in Austurvöllur Square when searching for people who knew Hannibal. Ellidi was brought in for questioning and remanded in custody as a result.

In the end a total of eight men were arrested after Fannar named the brothers. Prior to the arrests, it was thought inadvisable, in the interests of the investigation, for Fannar to be on the streets, so the police had applied for permission to detain him for breaking into the jeweller's. The only person he was allowed to see was the solicitor he had finally got around to hiring.

When Erlendur looked in on him in the cells at Hverfisgata, Fannar was in a terrible state, exhausted from being pumped for information about the brothers all the time, unable to sleep or eat. He now deeply regretted the burglary and the fact that he had snitched on Ellert and Vignir.

'I should have kept my mouth shut. They'll find out who grassed them up and then . . . shit! I don't know what I was thinking. What was I thinking?'

'I doubt you're even on their radar,' Erlendur said to reassure him. 'They would have been exposed sooner or later.'

'Yes, but it's happened *now*, and they'll find out it was me.'

'Try not to worry about it.'

'Do you think I'll be allowed to go home when it's over?'

'To be honest, I can't tell you,' said Erlendur. 'Probably. You'll be charged with burglary, but I don't know if you'll have to do time for that.'

'One of the cops said I'd avoid the nick if I helped them.'

'You shouldn't believe everything you're told.'

'Shit, I never should have blabbed.'

'You don't happen to know if the brothers were acquainted with a man called Hannibal?' asked Erlendur.

'Hannibal. No. Who's he?'

'They never mentioned the name?'

'They never mentioned anything except how much I owed them,' said Fannar. 'I only met them the once. Didn't usually score direct from them. All they told me was how big my debt was and how I could pay it off.'

'By breaking into the shop?'

'Yes.'

'Where do you suppose they got the idea from?'

'Saw it on TV, some series they're always watching. Thought it was cool.'

'What series was that?'

'Can't remember . . . bloke in a wheelchair . . . Don't watch TV myself.'

'*Ironside*?'

'That's the one.'

44

The brothers were briefly detained at Hverfisgata while the request to remand them in custody was being processed. They were silent, their faces grim, as they were led down the corridor and locked in. A homeless man who had begged to be admitted early that morning was the only other occupant of the cells. He had whimpered that he was worn out, hadn't had a proper night's kip in a bed with a roof over his head for God knows how long. The duty sergeant told him to try the Fever Hospital but he said they had turned him away. After some argument the sergeant gave in and let him sleep in one of the cells.

Erlendur knew that once Ellert and Vignir had been transferred to the prison at Sídumúli he wouldn't be able to get anywhere near them. If they decided not to cooperate and denied everything, they could end up languishing in solitary confinement for weeks. Erlendur didn't have the patience to wait that long. He happened to be at the station when he heard that Vignir was already on his way to Síðumúli, so, realising he needed to act quickly, he slipped down to Ellert's cell.

Ellert couldn't believe his eyes when he saw Erlendur in his police uniform. He recognised him immediately. Erlendur had told them nothing about himself, only that he had known Hannibal.

'You!' exclaimed Ellert. 'You're never a cop!'

'I'm in Traffic.'

'Traffic?'

'I'm not involved with your case,' said Erlendur. 'I hear you and your brother were picked up for drug trafficking but that's nothing to do with me. My only interest is in Hannibal – seeing as your case is under investigation anyway.'

'Our case? There is no case.'

'No, right. As I said, my only concern is Hannibal.'

'I don't follow. What's he got to do with it?'

'This changes things,' said Erlendur. 'Don't you think?'

'Things?' said Ellert. 'What things? Why the hell do you keep going on about Hannibal? And who made up this shit about us selling dope? That's what I'd like to know. Who the fuck is trying to frame us for that? Is it you? Did you make up that bollocks about Hannibal just to snoop round our house?'

'No.'

'So who's been spreading this shit about us?'

'I know nothing about the investigation beyond the fact that you're being charged with drug trafficking. And I don't have a clue what people have been saying about you. I wasn't snooping, either. I wasn't there on official business; my only concern was Hannibal. Did he know what you were up to?'

'We weren't *up to* anything,' said Ellert. 'Now you've really lost me.'

'Did he threaten you? Was that why you set fire to his cellar – to scare him off? Is that what it was all about?'

'I've nothing more to say to you.'

'I repeat: did you set his cellar on fire?'

'For Christ's sake, the bloody tramp started it himself!' snapped Ellert. 'How many times do I have to tell you? We saved him. What don't you understand? We shouldn't have bothered. Should've left the stupid bastard to burn. Then at least we wouldn't have you to deal with.'

'I reckon you got rid of him,' said Erlendur. 'He suspected you. He was thrown out of his home and held you responsible for that. I reckon he knew what you were up to and threatened to expose you. You had a lot to lose. One tramp more or less didn't matter. So one evening you and your brother went up to the pipeline where he was sleeping and attacked him. He fled to the flooded diggings where you two caught up with him.'

'What the fuck?' exclaimed Ellert. 'We had no idea where he went after he was chucked out of Frímann's place. And that wasn't our fault – he managed that all by himself. The stupid bastard set the house on fire! It had nothing to do with us. And he never threatened us.' As an afterthought he added: 'Not that I know why he would have wanted to in the first place.'

'Ever heard of a woman called Oddný?' asked Erlendur, changing tack.

'You what?'

'She went out partying the night Hannibal died. To Thórskaffi. Decided to walk home because the weather was good and she wanted to clear her head. She never made it.'

'What . . . what are you on about now?'

'Chances are that Oddný walked past Hannibal's camp that night,' Erlendur continued. 'Perhaps you recognise the name?'

'Oddný? Never heard of her.'

'Are you sure?'

'Sure? I'm positive!'

'Is it possible that she saw you two?' asked Erlendur. 'Or perhaps it was just one of you? Was it Vignir? Or maybe you sent a side-kick to do your dirty work for you. Was that it? Did you send someone else to drown Hannibal?'

'Oh, drop the bullshit. I don't have a clue what you're on about. Get out of here and leave me alone, you stupid prick.'

He stood up and advanced towards Erlendur. He was more of a mess than the last time Erlendur had seen him; after a night in the cell his eyes were bleary, his hair dishevelled. Erlendur was careful not to betray his unease. All along he had spoken in even, almost soothing tones, never raising his voice, never changing his expression.

'She tried to run away,' he continued, unperturbed, 'but she didn't get far. She was only about ten, fifteen minutes' walk from her home in Fossvogur. Maybe she started running in that direction when she saw you. You went after her. Perhaps she didn't get any further than Kringlumýri before you caught up with her. At least, there were no witnesses.'

Ellert regarded him in silence.

'What happened then?' asked Erlendur.

The other man did not reply.

'I know she was in the pipeline at some point,' said Erlendur. 'Did you take her there? Did you drag her? Or did she hide there until you found her?'

'Is this some new kind of trick psychology?' asked Ellert. 'Trumping up charges for a serious crime I've never even heard of to get me to confess to some minor shit? Is that what this is all about? Is that how it works? Think I'm going to piss my pants just because you talk a load of bollocks?'

'Did she hide in the pipeline?' asked Erlendur, ignoring him.

'You just carry on bullshitting,' said Ellert.

'Did you find her there?'

Ellert moved closer until their faces were nearly touching.

'What do you want with me if you're not even involved in the case? Why don't you just fuck off?'

'Wouldn't it have been enough to threaten Oddný? Did you have to kill her?'

For a second he thought Ellert was going to go for him but then the other man backed away. His face twisted in a smile and he returned to the bed, where he sat down and stared at the floor in silence.

As Erlendur walked down the corridor he heard an ugly cough from the other occupied cell. Seeing that the door was open a crack, Erlendur decided to check if the man was all right. He pushed it wider and saw the tramp lying on the bed, fully clothed, reminiscent of Hannibal the year before. There was a throat-catching stench of urine. The tramp was wearing a filthy overcoat, his woolly hat lay on the floor at the head of the bed and one of his waders had fallen off, revealing three pairs of holey socks, one on top of the other, in as many colours: black, red and green. On the table lay a pair of battered horn-rimmed glasses, held together with Sellotape.

The man coughed again and Erlendur asked if he was all right.

The bundle of rags on the bed stirred and raised his head to see who was there. Erlendur recognised him at once: it was Vilhelm. The man fumbled for his glasses and Erlendur pushed them into his hands. He put them on and stared at Erlendur. His eyes, magnified by the lenses, held no recognition.

'You're Vilhelm, aren't you?'

'Who are you?' asked the tramp, racked again by the ugly, rattling cough that Erlendur recalled from their first meeting.

'We met the other day up by the hot-water pipeline in Kringlumýri. Have you moved on?'

'The pipeline? I couldn't stay there. It's not fit for humans. It's a bloody dump. Sorry but I don't remember you.'

'Doesn't matter.'

'Did we meet there?'

'Yes, we did.'

'It's completely slipped my mind.' As Vilhelm sat up, the smell intensified and Erlendur retreated to the doorway.

'I was asking you about a man I knew called Hannibal who used to sleep in the pipeline. He drowned.'

'Oh, yes, Hannibal, that's right. He drowned. Drowned, poor fellow. No, no, I've moved on, but . . . I'm telling you, it's hard to find a place indoors. Though with the weather we've been having it's not been too bad. It's not so bad sleeping under the trees in the park. Better than the pipeline, at any rate. Like sleeping in a coffin that was. Just like a coffin.'

'Yes, well, anyway.' Erlendur turned to leave.

'You couldn't spare a few fags?'

'Sorry.'

'Are you going?' Vilhelm sounded as if he would have liked Erlendur to stick around.

'Yes. Things to do,' said Erlendur.

'What did you say your name was?'

'Erlendur.'

'It might be coming back to me now.' Vilhelm was obviously eager to spin out their conversation. 'Bergmundur came over after you'd left. Wanted to help me get a place at the Fever Hospital. Wouldn't hear of my camping in the pipeline. Kept going on about his Thurí. Funny how he's always been so crazy about that miserable cow.'

Perhaps Vilhelm was lonely and this was the first time he had talked to anyone for ages. Erlendur knew no more about him than any of the other vagrants in the city. The only one he had become acquainted with was Hannibal and he was still dealing with the repercussions.

'Right, well, you take care,' Erlendur said in parting.

'You gave me some change, didn't you?' said Vilhelm, gazing at him through the thick lenses.

'That's right.'

'Yes, I remember you. Took me a while to work it out. You weren't wearing that get-up then.' He indicated the police uniform.

'No.' Erlendur smiled.

'I couldn't understand what you were doing there. What you wanted from an old sod like me. You were asking about Hannibal, weren't you? You knew him. I remember you clearly now. I'm no fool. Have you found out what happened to him?'

'No,' said Erlendur. 'I'm no closer.'

45

They drove slowly through the centre of town. It was almost morning. The night had been quiet: they had answered a few call-outs but for the most part simply patrolled the streets, Marteinn and Gardar chatting away, Erlendur withdrawn and preoccupied. As they passed the entrance to Austurstræti, which had recently been pedestrianised, Gardar observed that it was ridiculous to close a street to traffic. Marteinn, playing devil's advocate as usual, pointed out that lots of streets were pedestrianised abroad. You had to consider people on foot too sometimes, not just drivers. Gardar said he'd never heard such a load of rubbish in his life.

On their way to the centre they had driven along Borgartún, where Gardar had shown them a vacant premises, formerly a cycle repair shop, which he reckoned would be perfect for a pizza place. It had two large picture windows facing the street. Gardar's cousin, who owned a fishing vessel and had plenty of money, was interested: he had eaten pizza in London so the concept wasn't completely foreign to him. But although Gardar was hopeful about getting him on board, other potential investors seemed to have less faith in fast food.

'You two can come in on it, if you like,' he offered.

Marteinn shook his head, full of doubt.

'What about you, Erlendur?'

'No, I've no interest in pissers.'

'Pizzas,' corrected Gardar. 'Pizzas! How many times do I have to tell you? Are you sure, Marteinn?'

'What are you going to call it?' asked Marteinn.

'Don't know yet. Something foreign. Cool and catchy. Something like . . . something American.'

'So not "Gardar's Pissers"?' suggested Erlendur.

Marteinn snorted with laughter. Gardar said there was no point talking to them. They'd be laughing on the other side of their faces when he rang them from sunny Mallorca once his business had taken off.

They drove along Pósthússtræti, past the Reykjavík Pharmacy, and turned into the section of Austurstræti that was still open to traffic. Their reflection appeared in the shop windows, undulating from one to the next under the illuminated signs like a flickering film. Twice that night they had been summoned to deal with punch-ups; at one of the parties they'd arrested a drunk, who was spending the rest of the night in the cells.

Just as they were leaving the centre of town, an alert came through about a domestic incident in the Bústadir district. Erlendur recognised the address immediately. He put his foot down and turned on the flashing lights, though there was no other traffic, and before they knew it they were storming along Miklabraut.

'Weren't we there not so long ago?' asked Marteinn.

'Yup,' said Erlendur.

'Wasn't the woman out cold on the floor?' said Gardar.

'Right again.'

'What's the matter with these people?' Marteinn sighed.

Erlendur accelerated but his path was soon blocked by two cars travelling side by side. When he switched on the siren, one of them pulled out of the way, and within a few minutes they had reached Bústadavegur. By then Erlendur had turned off the siren to avoid waking the residents. They parked in front of the house and saw the next-door neighbour waiting for them in his dressing gown at the kitchen window. As on the previous occasion, he was the one who had reported the disturbance. Seeing them climbing out of the van, he hurried to his front door.

'It's stopped now,' he said. 'Perhaps they've gone to bed. He was making a hell of a racket. Screaming at her like a maniac. I was frightened . . . I thought he was going to kill her. Otherwise they've been fairly quiet since last time. Maybe a bit of shouting once or twice but nothing much apart from that.'

'When did the noise stop?' asked Gardar.

'Almost as soon as I'd called you. So . . . maybe it was a waste of time.'

'Can't be much fun living next door to this,' said Marteinn.

'Seriously, we're thinking of moving. But he's such a nice guy at other times. Works in the garden, chats to us and so on. I simply don't get it.'

No one answered the doorbell or when they knocked. Erlendur checked whether the door was locked and then made his way cautiously inside.

'Police!' he called, but received no reply.

He called again, to no avail. By now they were all crowded into the entrance hall. A deathly silence reigned in the house. Heavy curtains covered the windows in the sitting room, which lay in semi-darkness. The kitchen door was closed and the passage empty. Erlendur remembered that the couple's two sons had been sent to the country for the summer.

'Hello, is anybody home?' he shouted. 'Police!'

They listened and after a moment heard muffled sobbing coming from the sitting room. Erlendur followed the sound and as his eyes adjusted to the gloom he made out a figure rocking in a chair by the window. When he drew closer, he recognised her; it was the woman he had found lying unconscious on the floor last time.

Gardar and Marteinn remained in the doorway; her husband was nowhere to be seen.

'Are you all right?' asked Erlendur.

The woman merely carried on her sobbing and rocking.

'Where's your husband?' Erlendur knelt down beside her.

She said nothing, and it was as if she could neither hear nor see him, as if she were alone in the world, alone with her thoughts. She sat hunched up in the chair, rhythmically swaying back and forth.

Not until Erlendur touched her arm did she become aware of his presence. She flinched and turned her head to look at him. Only then did he see that she had been assaulted. One eye was masked by the swelling and bruising; her upper lip was puffy and split. Her nose had been bleeding too and her arm was obviously sore where he touched her. He wondered if it was broken. Beneath the new wounds the traces of older beatings were still apparent.

'He always took care not to mark my face,' she whispered into the gloom. 'But the other day . . . and now, it just didn't seem to matter any more.'

'Where did he go?'

'They gave him the sack,' she murmured, so quietly that he could hardly hear her. 'Said they were restructuring and . . . there was no room for him any more.'

'Where's your husband?'

'So they gave him the boot.'

It was as if she still couldn't hear Erlendur.

'He didn't want it to show,' she whispered. 'Didn't want people to know. Hit me where nobody could see. Even the boys. But they knew . . . they knew what was happening. They're such sweet boys, both of them. He can be like that too, sometimes. He can be sweet.'

Erlendur nodded.

'But now he . . . he's stopped caring,' she said. 'It doesn't matter to him where he hits me.'

'Do you feel up to coming with us or would you like us to call an ambulance?'

'He doesn't care any more.'

She turned to face Erlendur again.

'I must look terrible.'

'We need to know where he is.'

'Maybe I could go to my sister's,' the woman whispered. 'I can't live here any longer. Can't stay in this house. She doesn't know. I'll have to talk to her. She . . . I've never told her. Or anyone. I've . . . no one . . .'

'Do you feel up to coming with us?' Erlendur repeated. 'We can take you to Casualty. Can you stand?'

'I can't live here any longer,' the woman said again. 'The boys are coming home tomorrow and . . . God, they mustn't . . . what am I to tell them?'

'Perhaps you should talk to your sister,' suggested Erlendur. 'Do you know where your husband is?'

'Who?'

'Your husband.'

'What about him?'

'Do you know where he is now?'

'Yes, of course.'

'Where?'

'He's in the kitchen.'

'In the kitchen here?'

'Yes.'

'What's he doing there?'

'Lying on the floor.'

'On the floor? Why?'

'I think he's dead,' said the woman. 'I washed the knife. It was all bloody. I hope that was all right.'

Erlendur rose slowly to his feet and walked back to the doorway where Marteinn and Gardar were waiting.

'Where's the husband?' asked Gardar.

'In here.' Erlendur opened the door to the kitchen. It was small; the harsh ceiling light illuminated the fridge and cooker, a round table and four chairs. On the floor by the sink lay the man who had been so reluctant to let them in last time. A large pool of blood had collected beneath him. It looked to Erlendur as if he had been stabbed at least three times in the stomach. The knife, newly washed, was lying on the draining board.

The woman stood behind them, looking at her husband, who lay as she had left him.

'I washed the knife,' she repeated. 'I hope that was all right. I must clean the floor as well. I must clean it before the boys come home.'

Erlendur bent down and felt the man's neck.

'He's still alive!' he exclaimed, his fingers on the weak pulse. 'He's still alive. Call an ambulance. And a doctor. Now!'

He grabbed a tea towel that was hanging by the sink, tore off the man's shirt and did his best to stop the bleeding. Gardar and Marteinn were rooted to the spot, gaping horrified at the woman in the glare of the kitchen light. She stood beside them, abject, frail, her face disfigured by her husband's fists. It was the most distressing sight they had ever seen.

'Now!' yelled Erlendur. 'For Christ's sake, call a doctor!'

46

They finished their shift and said goodbye in the station yard, still badly shaken from the last call-out of the night. Marteinn had his car and offered to give the others a lift home, but Erlendur said he would walk. He watched them drive out of the gate. The three of them had sat in the coffee lounge for a long time after they came off duty, talking about the woman, her husband and their two sons. About the violence that had gone on in their home, as it did in so many others. About the helplessness of the victims. The shame that must be associated with such incidents. The dirty family secrets.

It looked as if the husband would live. He had lost a great deal of blood but the stab wounds had not proved fatal, and he had been taken straight to the operating theatre where he was now undergoing emergency surgery. The woman's injuries had been treated in Casualty and she was being kept in hospital for further tests.

'Can I get a bed?' Erlendur heard a voice ask behind him, and turning, he saw that Vilhelm had stolen into the yard.

'It's not a hotel, you know.'

'You don't say,' said Vilhelm.

'I suppose you'd like breakfast in bed too?'

'Wouldn't mind.' Vilhelm rolled his eyes behind the thick glasses. 'Coffee and toast? I wouldn't turn my nose up at that.'

'Come on then,' said Erlendur. 'The cells are all empty apart from one where a prize moron's sleeping it off. Tried to take a pop at us last night.'

'Didn't have much luck then.'

'No.'

He escorted Vilhelm down to the detention unit and showed him into one of the cells. The brothers, Ellert and Vignir, had both been transferred to Síðumúli. There was no sound from the idiot who'd ruined the party last night. Roaring drunk, he had kept swearing at them until finally he went for Gardar. Right now he was sleeping like a lamb but presently he would have to contend with an almighty hangover.

Vilhelm thanked Erlendur for the favour and got himself ready for bed. He seemed utterly exhausted and grateful for a rest. As he carefully laid aside his broken glasses, Erlendur enquired what had happened to them.

'That was Bergmundur.'

'What did he do?'

'Trod on them. Deliberately.'

'Why?'

'Because he's a dickhead.'

'Did he do it for a laugh?'

'I said something about Thurí that got his goat.'

'So he broke your glasses?'

'He knows I'm blind as a bat without them,' said Vilhelm. 'He's clever that way.'

'How do you mean?'

'Attacking people's weak points. He's a mean bugger. I've often said so. In his hearing too. I'm not scared of him. Not scared of anyone.'

Vilhelm lay down, and, leaving him to his rest, Erlendur went out the back of the police station into the morning sunshine. He decided to walk down to the seafront before heading home. It felt good to purge himself of the night's sordid experiences, to breathe in the clean salty air and lift his eyes to the faraway horizon as he used to as a boy out east. He had grown up between the highlands, with their moors and mountains that could exact such a cruel price for the slightest mistake, and the fjord. He remembered the heavily laden boats coming in to land at the little fishing village near his home, the swarm of gulls that attended them, the bustle on the quay, the shouts of the sailors. His mother had worked in the fish factory and he recalled the long shifts, the razor-sharp knives and the big women in their white aprons admonishing him not to get underfoot. He looked back with nostalgia, regretting that he no longer lived beside the sea.

He had been standing for some time gazing at the sunbeams glittering on Faxaflói Bay, when his thoughts snagged on something Vilhelm had said, both on his last stay in the cells and again just now. He had referred to his stint in the heating conduit and to Bergmundur's visit. Erlendur began to think about Thurí and why on earth Bergmundur would have broken Vilhelm's glasses.

'Wanted to help me . . .' Erlendur whispered to himself.

After brooding for a long while, eyes staring, unseeing, over the bay, he turned and walked back up to the police station.

When he opened the door to the cell, Vilhelm was fast asleep. Erlendur prodded him, but the tramp was dead to the world. Erlendur had to grab hold of him and shake him before he finally began to surface. It took his sleep-fuddled brain some time to work out where he was and who was so insistent on rousing him.

'What's going on?' he asked, sitting up.

'I'm sorry,' said Erlendur, 'but I have to ask you about something you told me yesterday.'

'What . . . what's that? Yesterday?'

'Why didn't Bergmundur want you to stay in the pipeline?'

'Come again?'

'You told me yesterday that Bergmundur had been to see you. Around the time I ran into you there.'

'Oh, yes.'

'You said he wanted to help you get a place at the Fever Hospital. That he didn't want you to go on sleeping in the pipeline.'

'So?'

'Wasn't that rather strange?'

'What?'

'Bergmundur being concerned about you like that. Being so considerate. Wasn't that unusual for him?'

Still bemused, Vilhelm now looked irritated as well.

'Did you wake me up for that?' He put on his glasses.

'Please try to remember. Then I won't disturb you any more and you can go back to sleep. We had a chat yesterday. You told me Bergmundur had come to see you by the hot-water pipeline shortly after I left. Remember?'

Vilhelm nodded.

'Why was that? What did he want?'

'He was talking about Thurí,' said Vilhelm, making an effort to recall what he had or hadn't said to Erlendur the day before. 'Then he asked if I had any booze and if I wouldn't rather go to the Fever Hospital.'

'What exactly did he say?'

'How on earth would I remember that?'

'Please try.'

'He said I couldn't possibly doss down in the pipeline. Said it was crazy. He'd help me find somewhere else. If I was sober, I stood a fair chance of getting a bed at the Fever Hospital. That sort of thing. At least, that was the gist of it.'

'Wasn't that unusual? Unlike him, I mean?'

'It was the first time he'd behaved like that,' agreed Vilhelm. 'The stupid git was almost friendly.'

'Did you go with him?'

'He wouldn't let up till I agreed to go into town with him. Wouldn't stop hassling me. Let me sleep at his place. You could have knocked me down with a feather.'

'So he was determined to get you out of the pipeline?'

'Yes, said it wasn't good for my health.'

'But, as far as you're aware, he'd never bothered about your welfare before?'

'Never. Took me aback, I can tell you. I thought it was nice of him to care what happened to me. Because he's not the type. Normally he only cares about number one.'

'But then he broke your glasses?'

'Well, I called Thurí a bloody whore. He went mad. I shouldn't have slagged her off like that. At least, not to him.'

'What sort of relationship did he have with Thurí?' asked Erlendur. 'They weren't always a couple, were they?'

'No, no one can put up with Bergmundur for long.'

'Did she start seeing someone else?'

'Er, yes. Didn't you know?'

'It was Hannibal, wasn't it?'

'Yes, your friend Hannibal. They were inseparable.'

'I presume Bergmundur wasn't too happy about that.'

'He couldn't stand Hannibal. Couldn't stand him. And Bergmundur never gives up. He's a hell of a stubborn bugger. Only the other day I heard they'd taken up with each other again.'

'Do you reckon he was jealous of Hannibal?'

'Not half,' said Vilhelm, stretching. 'That's what he's like. Are you asking if he could have hurt him?'

'What do you think?'

'Never occurred to me. It was an accident, wasn't it? Hannibal drowning?'

Erlendur shrugged.

'You know he . . .?'

Vilhelm broke off. He was wide awake now.

'What?'

'Of course, Bergmundur was much stronger than Hannibal – bigger, younger and stronger.'

'You mean he could have overpowered him?'

'Easily. Hannibal would have been no match for him. It was probably him who . . .'

'What?'

'You know about Bergmundur? About what he did?'

'No, what do you mean? What did he do?'

'Óli claimed to have seen him.'

'Óli, who's Óli? What did he see?'

'Ólafur! He dropped dead in Nauthólsvík,' said Vilhelm. 'You must remember him. His name was Ólafur. Heart attack, wasn't it? Lying by the road to Nauthólsvík. Gave up the ghost halfway.'

'Oh, yes. What about him?' Erlendur finally called Ólafur to mind; the tramp who had been found dead recently. 'What about him? What did he see?'

'Bergmundur, of course,' said Vilhelm. 'The night Hannibal's place caught fire. Óli told me he'd spotted Bergmundur loitering near the house that evening. Óli was sure he'd started it. In fact he was certain.'

Erlendur sank down on the bench beside him.

'He saw Bergmundur?'

'He was certain about it. Quite certain.'

Erlendur remembered the comment Vilhelm had made at their last meeting about living in the pipeline.

'Like sleeping in a coffin,' he murmured absently.

'What?'

'You said the pipeline was like a coffin.'

Vilhelm stared at him owlishly.

'Too right. It was like lying in a coffin, sleeping there. Like lying in a bloody coffin.'

47

Thurí was not in her room in the west of town; Svana at Póllinn said she hadn't been in recently; none of the usual suspects in Austurvöllur Square had seen her either, and she hadn't shown her face at the hostel on Amtmannsstígur. Erlendur was running out of places to look. He climbed up the green mound of Arnarhóll, another popular gathering place for drinkers. There were three of them sunning themselves at the top, smoking and sharing round a bottle of *brennivín*. Erlendur noticed two more sea-green bottles of this favourite tipple lined up on the ground between them. They must have got their hands on some cash. One had taken his top off, revealing a torso so emaciated that you could count his ribs. Another man, small and skinny, with a flat cap on his head, was singing a snatch of Steinn Steinarr's verse about Cadet Jón Kristófer of the Sally Army. They couldn't have been enjoying themselves more in the balmy weather.

'Any of you spotted Thurí from up here?' asked Erlendur,

squatting down beside them. His feet were sore from trekking all the way to the west of town and back again. He had banged on Thurí's door and then her window, but no one was home.

'Thurí?' said the bony man, scratching his armpit. 'Haven't seen her.'

'Bergmundur, then? Run into him lately?'

'No, not seen him either,' said the small man, lifting his cap and clawing at his head.

The others agreed that they hadn't seen them.

'Are they back together?' asked Erlendur, stretching out his legs.

'Wouldn't know,' said the third man, morosely. He was fat and bearded, and evidently worried that Erlendur was trying to cadge a drink. 'Why the hell do you care, anyway?'

'I hear he's as crazy about her as ever,' said Erlendur.

'He's an arsehole,' said the bony man, still scratching his armpit.

'He once beat the crap out of Tommi here,' commented the surly man, looking slightly mollified at the memory of another's misfortunes. 'So he doesn't have a good word to say about him.'

'Nobody has a good word for that jerk,' retorted the man they had referred to as Tommi.

'What have you got against him?' asked Erlendur. 'What happened?'

Tommi ignored him.

'Thurí always used to oblige in return for gifts,' explained the surly man. 'Always had done. Didn't have to be much.'

'Like a bottle of meths?' prompted Erlendur.

'Not even that. So long as Bergmundur didn't get wind of it. Once Tommi here went to see her with . . . what was it you gave her, Tommi? Something ridiculous, wasn't it?'

'Bus tickets,' said Tommi.

'Bus tickets?' Erlendur echoed.

'A ten-trip card I nicked.'

'Tommi's never had much luck with the ladies,' said the fat man, beginning to enjoy himself.

'What would you know?' countered Tommi. 'Who'd want to screw an ugly git like you?'

'When Bergmundur heard about it he tracked Tommi down and made him eat the tickets before kicking the shit out of him. Said if he ever went near Thurí again he'd murder him.'

'When was this?'

'About five years ago.' Tommi stopped scratching and squinted up at the sun. 'Knocked my tooth out,' he added, tugging at the side of his mouth to show the gap.

Since he was missing at least four teeth, Erlendur had no idea which one had fallen victim to Bergmundur's fist.

48

This time he took a small spade and a powerful torch with him to the pipeline. He had borrowed the spade from his upstairs neighbours who took care of the garden; the torch was police property.

Bergmundur's name cropped up in a number of police files. He had a long criminal record for a variety of minor offences, as well as affray and theft. Erlendur thought back to their chat on Arnarhóll, when he had been suckered into buying meths for him, and recalled that Bergmundur was convinced Ellert and Vignir had set fire to Hannibal's cellar. It was Bergmundur who had claimed Hannibal had dangerous information about the brothers; Bergmundur who had implied that they had finally caught up with Hannibal and silenced him for ever in Kringlumýri. It looked as if Bergmundur had been deliberately trying to mislead him.

It was late evening when Erlendur set off for the pipeline, after failing to trace either Thurí or Bergmundur. Perhaps it no longer mattered. He had resolved to take the earring and the results of all his detective work to CID in the morning and let them handle the rest. He would explain to Rebekka. He would like to have spoken to Thurí too before handing over the case but it was as if the ground had swallowed her up. He wanted to question her about her relationship with Hannibal towards the end and about Bergmundur's reaction to it. About whether or not the two men had got on. About exactly what she knew about the events on Kringlumýri and when she had figured it out. Was it coincidence, for example, that she had visited the conduit after Hannibal's death and come across the earring? And had she known about the fire? Known that Bergmundur had been spotted near Hannibal's cellar that evening? According to the drinkers on Arnarhóll, she could twist Bergmundur round her little finger. It was strange that he remained so infatuated with her, even after she went off with Hannibal. Clearly he felt an urge to protect her, an urge that could make him violent. And he believed in vengeance, not forgiveness.

Erlendur approached the hole in the pipeline casing, Hannibal's last refuge. The spade had a short handle and a good-sized blade, which was just what he needed inside the tunnel; the torch was more like a large lantern, really, with powerful batteries that would last all night if required. It was overcast but still. Veils of rain were drifting across the Bláfjöll range. There was nobody else around.

He switched on the torch, then squeezed in through the opening. According to Thurí, she had found the earring a little to the left of the entrance, so that is where he began his search. The soil was a combination of earth and gravel, which the small spade sliced through easily enough. He thrust the spade into the ground several times until he had broken up the surface, then continued until he'd dug a hole at least half a metre deep. After that, he wormed his way a little further into the tunnel and repeated the process.

He kept at it, kneeling, back hunched, working his way metre by metre along the tunnel, the light balanced on top of the pipes. As he moved on, he banged the blade on the pipes to clean off the dirt, then broke up the soil and drove in the spade, making one hole after another, finding nothing.

Eventually, glancing behind him and calculating that he was about ten metres from the opening, he decided it was time to turn round and start his search in the other direction. In spite of this, he carried on for another two metres before concluding that he had dug enough holes on the left-hand side. There was sufficient room to turn and crawl back on all fours to the entrance. Nevertheless, the cramped space was getting to him, so he decided to take a break. Once outside he stretched, then sat down with his back to the pipeline, facing Mount Esja to the north. This is how Hannibal must have sat during his stay in this odd choice of home, in a sort of exile within the city. The idea was somehow attractive: Hannibal's situation had been far from enviable, yet in his own way he had been free.

After a short break, Erlendur climbed back inside the conduit and started driving the spade into the ground on the other side. He pushed the torch along in front of him, crawled a bit further, scraped out a hole, moved on, dug out another hole, progressing deeper into the tunnel little by little. Before long he observed that the soil was looser and the spade was sliding in more easily. About seven metres from the entrance, he encountered some resistance.

Shining his light into the hole revealed nothing, so he began to scrape away more earth, and felt further resistance. It couldn't be a rock, he knew, because there was no recoil from the spade, no clink of metal on stone. He illuminated the ground around his hole, yet could not detect any signs that the soil had been disturbed.

Propping the lantern on the pipes again, he carefully began to remove earth from a wider area. He made small incisions with the spade, approaching the task with extreme caution so as not to destroy any evidence. There was no sound apart from the booming of the pipes and the metallic scraping of the spade. He took a short break and peered further into the tunnel. The glow from the torch rendered the darkness even blacker, and he felt as if it were pressing in on all sides. The spoil was now heaped up along the pipes, so he began to pile the loose dirt against the concrete wall to his right instead.

Back bent, still on his knees, he continued to scrape away until suddenly the blade stuck fast. He jerked back his hand. Then, nervously, he picked up the torch; it revealed a piece of cloth sticking out of the earth. Leaving the spade where it was, he began to clear away the soil with one hand. It looked to him like the collar of a jacket. Next he saw what appeared to be tufts of hair, and then he caught sight of an object he recognised.

Erlendur picked it up gingerly, wiped off the dirt and held it up to the torch beam. It was an earring, consisting of two linked hoops. Suspended from the lower, slightly smaller, hoop was a tiny white pearl.

He had found Oddný.

Once he uncovered more of the body, he could see that nature had done its work. He glimpsed a shoulder bone and a hand, picked clean, before he abandoned the task. An overpowering sensation of horror and nausea assailed him and he knew he could not stay there a moment longer. He had to get out of this ghastly place, out of the pipeline, out of the darkness closing in on him from every side.

As he was turning away, Erlendur's gaze fell on the hand again, and he noticed that it seemed to be concealing something, as if the fist had closed over it at the moment of death. Moving nearer, he lifted the bony fingers with extreme care and managed to prise the object from their grasp. He cleaned off the soil, examined it and was instantly lanced by the realisation that his decision to search the pipeline for Oddný's grave had been based on entirely the wrong suspect.

He held the tiny object up to the light. Oddný was not the only person who had lost something that fatal night.

49

Early next morning Erlendur left home and walked down to the CID offices on Borgartún. He had not slept a wink. After leaving the pipeline, he had showered, changed his clothes and eaten a quick breakfast. He could, of course, have called to report the body as soon as he got home, but he believed there was no urgency. A few hours would make no difference, and besides he wanted to beg a favour of the detectives.

When he asked to speak to Hrólfur, he learned that he was on holiday, but he could see Marion Briem instead. He knew the name well; Marion was the driving force in CID. They had crossed paths two or three times since Erlendur joined the force. He learned that Marion had recently returned from a long sabbatical in Denmark and so had not been involved in Oddný's case.

Marion, who was taking off a coat when Erlendur knocked on the door, recognised him immediately.

'Erlendur, isn't it?'

'Yes.'

'Not in uniform?'

'I'm off duty,' Erlendur explained.

'I see. What brings you here?'

'I want to report a murder.'

Marion put down the coat, trying to conceal any sign of astonishment.

'What do you mean?'

'In fact, I believe it's a case of double murder,' Erlendur said. 'One of the victims was a woman called Oddný. The other was a vagrant I knew, called Hannibal. He was unlucky. It looks as if he was the wrong man in the wrong place. The woman was the main target. They both died at around the same time in Kringlumýri. And I'm fairly confident that the murderer was the same in both cases.'

'Oddný, isn't that the woman who went missing last year?' asked Marion.

'Yes. And Hannibal's the man –'

'Who drowned in the flooded pit.'

'Correct.'

'Hrólfur told me a junior officer had come in and asked a lot of strange questions about those two,' said Marion. 'I take it you've found the woman.'

'She's buried in the hot-water pipeline not far from the diggings. The pipeline was Hannibal's last refuge. Oddný probably tried to hide there, which is how Hannibal got mixed up in the whole thing. It cost him his life.'

'Have you been conducting a private investigation?' asked Marion.

'I knew Hannibal,' Erlendur explained. 'His sister asked me to find out how her brother drowned. I've been meaning to report my discoveries. Then this morning I found Oddný. I've worked out who the killer is too. But I wanted to ask you a favour.'

'Which is?'

'I'd like to be granted a few minutes with him before you take him away.'

The house in Fossvogur stood at the bottom of the valley, a boxy, modern structure, its immaculately tended garden now in full bloom. The verdant lawn was freshly mown and neatly edged; pansies and peonies flowered in tidy rows along the walls of the house. The red garage door was closed. It was still early and the morning breeze held the scent of summer and the promise of a glorious day.

Erlendur approached the front door and rang the bell. There was a lengthy wait before Gústaf opened it.

'You again,' he said. 'What do you want? And what . . . why are they here?'

'I asked them to come with me,' Erlendur replied.

In the drive behind him was a patrol car containing two uniformed officers. A new-looking, unmarked vehicle was parked beside it. Marion Briem stepped out, accompanied by two plain-clothes detectives, their eyes on the house. Another team of officers had been deployed to the pipeline, where a section of the wall, and the concrete slab on top, would be removed to provide easier access to the body.

'They're detectives from the Reykjavík Criminal Investigation Department.'

'Criminal Investigation . . .?'

'They want to talk to you, but they've agreed to give me a few minutes with you first.'

Gústaf peered down the road as if principally afraid that his neighbours would witness this visit. Police cars were a rare sight in this area.

'What do you want with me? I'm about to leave for work. I haven't got time for this.'

'It won't take long,' Erlendur assured him. 'There's just one small matter I want to ask you about.'

'Do they have to park in the drive?' asked Gústaf.

'It won't take a moment.'

'Well, let's get it over with, then,' sighed Gústaf, realising that, whatever he said, Erlendur was not going to back down. 'I'm already late for work.'

They went no further than the hall. Gústaf closed the front door behind them. Erlendur could smell toast and coffee.

'How dare you show up unannounced like this?' Gústaf snarled. 'Turning up with all these cars at the crack of dawn, as if it were some major incident. As if I were a dangerous criminal!'

'Oh, I don't think you'll be making any complaints,' said Erlendur. 'Any more than you did the last time I visited you and came pretty close to blaming you for your wife's disappearance.'

'I saw no reason to,' protested Gústaf. 'I can't go around reporting every nutter who makes crazy accusations against me.'

'Fair enough. But of course you were keen not to attract any attention either.'

'I don't know what you're referring to. What do you want? Why won't you stop harassing me?'

'Last time we spoke – it's in the case notes too – you stated that you attended a Lions Club meeting the evening Oddný went to Thórskaffi. Is that correct?'

'What are you getting at now?'

'Is that correct? That you were at a Lions Club meeting?'

'Quite correct. It's common knowledge.'

'And you came straight home from the meeting. Shortly after midnight, I imagine?'

'You know, I don't have to talk to you,' said Gústaf. 'You're not even involved in this case. It's none of your business. Why don't you get out of my house and take your colleagues with you?'

'An acquaintance of mine died in the peat diggings that night,' said Erlendur. 'His sister's terrified that he'll be blamed for your wife's disappearance. She's desperate for that not to happen. Did you change your clothes after coming home from the meeting?'

'Change my clothes? No . . . I can't remember. What kind of question is that? Did I change my clothes?!'

'You were wearing a nice suit, weren't you?'

Gústaf said nothing.

'And a white shirt? Perhaps a new white shirt?'

Gústaf returned his gaze in obstinate silence, refusing to answer.

'Did the sleeves have buttons?'

No reply.

'Or were you wearing cufflinks?'

'You'd better get out of here, all of you.' Gústaf made to open the door.

'Were they Lions Club cufflinks, by any chance?'

Gústaf gaped at him.

'I don't own any cufflinks myself and don't know how they're worn,' continued Erlendur. 'But I do know that you lost one. Just like your wife lost an earring. Ring any bells?'

The other man remained silent.

'When did you notice it was missing?' asked Erlendur. 'Or didn't you notice?'

He could see that Gústaf was rattled. Erlendur had entered the pipeline fully convinced that Bergmundur had killed Oddný. He had been equally confident that the tramp had finished off Hannibal. That he had hunted Hannibal down in revenge for the fact that he had stolen his Thurí. Their encounter had ended with Bergmundur forcibly drowning Hannibal in the diggings. Oddný, witnessing the crime, had fled and hidden in the pipeline, where Bergmundur had found and murdered her.

Now, however, he knew that Bergmundur was innocent of her death.

'Did you think you'd lost the cufflink somewhere else?' he asked.

'You can't come here and . . .'

Gústaf was casting around in vain for something to say.

'You must have been frantic when you couldn't find it.'

'But I haven't –'

'Is this your cufflink, by any chance?' Erlendur fished in his pocket and pulled out the object he had found in Oddný's hand. It was sealed in a small plastic bag, which Erlendur held out for Gústaf to examine. He had cleaned off enough of the dirt to reveal that the cufflink was silver-plated, with diagonal stripes and the Lions Club crest in the middle.

Gústaf took a step backwards.

'Why don't you take a closer look?' suggested Erlendur. 'Check it's definitely yours?'

Gústaf shook his head in disbelief.

'Did Hannibal stumble on you and your wife?' said Erlendur. 'Did he see what you'd done? Catch sight of your face?'

The other man avoided his eye.

'Did you think she'd never be found? That they'd seal up the hole in the casing and she'd stay hidden in her grave for all eternity?'

Erlendur advanced towards Gústaf, who was standing there as if turned to stone.

'Answer me!' he shouted.

Gústaf flinched.

'I didn't mean . . .' he mumbled almost inaudibly. After all this time his defences were finally crumbling. 'I didn't trust her. I thought she'd started seeing that creep again . . . that bastard. And she told me – told me when I caught her – that she'd slept with him and was planning to do it again. Planning to leave me. And that she hated me. I was a monster and I disgusted her.'

'When you caught her?'

Gústaf searched Erlendur's face for any sign of understanding.

'I chased her. She came home and we had a row and she ran out and . . . I went after her. I didn't mean . . . I hit her in the face . . . I didn't mean to kill her – it was an accident. And when the man saw, when he saw me I . . . I completely lost my head. Lost control. I had no idea what to do.'

'Where did Hannibal appear from? Inside the pipeline?'

'I don't know. Probably. I had no clue he was there. Didn't think anyone was around. Then suddenly he popped up. By then it was too late. He saw what I'd done.'

'So you went after him?'

'He saw me,' repeated Gústaf. 'He saw what I'd done to Oddný.

I couldn't let him report me to the police. I couldn't. He ran towards the diggings. What was I supposed to do? What could I have done?'

Gústaf's gaze was riveted to the cufflink.

'I've been looking for it ever since,' he said. 'I didn't know where I'd lost it. Didn't know where it was. I was going crazy. Turned the house upside down, searched up by the pipeline, inside it . . . I had a horrible feeling it was there. Was terrified I'd dropped it there.'

'I found it with Oddný.'

'Where . . . where exactly?'

'In her hand.'

'Oh my God,' whispered Gústaf.

'I found her last night, where you buried her.'

'I . . . I never dared look at her. I regret it so much . . . what I did. I –'

'You must have been keeping an eye on the pipeline,' said Erlendur. 'Especially as it was still open.'

Gústaf nodded.

'I went there often, mostly at night of course – I didn't want anyone to see me. It's like an open grave. They'll never get round to mending it. Never mend that horrible hole in the casing.'

50

Later, once Erlendur had learned the whole story from the detectives who had taken over the case, he went to see Rebekka and told her that he finally had an answer for her. It was pure chance that Hannibal had witnessed Gústaf's crime.

Oddný had gone home after all that night, to be met at the door by her furious husband. He had been waiting up for her, suspecting her of cheating on him. Because she was drunk she gave him an earful. They had a violent row, in the course of which he had threatened and slapped her. She had fled out of the house and run up the Fossvogur valley towards Kringlumýri.

'The poor woman.'

'There's no way of knowing where she was going; Gústaf didn't know,' said Erlendur. 'Perhaps she was thinking of returning to her friends. I couldn't say. Gústaf followed some way behind and, according to his statement, saw her climb up on the hot-water conduit. By then she had slowed down, so he was able to creep up behind her and grab her, not far from the hole in the casing where Hannibal was living. They started quarrelling again and he hit her. She fell off the pipe-line, he leapt after her, seized her by the throat and banged her head against the concrete until he realised she was dead, and –'

'Please, spare me the details,' Rebekka interrupted. 'I don't want to hear.'

'Sorry,' said Erlendur. 'I didn't mean –'

'What happened next?'

'Just then Hannibal appeared from inside the tunnel, clearly felt he was no match for a man who had completely lost his mind, and fled in the direction of the peat diggings. Gústaf ran after him, caught up in no time and pushed him into the pool, then waded in after him and held him down until he . . . until he reckoned it was enough.'

'Oh, sweet Jesus,' murmured Rebekka.

'He left Hannibal in the water and ran back to where Oddný was lying by the pipeline. By then he was beginning to calm down but it never occurred to him to give himself up and confess his crimes. Instead, his first thought was to hide the body. He pulled it in through the opening and hid it in the darkness deep inside the tunnel, then raced home. He didn't notice that one of her earrings had fallen off and landed under the hot-water pipes, though later he discovered he'd lost one of his cufflinks but didn't know when or where. He waited in a state of frantic anxiety for the police to find Oddný's body when they went to clear out Hannibal's belongings, but nothing happened. It didn't cross anyone's mind to explore further inside the tunnel.'

Rebekka sat quietly during Erlendur's account. This time she had invited him round to her pleasant flat in an apartment block on Álfheimar. Later that day he had a date with Halldóra: they were going look at places to rent together.

'Long afterwards, when the fuss had died down – the police had taken no action over Hannibal's death and were treating Oddný's as a probable suicide – Gústaf crept back to the pipeline at night, carrying a torch and a small spade, to bury the body. He couldn't bring himself to move it from the tunnel, so he had no real alternative. Apparently, he avoided looking at her as far as possible and never noticed the cufflink in her hand.'

It had also emerged during an interview, as Erlendur now informed Rebekka, that Gústaf had expected the district heating company to repair the hole in the conduit casing before long, thus perfecting the final resting place he had chosen for Oddný. But months had passed without any sign of activity. He had even made an anonymous phone call to the company to complain. It had achieved nothing.

'Was that all he cared about?' asked Rebekka.

'Well, naturally, he wasn't in his right mind,' said Erlendur. 'I think that's gradually coming home to him now.'

'So this Bergmundur had no part in the affair?'

'None at all. Mind you, he held such a grudge against your brother for his relationship with Thurí that he was almost certainly behind the arson attack on the cellar.'

'What about Thurí?'

'I don't know,' said Erlendur. 'I haven't seen her.'

'Think she'd be willing to meet me?'

'Is that what you want?'

'Yes, I'd like to talk to her. About Hannibal.'

'I'm sure it would help you,' said Erlendur. 'She's all right. Once you get to know her.'

51

Erlendur tugged at his tight shirt collar under his uniform jacket. It was the end of July and the weather was sweltering at Thingvellir. The lake was like a mirror. People were out in rowing boats and children were playing barefoot on the shore. Traffic snaked around the festival site where the sun shone blindingly on the city of tents that had been pitched on every flat piece of ground at the foot of the Almannagjá ravine.

He had been on duty since early that morning, with only a fifteen-minute break to bolt a sandwich and wash it down with bad coffee. The police facilities were close to the festival organisers' tent. They'd had to deal with several unexpected incidents, including a protest against the NATO airbase at Keflavík. The protestors had been swiftly and forcibly removed from the brink of the ravine. Their banner, which bore the familiar war cry of *Iceland Out of NATO – Army Go Home*, had been bundled up and chucked into the police van. The episode had caught the police completely unawares. For the most part they had been busy directing traffic – a mixture of cars and pedestrians – and trying to keep the peace among the thousands who had massed at Thingvellir to celebrate eleven hundred years of settlement in Iceland. Erlendur, who hadn't been involved in the arrest of the anti-NATO protestors, heard about the events second hand as he was snatching his lunch.

The most he had to deal with were some evangelical Christians who were circulating their propaganda, in the form of pamphlets printed in English, all over the festival site. A middle-aged atheist, who had downed a few too many, had begun by rebuking the children of Jesus, then took a swing at one. His victim, a blond, bearded youth of about twenty, wearing a peace sign around his neck, was determined to offer the other cheek. Witnessing the scuffle, Erlendur drew the drunk aside and threatened to eject him from the festival if he didn't leave the Christian brigade in peace. Realising that this was no idle warning, the man had swallowed his objections.

Erlendur had been deliberately inching his way closer to the stage by the Law Rock so he would not miss the moment when the poet Tómas Guðmundsson, a slim figure with a large head, stepped up to the podium to recite the commemorative ode. He allowed himself a break from his duties to listen to the poet whose work he had enjoyed from a young age. As the sun drew a halo around the speaker, Erlendur looked out over Thingvellir to Mount Skjaldbreiður. They could not have asked for better weather and there was genuine elation all over the old assembly site. People wandered between performances and refreshment tents festooned with Icelandic flags and balloons, as they listened to male-voice choirs singing folk songs and their heads reverberated with the joyous fanfare of trumpets.

The nation had come together to celebrate. Icelanders from all walks of life: long-haired, free-thinking hippies in peasant smocks, respectable ladies in light summer dresses with backcombed hair and handbags on their arms, men in hats and new Sunday best, their lapels as wide as cod fillets; farmers and big businessmen, labourers and fishermen, wholesalers and shopkeepers, people from the city, villages and countryside, all united on this glorious day, determined to pay homage to whatever Iceland represented for them.

After listening to Tómas Guðmundsson, Erlendur continued on his way, heading in the general direction of Hótel Valhöll where earlier in the day he had formed part of the guard of honour. Many of the foreign dignitaries – ambassadors, government ministers and royals – had arrived in gleaming limousines and processed like film stars to the humble hotel. He had donned his regulation white gloves and raised his hand to the peak of his cap, eyes fixed dead ahead, as if detached from the whole business. All the while he had kept a lookout for potential trouble-makers, but none of the crowd who had collected to watch the spectacle had any such intention in mind.

Now he stopped by the hotel to catch up with Gardar and Marteinn, who were also on duty. They were full of the protest up by Almannagjá. It had caused a certain amount of consternation among the police since they were responsible for ensuring that everything went smoothly.

'Bloody Commies!' said Gardar.

Erlendur sauntered over to the campsite where thousands of people had pitched their tents in the preceding days, taking advantage of the fine summer weather. The campers had packed stoves and tinned food, burgers, saucepans, coffee pots and bread bins. Lots of them had brought along a little something to fuel the festivities and toast the occasion in style. It had all gone peacefully, as befitted such a place, apart from the odd fight over the stupidest provocations.

He wended his way between the tents, where women were making coffee and sandwiches with pâté or smoked lamb while their menfolk lounged in their vests on deckchairs, smoking, or reading the papers they had brought from home. There was a buzzing of transistor radios as people followed the festival programme. A choir was singing 'I Will Love My Land'. One man had a bottle of illegal spirits, which he hid as Erlendur approached. He turned a blind eye.

'Hello,' a reedy voice said behind him.

Turning, he saw Marion Briem dressed in full regalia for the occasion, looking as uncomfortable in the heat as Erlendur was himself.

They shook hands.

'You should have a word with us in CID if you ever feel like a change,' said Marion. 'I've been going through your reports regarding Hannibal and Oddný and noticed that you broke every rule in the book.'

'I'm sorry, I didn't mean –' Erlendur began.

He had received a stiff reprimand from his superiors for failing to turn the investigation over to CID when he found the earring. He had nearly lost his job.

'No, I'm impressed,' said Marion. 'No need to apologise to me. I spoke to the sister of your friend Hannibal.'

'Rebekka?'

'She gave a good account of you. Get in touch with me if you're interested in doing more of this kind of sleuthing.'

With that, Marion disappeared into the throng. Erlendur gave his collar another tug, thinking how good it would be to shed his uniform once he came off duty. Not that he would be free of it for long, since all next week he would be back on the Reykjavík night shift.

52

He halted in front of the house and stared up at it before continuing on his way through the lightly falling rain. He had often retraced these steps, lingering briefly in this street. The girl's family no longer lived here; they had moved out more than ten years before. He was not sure which room had been hers but liked to imagine that it was the one with the pretty attic window, that it was there she had awoken to a new day and got ready for school, before yelling a quick goodbye to her parents because she was running late. Cheerful as ever, according to their account.

The house had changed owners twice since then. A young couple lived there now and Erlendur wondered if they were aware that it had been home to the girl who had disappeared on her way to school. He doubted it. People came and went without dwelling too much on the past; they built new lives, shaped a new future. The cycle of life. Time waited for no man.

He was filled with the old sense of sadness as he followed the girl along the street for the last time. They walked towards the site where Camp Knox had once stood, like a bleak memorial to the occupation and the nation's impoverished past. There he stopped and watched her go on, her outline fading into the softly falling rain.